Just
Friends

Just Friends

Billy Taylor

Just Friends
Copyright © 2016 by Billy Taylor

Book design by Maureen Cutajar
www.gopublished.com

ISBN-13: 978-1530511518
ISBN-10: 1530511518

For my family x

APRIL 16TH

Today is a special day for two reasons. The first is that it's the twelve-year anniversary of meeting my best friend, Ethan Knight. The second is that it's the nine-teenth birthday of my best friend, Ethan Knight. Before I go on, the story of how we met should be told.

My parents and I had moved house; the small house we lived in had become too small. I was six and had started at my new school with a whole load of kids I'd never met. Ethan and I were in separate classes during my first week of school, so we didn't meet. Until one day, his dad asked my parents if I wanted to go to his seventh birthday party. Ethan's dad knew I was new in school so it should be a nice opportunity for me to try to make new friends. It was the last thing I wanted to do because I was a stubborn child, but looking back on it now, I'm glad my parents forced me to go. Meeting Ethan is my favourite childhood memory.

I was still frowning at my freckled cheeks in the mirror even after they had dropped me off. I tied my long, dark blonde hair up in the mirror. My mum had spent forever brushing it, but I hated having my hair brushed when I was younger. I ventured into the kitchen and grabbed a slice of cake that had been placed on napkins along the side. It was an indulging chocolate fudge cake. I swear each slice was the same size as my face. I popped it onto a plate. I was a clumsy kid and knew I'd drop cake somewhere. The other kids in attendance were all screaming and running around in the garden. Meanwhile, I was sitting on the sofa inside, eating Ethan's birthday cake, alone.

After two or three minutes of silence, a boy came running past wearing a top hat, cape, and white gloves. Don't forget the magic wand. I'd never met Ethan before so I had no idea who I was looking for to say happy birthday to. After he ran through the kitchen, he casually walked backwards, poking his head around the corner, staring at me. I gave him an awkward smile and wiped my fingers and face with my napkin.

"Who are you?" he curiously asked, strolling over.

"I'm August, happy birthday by the way," I said with a mouth full of cake.

He removed his top hat, allowing his long brown hair to fall across his forehead, half covering his eyes. He extended his right hand towards me and said, "Pleased to meet you, August. Do you want to see a magic trick? I've been practising all day."

I paused and examined his appearance. He was so small. I was taller than him at this stage. He was wearing the pearliest white tie I had ever seen. Not that I'd seen many of them, but that tie could've advertised teeth whitening.

"Ok," I said, shaking his hand.

I moved the plate off my lap and onto the sofa cushion beside me. He removed his gloves and threw them over his shoulders onto the floor behind him. He then stuck his hand into his hat and pulled out a deck of cards. Retrieving them from the pack, he fanned them out in front of me.

"Before you pick a card I want you to think of a number between one and ninety-nine for me, please."

I frowned at him, leant back on the sofa and hummed.

After a few seconds of consulting in my head I chose the number seventy-three.

"You got one?" he asked, raising an eyebrow at me.

"Yes," I replied, gripping my knees.

Magic bewildered me growing up. Although not as much as the guys who could make balloon animals. Those guys were literal geniuses. He shuffled the deck in an emphatic fashion before fanning it out in front of me. I perused amongst them cautiously; I didn't want to make it too obvious.

"We don't have all day you know," he said, nudging the cards closer.

I hadn't wiped my hands properly after eating the cake, and my smudgy fingers marked the card of my choice in chocolate cake. I selected my card and turned it over. And there it was, the seventy-three of hearts. Well, a seven of hearts with a three drawn next to the seven in black marker pen. Still, I found it astonishing.

"How did you do that?" I asked with a grin.

"A magician never reveals his tricks, August. However, nothing is over yet." He pulled a lighter and a black marker pen from his pocket and waved them around in front of me.

"Will you write your name on the card for me, please?"

I rubbed my hands on the napkin again to prevent any further cake prints on the card. I didn't have a signature or anything fancy at six years old, so I wrote my name and drew a smiley face next to it. My fingers were still greasy so my handwriting appeared messy.

"I will now set this card on fire, doing so will move the card into your shoe... ready?" he said, holding the lighter up to the bottom of the card.

"Wait... you're setting my shoe on fire?" I asked.

"Why would I set your shoe on fire, August?" he replied, blank faced.

"You said you're going to set the card on fire and put it in my shoe."

"This card will go into your shoe after I've set it on fire, it won't be on fire in your shoe. Ok?"

We looked at each other, confused.

"Can I take my shoe off first? I don't want it to burn my feet."

He flapped his arms by his side. "August, the fire will come nowhere near your shoe or feet, ok?"

I cheekily grinned at him. "I was just kidding!"

He angrily smirked at me and flicked the lighter on underneath the card. Suddenly it went up in flames and within a second or two dissipated into thin air. It didn't even leave a mark on the cream carpet. I flicked off my shoes; to my disappointment there wasn't a card there. Ethan snatched at my shoes and stuck his hands inside them.

"Where is it?" he whispered, sticking one of my shoes right into his face and peering into it.

"I still liked it," I said, trying to encourage him.

He dropped my shoes by my feet and walked away. Before I could ask him to stay, he'd gone. I suddenly became so alone and wished for his return. Moments after feeling sorry for myself, he ran back in with two cartons of juice in his hands.

"I got juice," he said, throwing one towards me.

I flapped at it and pushed it away from me. I'm terrible at catching things, even now at eighteen years old. He giggled at me, scooped it back up, and placed it back into my hands and slumped beside me on the sofa. I unhooked the straw from the back and pierced the foiling, then sipped away at the black currant juice. I looked over at him; he was observing me with delight.

"What are you looking at?" I asked, shuffling myself away from him.

He smiled. "You're very pretty."

Such a statement *may* have startled me and I *may* have spat out the juice in my mouth over him. I tried to raise my hand and stop it, but my reactions were far too slow. He saw what was coming and closed his eyes to prevent the juice from entering them. There was a brief silence between us where I assumed I was in the worst possible trouble, ever. I watched in despair as the juice dribbled down his face. He laughed and wiped his eyes. "Thanks."

"I'm so, so sorry, I didn't mean to do it!" I shouted.

Ethan stood and shook himself. "Oh no, my tie!"

He grabbed it and attempted to wipe away the juice sprayed across it, but it smeared, making it worse. "Ah, this was Mum's tie."

He ran off into the kitchen, stood on the stool in front of the sink and rinsed water over his tie, scrubbing at it furiously.

I rushed behind him. "I'm sure she'll have another one." My pathetic attempt at reassuring him. I was a kid, so I wasn't superb at many social matters yet.

"This was her only one. Don't worry, August, my dad will clean it later."

I watched the purple-coloured water flow down the drain, and guilt engulfed my emotions. "Is your mum here? I'll go apologise now and say it was my fault." I asked, gripping his arm.

He looked at me from atop his stool and smiled. "She died not long after my birth."

I tucked my hair behind my ears and looked to the floor. I've always done this when I'm nervous or embarrassed. Or in this case, both.

"I'm sorry," I said to the floor.

"Oh it's ok, I sometimes just wish I could have met her. I'm sure she was a nice lady."

Ethan's dad then came into the kitchen. "Hey bud, what happened to you?" he asked.

My eyes bulged up at Ethan. I needed to avoid getting into trouble straightaway.

"Oh, the juice pouch had a leak in it and when I squeezed it, it sprayed onto me," Ethan replied.

At the time I thought he'd saved my life. His dad's face dropped as he saw the tie. It would've had significance to him too since it was his wife's. "I'll see if I can get that cleaned up later, kiddo." He ruffled Ethan's hair. "Hey! Hop off your stool and have a photo with your friend here. September, right?" Ethan's dad's mood suddenly changed, pulling a camera out from his back pocket.

"August," I corrected moodily.

"I'm winding you up, August, stop being so grumpy!"

I smirked through my sulk. Ethan hopped off his stool and put his arm over my shoulder as we posed for the photo.

We've been best friends ever since that day, and we still have a photo taken together every birthday, and Christmas as well. It's our little tradition. I gave Ethan my old school tie to replace his white one. It was a maroon and dark navy diagonally striped tie, and then I made my mum take me shopping to buy him another white one. I arrived at the party without a present, so it was the right thing to do. We didn't find a white one, so we bought him a plain black one instead. His dad managed to get the stains out anyway. Every birthday and Christmas since, I have bought him a tie. It started off as a joke, but then it became a genuine thing.

Choosing a tie for his nineteenth birthday I found difficult. After long searches online, I decided upon a plain black tie with his initials stitched into it in white. He appreciated it more than I expected. This morning, when he knocked on my door to walk me to college, he wasn't wearing a tie, as he knew he would receive one, since he'd received a tie on his birthday every year for the last twelve years. I tied it for him and patted his chest once I'd finished.

"Very smart," I said and hugged him, wishing him happy birthday.

You'd think for his birthday we'd organise a huge gathering and have a crazy party with our large group of friends. But we have no friends. One other friend to be exact, Max Parker, or Maximus; it depends on how much he likes you. Max was the only one we'd allow in our circle of friendship. We run a tight shift. Max and I insisted we take Ethan to a bar to celebrate his birthday. Drinking isn't something we look forward to. We don't go out often so we thought it would be fun. Our idea of a night out—or in—is to order pizza and sit inside watching a movie, or Ethan will show off one of his new magic tricks. Yes, twelve years on, he is still performing magic. He's exceptional at it now. He's made the impossible appear possible.

So, Ethan, Max, and I found this new bar not too far away from our homes, and we sat and drank. Rather responsibly, too. It was a casual evening, but things would soon get out of hand.

"Shall I get us another round?" Max asked, already standing to make his way to the bar. We were all on the verge of entering the quite drunken state, and I think Ethan and I both recognised this.

"I think it's time to go home now, bud," Ethan said, glancing over at me in search of support with his comment.

I nodded. "I think it's time to go, too, Max."

Max wafted his hands at us. "Fine, let me go to the loo first."

"Have you enjoyed your evening?" I asked Ethan, resting my head on his shoulder.

"I have indeed," Ethan replied, sipping down the last of his drink.

We sat there in silence for a minute or two before I saw Max return out of the corner of my eye. He was holding a tray full of shots like your parents would hold a birthday cake. He sang "happy birthday" as he placed the tray down in front of us. He had the silliest grin on his face and raised his eyebrows to show how pleased he was with himself. Ethan and I sighed in unison. The tray was full with shots, and I mean full.

"Jesus, how many did you buy, Max?" Ethan asked, analysing the tray.

"Well, I made a deal with the barman and got six shots for ten pound, so I got us six each!"

He passed Ethan and me a small shot of red liquid.

"Bottoms up," Max said, wafting his brown-black hair off his forehead and tilting back his head, downing the shot.

Ethan and I paused before clinking glasses and downing ours. The next thing I knew, Ethan was carrying me in his arms. I must have passed out, too drunk to show embarrassment, and then I was sick. Ethan isn't my best friend, he's more of a...guardian angel. He's always there to guide me and look over me, or catch me when I fall. In this case, carry me home because I was too drunk to do so myself.

I woke up the next morning lying on Ethan's bare chest in his bed. I jumped up at once, tripping and falling out of bed, dragging the bed quilt with me. It wasn't the smartest move. I'll admit my head felt as if it was going to explode. I gripped my forehead as a blinding pain shot through it. My head spun while I stared at the ceiling.

"Twelve years and we finally slept together!" Ethan said, rising upright after being awoken by my clumsiness.

"No!" I shouted at him in despair. "We didn't!"

He wafted his arms at me. "No, you moron, we didn't. You kept saying you were cold, so I stayed with you. You should see your face right now!" Ethan replied, bursting into laughter.

I threw a pillow at him and returned to clutching my head.

APRIL 26TH

Just before midday, I dragged myself out of bed, forcing myself to do something productive with my Saturday.

"What are you two doing?" I asked as I entered the living room to find Ethan and my adorable little sister, Madeline, sitting on the floor with a couple of arts and craft boxes out.

"We're making friendship bracelets," Madeline replied, adding a couple of beads to the tiny tube in her tiny hands.

"Aw, how cute," I replied, crouching beside her and brushing her beautifully long ginger hair aside to kiss her freckled cheek.

"Good morning, dear," Ethan said, pushing his cheek in my direction.

I squinted at him for a moment. "Fine, you can have one as well, morning." I crouched over and kissed his cheek.

He was still wearing the new tie I had bought him for his birthday. He always has a couple of weeks after his birthday where he doesn't take off his new tie.

"So are you making me one?" I asked, feeling left out.

"If you weren't nocturnal, maybe you could have made one with us," Ethan replied, nudging me with his elbow.

"I'm one step ahead of you; I've nearly finished yours now, August," he added, awkwardly flapping with a bracelet in his hands.

"Need a hand there?" I asked sarcastically.

He looked me dead in the eye. "I got it."

I noticed Mum and Dad weren't around and since it was a Saturday they shouldn't be working. "Where are Mum and Dad?"

Madeline tied the friendship bracelet together with her teeth. "They asked Ethan to babysit while they went shopping or something."

I frowned. "Well, why didn't they ask me? I can babysit you. I always do."

Her cute eyes flicked up and glanced over at Ethan. "He's not here to babysit me."

I rolled my eyes at them. "How long have you been waiting to say that?"

She grinned. "Like an hour."

She giggled, then Ethan laughed. I sulked at them both.

"I get yours, he gets mine, and you get his. See?" She slid the bracelet along her wrist and raised it to my face. It was miles too big for her, but I was sure that wouldn't bother her. *She'll grow into it* as my dad would say. The well-arranged multicoloured bracelet was spectacular. She twizzled it around to show me the side that had AUGUST spelt out. A different-coloured plastic bead separated each letter. Ethan lifted his wrist to show me his. It was white and black, spelling out MADDIE. Only Ethan is allowed to call Madeline Maddie. She demanded everyone else call her Madeline.

"Finished!" Ethan shouted, holding the bracelet in front of me.

Mine was pink, hot pink. It fit perfectly, obviously spelling out ETHAN. It's sweet now that we have our own friendship bracelets.

MAY 1st

"**G**ood morning, dear," Ethan said as I opened the front door to him. We always met before college, mainly beside the tree outside college, or Ethan often popped by my house and walked me there. He was wearing one of his tartan ties today. He has a few now. They make him look quite smart. I bought him this one for our sixth Christmas together.

"What do you want?" I sarcastically replied.

"I'm here to walk my delightful best friend to college."

Madeline came rushing to the door, pushing past me and cutely wrapping her arms around his waist.

"Hey, you," he said, patting her head.

"Are you still wearing your bracelet?" she asked, releasing her grasp from around him.

He dangled his wrist in front of her. "Of course I am!" He knelt down and kissed her cheek. "You best go and get ready for school, you. Don't want you to be late, do we?"

She sighed, then returned inside and raced back upstairs. I adored how well Ethan and Madeline got along. He had been so nervous when he first met her. She was such a tiny, delicate baby. He's loved her endlessly since that moment.

My mum then came to the door. "Hello, Ethan, how are

you? Have you two admitted you're both perfect for each other yet?"

"I'm well, Mrs. Bishop, I trust you're well, too. As for August, she's too...boring for me, like a cat. I'm more of a dog person," Ethan replied with a smug look upon his face.

"Well, this chat is fabulous, guys. I do wish we could continue it, but we must dash," I announced.

"Let me grab my bag and we can go," I said to Ethan, who nodded in acknowledgment.

My mum grabbed my wrist before I rushed downstairs. "Stop being boring," she said, raising her eyebrows at me.

I rolled my eyes at her and laughed. She didn't mean it because she thought I was boring; she said it because she wants us to be a couple.

MAY 16TH

Since it's the weekend, Ethan asked if I wanted to stay at his house since his dad is hardly around. He's occupied by travelling constantly to gamble. Apparently he's been doing well lately, but drinking has now become a big problem in his life since the end of last year. Ethan claims he said it helps him make risky decisions he wouldn't when sober. I'm not sure why he's drunk when he's home then, if that's the case. Ethan's dad is only home once every two or three weeks. The image I am painting of Ethan's dad isn't pleasant, I know. It wasn't always like this. It's only been over the past year or so that he's become a proper gambling addict. He's gambled for a long time, but not like this. I'm not sure what caused him to become this way; maybe he doesn't even know. All that concerns me is that Ethan is ok. As long as he's ok, then I'm ok.

Ethan ordered pizza, and it was delicious. I only eat plain pizza. Ethan's favourite is pepperoni. Since I hated the smell of pepperoni he decided to join me in eating the plain pizza. We sat and watched an episode of Patrick Miller's chat show. I live for his show. It is my dream to appear on it. He always interviews the coolest people and he has a great sense of humour! I love how Patrick is always smiling, too.

"Do you want something else?" Ethan asked, passing me the last slice.

"No, thank you," I replied, nurturing my stomach and flopping out along the sofa. I shouldn't have accepted the last slice of pizza.

MAY 22ND

Ethan, Max, and I ate outside at lunch. The sun was shining so we ventured out to make the most of the rare warmth. The only decent empty seating area was the rickety old wooden bench near the tree I meet Ethan at each morning if he doesn't meet me at my house. As we sat down, Ethan pulled an apple from his rucksack. He shut his eyes and looked up towards the sun, allowing it to shine upon his face. Today he was wearing his hilarious dog tie. A springer spaniel tie if we're being exact, which I bought him for his fourteenth birthday. His tie has a black background and at the bottom is a cartoon sketch of a dog sitting on grass outside its kennel, smiling at you.

"So last night I came up with a simple, yet clever new trick to show you, my dear," Ethan said, holding the apple up in front of me.

"Oh, I see. What happens in this one, may I ask?"

I snatched the apple off him, biting into its succulent core, wildly chewing it directly in front of him and cheekily grinning afterwards.

"Well...one will require the apple back first to perform one's trick."

I rolled my eyes at him and passed him the apple while maintaining a sarcastic look. He frowned at me before holding up the apple. Showing the side that had the bite mark, as if I'd never seen it before. Then he casually launched it a few feet into the air, reclaiming it in his hands as it fell. He paused before spinning it around, to reveal the bite mark had disappeared.

"Not your best work, but, I shall admit, I am impressed. Am I going to be shown how this one is done?" I asked out of repetitiveness. The secrets to his tricks were kept a secret, as they should be really.

Ethan squinted at me for a second. "Ah all right, I can part with the secret of this one, since it's so simple." He took a second to gather his explanation. "It helps if you have two identical apples, good sleight of hand, and voilà, the apple is replaced."

I remained puzzled. "So what happened to the other apple?"

He took a bite out of the apple in his hand. "Check your lunch container, my dear. Then all shall become clear."

I looked at my lunch container anxiously. I lifted the lid with one eye open, squinting with the other. And there it was. The apple I had bitten. I looked back at Ethan, smiling in bewilderment. "Well played, Mr. Knight. Well performed, might I add? You set me up. You knew I'd ask for it to be explained as I always do."

Ethan tilted his head in acknowledgment.

When I got home, I thought the trick over, while watching TV with Madeline and plaiting her hair. I realised that the trick was actually very clever. Simple, but clever. How he got the apple into my container I'll never know.

MAY 23RD

Imet Ethan outside college by our tree this morning. He stood with his back against the trunk as I approached.

"Good morning, dear," he said as he gave me a firm hug.

"Good morning to you, too," I replied.

Today, he wore his elephant tie. A white tie covered in a pattern of tiny miniature grey elephants. I bought it for our eleventh Christmas together. It surprises me how well I remember each one I buy him. This tie is ranked in his top ten favourites. It may not sound like a big deal; however, if you knew Ethan and his tie collection, you'd understand it's a big deal. We'd not taken five paces into college before calls of "Breakfast" from Verity came our way. Verity is a girl from college who has a massive crush on Ethan. She calls Ethan Breakfast because he's so delicious, she doesn't need anything else to eat in the morning. Embarrassing, right? After a while we had gotten used to it. Most of her friends call Ethan Breakfast, too. As he walked me to first period, which he insists on doing, they walked by checking him out from head to toe with no level of discretion. It doesn't seem to bother him.

As much as I love performing arts, I lacked the energy to take part with any enthusiasm today. I wanted to go home, return to my bed, and sleep. It's very rare for me to say otherwise. Ethan and I fist bumped as we arrived outside my PA class.

"Catch ya later, dude," I said before entering.

I'd just placed my bag on the back of my seat when a junior student walked in, explaining that Ms. Andrews, my performing arts teacher, was off sick and our replacement teacher would be along soon. This news saved me. I'd never been happier. Not about Ms. Andrews being unwell. Although now I had two periods of doing whatever I pleased, which I didn't waste: I got myself nestled in the corner with my earphones in and read my Hallway magazine I had stolen from Madeline earlier. Eleanor Walden— the main subject printed amongst hundreds of articles—the actress, taking the world by storm. Without question the most beautiful woman the lord has ever created. There's another section about Natasha Thompson, the stunning model, too. But I paid little attention to her since I'm more into actors and actresses. Back to Eleanor Walden...words don't describe how much I envy her, the perfect complexion, figure, career. She's a goddess. Her beautiful brown hair and eyes entice me. She's everything I aspire to be. The interview inside included her controversial on-and-off relationship with former co-star Cole Palmer. I didn't envy her relationship. Cole often disrespected her and cheated on her many times. I don't know Eleanor personally, but I know for sure she deserves to be treated with more respect than Cole showed her. I hope she finds her happiness one day; she seems like a nice girl.

Ethan and Max waited for my exit as I stepped out.

"Hey, losers," I said as I walked over to them.

"Ethan and I nearly burnt off our eyebrows in science. I thought it'd be a good idea to spray deodorant into this chemical thingy and it didn't react well," Max replied.

I giggled at their childishness and shook my head.

"*This chemical thingy* will not get you a good grade in your exam, Maximus," Ethan hinted.

He opened the college doors for us to head outside. We reclaimed the unoccupied bench we sat on yesterday. We almost sat down before calls of "*Breakfast!* Hey, *Breakfast!*" came our way. Verity enthusiastically trotted over. Verity is actually quite pretty. She has blonde hair, which she always ties up in a messy bun, and she has a beautiful smile. She doesn't wear too much makeup, and she's always dressed well. If someone said she was the hottest girl at college, I'd probably agree with them. I sound like I have a crush on her, but I don't, I most certainly don't. I'm sure we'd talk to Verity more often, but we don't like her friends; they're too stuck up. So we have the odd chat in passing. I don't think I'd allow her into our group because, like I said, we run a tight shift.

"I've been looking for you," she said with a huge smile on her face.

Ethan said nothing, just acknowledged what she said and waited for her to continue. "I'm having a party tonight at my place. Would you like to come? It's sorta being planned last minute. August, Max, you're also welcome to come along if you wish." Her smile had now grown into a grin and it worried me how long she held it for. Ethan looked over at us with an unsure expression on his face.

"I guess it'd be cool to check it out, right, guys?" he asked, searching for our agreement with his decision.

Max and I smiled and nodded.

"I guess we'll see you tonight. What time?"

"That's great! 9:00 pm. Get there for 9:00 pm."

She extended her cheesy grin before leaving. Max leant towards Ethan with a sarcastic expression already poised. "Well, you handled that with ease, Breakfast." Max switched towards me. "Are we going to go?"

I shrugged. "I guess we'll need a sober designated driver." I pointed to Max as I spoke. "It'd be nice to go out for an evening. We can always leave if we're not enjoying it, or whatever." I waved my hands around to show I wasn't being serious but some seriousness remained.

"I hope I don't have to carry you home. Being sick on isn't how I intend to spend my evening again," Ethan replied.

I punched his arm and sarcastically laughed.

When college came to an end, I was exhausted. All these essays and rehearsals for our final assessment wear me out. We only have to prepare a couple of scenes from our favourite play, but we've practised and repeated them so many times. My partner for the assessment, Daniel, agreed to do *My Fair Lady*. It's our favourite play, and now we hate it. Daniel and I get along, but he doesn't like to chat; he just likes to rehearse and rehearse and rehearse. So I don't really know anything about him, apart from that he likes to rehearse. I can't wait until it's over. I hope my parents have booked a holiday to somewhere sunny. A holiday would be perfect right now. I sat at the base of mine and Ethan's meeting tree, and imagined I was sunbathing in Spain. I admired the sky while I had time to spare. I love how calm it is, and how it slowly passes by. It's just so peaceful. I wanted the shade from the tree to protect me from the blistering sunlight, but the branches didn't cover that far. So I had to hold my hands over my eyes to avoid giving myself a migraine from constant squinting. I loved listening to the leaves rustle in the wind. Other than listening to rainfall, rustling leaves is my favourite natural sound. A short time after my encounter with Mother Nature, Ethan walked over and graced me with his presence. He looked upon me, dropped the rucksack off his shoulder, and sat down beside me. I shifted over, creating some more space.

I lifted his arm, placing it over my shoulders so I could tuck into him and rest my head on him.

"Tough day, huh?" he asked.

"I'm *so* tired, I swear I could fall asleep for a decade," I murmured.

"Wow, you must be tired because that's a rather long time, especially if you're waiting for a delivery." He laughed at his comment.

"You're such an idiot." I sniggered but was too tired to maintain it for more than a second or two.

"You don't have to come later if you don't want to. Max and I are big boys now. We can take care of ourselves, believe it or not."

"No, no. I need a short nap when I get home. Then I'll be fine." I smiled up at him. Our eyes met. His brown eyes lit up in the sunlight as I lazily stared into them. Ethan lifted his left hand and tucked my hair behind my ear before bringing his hand down to the edge of my chin, squeezing my cheeks together.

"So adorable," he blubbered.

I innocently rolled my eyes at him as my face remained in his hands.

I don't want to imply I'm making an effort for Verity's party. Although I don't want to imply that I'm not making an effort for Verity's party. Does that make sense?

I watched an episode of Patrick Miller's show before drifting off to sleep. My outfit was laid out anyway, in case an emergency quick-change was required. I don't wear much makeup, so I didn't need to worry about that, only mascara and eyeliner. Foundation makes my face feel horrible and blotchy, and I like to stay as natural as possible also. That's how my mum raised me, so it remains that way.

A car horn blazed from outside, awakening me from my nap. I realised my nap had lasted a lot longer than I intended. I shot to my feet and threw my clothes off and snatched at the ones I laid out. I struggled to jump into my jeans; whoever was downstairs must have thought I was trying to jump through the floor. I eventually slotted into them and surrounded myself with a cloud of deodorants and perfumes. I put on my black leather jacket that had been lying in my wardrobe for a while. The car horn blazed from outside again. I hopped out of my room as I pulled on my boots and sprinted down the stairs, jumping the bottom two steps. I shouted good-bye to my parents, who sat at the dining table. I slammed the door shut, catching the edge of my jacket in it. The perfect way to start my evening.

"Sup, bro," Max said as I paced up to the car.

"Maximus," I replied, tilting my head in acknowledgment and hopping into the backseat of his truck. Ethan had taken passenger alongside Max. As I was fastening my seatbelt, Ethan turned around. "Miss Bishop."

"Mr. Knight," I replied with a thumbs-up.

Max is a surprisingly good driver. Sure, the truck jolted at the start of our journey; he was a little nervous. It's the first time we had been in his truck with him. It was nice. I wish I could afford a car. I've passed my test and everything, but I never manage to save enough money to buy one of my own. I drive my parents' cars when they're free, until I can afford one or have one bought for me. Ethan and Max were strangely quiet in the truck during the journey to Verity's. I'm sure they're both anxious about how the night was going to pan out. I gazed out of the window, focusing on the streetlights flowing by.

I must have dozed off for a few minutes, as Max banking the truck on the curb woke me. He probably hoped for a smoother arrival. Still, he stuck the handbrake on as if sharply banking the curb was his exact intentions. I reached for the door handle before Ethan beat me to it from the other side.

"Me lady," he said, offering his hand to help me out of the truck.

Ethan's outfit didn't really surprise me: black fitted jeans and a white shirt with the sleeves rolled up to the hinge of his elbow. His typical everyday outfit except for his trainers; they'd been replaced. He'd exchanged them for his smart black shoes with pointy ends, accompanied by the black tie with white spots that I bought him for his thirteenth birthday. I pulled the back, tightening and readjusting it for him. Max walked around to our side of the truck and huddled us in.

"Right, team, remember no man gets left behind or abandoned. I'm not drinking tonight, so please try to keep your behaviour to a mature level. I don't want to embarrass you guys tomorrow with stories of unsuitable things you did while you're nurturing your aggressive hangovers."

Ethan laughed and put his hand on his shoulder. "I doubt we'll even have that much tonight, my man. We're going to enjoy this on a sensible level."

Max nodded sarcastically. "Whatever you say, sergeant. Right, let's roll out, team."

I couldn't help but smile at them for being such dorks. They really spent too much time watching movies. I was genuinely expecting them to commando roll and crawl up to the front door while I walked behind them, questioning our friendship.

"Breakfast, hey, you made it! I assumed you weren't coming!" Verity said, throwing herself at Ethan, wrapping her arms around him as she opened the door. "There's booze in the kitchen and downstairs. Try not to make a mess please. It'd help me out when it comes to cleaning afterwards."

She already appeared rather drunk, swaying from side to side. It was only 9:17 p.m. Seventeen minutes behind schedule. They must have started early. She grabbed Ethan's wrist. "Come, let me show you around!"

Before Ethan could turn around to say anything, Verity had already dragged him away. Most of the attendees must've been downstairs in the basement. The bass from the music vibrated the floor below us. Almost shooting you off your feet. Max and I weren't really in the mood to have bleeding eardrums this evening. I wandered around Verity's living room while Max went into the kitchen to grab us a drink. It was surprising to see how welcoming Verity's home was. I mean, it's beautiful. Her parents have great taste. It was like stepping into page twenty of a furniture catalogue. Everything was perfectly positioned. I wanted to slip off my boots and scrunch my feet into the luxurious cream carpet. As I stood and stared down at the carpet, debating whether to take my boots off and scrunch my feet into it, something caught my eye. It was a framed photo booth picture of what I assumed to be Verity's parents. I walked over to it, wanting to examine it further. They appeared to be around the same age as me. It made me feel all warm and funny, to see them together at such a young age and still be together now. That rarely happens anymore; everyone's too busy cheating on one another. I hope they're still as happy now as they were in those photos.

Max reentered the room accompanied by two tall glasses of orange juice. "Don't worry, I checked the carton, it's not from concentrate." Max once gave us a big speech about how he hated concentrated orange juice and forbade Ethan and me to drink it. I haven't touched a single drop since.

"What are you looking at?" he asked, nodding towards the framed picture.

"I'm guessing it's Verity's parents. I thought it was kinda cute, they're so young." Max didn't seem to share the same emotion as me. "She's hot."

"I suppose so." I sighed. To be honest, Verity's mum was gorgeous. She and Verity could be twins. Her mum's hair is just wavier and darker.

"Shall we find Ethan?" I asked.

I was expecting him to have rejoined us by now. Max nodded.

Ethan's voice echoed throughout the room as we descended the staircase to the basement. "Pick a card, any card please." He'd been here no longer than fifteen minutes and he'd already started performing magic tricks. Max and I gathered around the crowd of fifteen or twenty people that made up the basement population. They had formed a circle around two sofas where Ethan was sitting across from Verity, holding out a fanned deck of cards towards her. She chose a card from the deck after peering amongst them for several seconds.

"Show everyone the card, but make sure I don't see it. Return the card to a different place in the deck," Ethan announced as he placed his hands over his eyes. She held the card up so everyone could see. It was the three of diamonds. She struggled to return the card back to the deck so used her other hand in support.

"Is August here?" he asked, standing up as he surveyed the room.

He eventually found me at the very back.

He pointed at me. "Come forward, please."

I crossed my arms, slowly making my way towards him.

"Be a dear and shuffle the cards for me, please," he whispered in my ear. Even after all these years I'd spent with Ethan, I always struggled to shuffle a deck of cards to a decent standard. Nevertheless, I unfolded my arms, snatched the cards off him, and poorly shuffled them before handing them back. He thanked me and returned to his seat on the sofa. Ethan grabbed Verity's hands, placing the deck between them, and placed his hands on top of hers.

"Your card has now vanished from the deck."

She stared at Ethan before she forced open her hands and searched through the deck for her card. It wasn't there, of course.

"How did you do that?" Her drunken state seemed to enhance the amount of disbelief. Before Ethan could reply with the corny line, *magic,* I interrupted. "Check your shoe, Verity." She stood without questioning my odd comment. Flicked off one of her little blue slip-on pumps, right foot first. The vanished card wasn't there. After discovering its emptiness, she quickly flicked the left pump off into her hands. A look of distress spread over her face. She reached into her pump, pulling out a card. It was the three of diamonds in all its glory. Describing Verity as excited would be an understatement.

"Oh my God, oh my God. How did you do that? That's *amazing*!"

She turned to her friends, handing them the card. They all snatched at it like it was a souvenir for them to keep. The circle gathered around went wild—clapping and cheering. Ethan bowed before offering his hand out to me. It made me blush, but I took a small curtsy.

"Thank you, everyone. I am humbled by your appreciation and applause," Ethan announced as if he'd just won a major movie award. Random shouts of "another" appeared from around the circle. In support Max and I joined them. Ethan held up his hands. "All right, all right. Will somebody pass me two beers from the fridge over there please? Bottled, not canned, otherwise nobody will see the trick." It seemed before he could finish his sentence somebody had sprinted across and brought him what he asked for. "Verity, will you inspect these for me please? Check they're normal?" He handed the two bottles to her; she lifted them up to the light, tilting her head and wincing at them.

"Yep, they seem good, Breakfast."

"So two normal bottles of beer, everyone. I will now freeze them both, using only my hands."

He held the bottles five or six inches apart. He paused for a second before jolting the bottom of each bottle against each other rather hard. It made me jump because I expected them to smash. Everyone stared at them for a few moments before Ethan held them up for all to see. The circle remained silent as they waited to find out if it had worked or not. You could see something rising inside each bottle. Ethan handed Verity a bottle. "What! It's frozen! What, how?" Her excitement exploded. "It's frozen! That's *incredible!*" Ethan passed the other bottle around the crowd. When it got to Max and me, we couldn't believe our eyes. It'd frozen solid. He couldn't have switched them or have hidden them up his sleeve. It would take time for me to figure this one out, not that I'd ever figured any out.

The circle dispersed, and the music turned up again. Ethan sat down on the sofa to compose himself, running his hands through his hair. Max and I shuffled through everyone to get over and check up on him.

"You ok, buddy?" Max wrapped his arm around him as we slumped onto the sofa.

"Yeah, Verity and I have been taking shots, not the best idea after what happened last time!"

Ethan wrapped his arm around me. "August, come do shots with me, it's fun." He got to his feet and tried to pull me up to join him.

"I'm fine with my orange juice, Ethan, you go have fun."

I figured Max would need a hand helping Ethan to the

truck. It wouldn't help if Max had to carry me out, too. Ethan flapped his arms at me and wandered over to Verity, who had occupied the table where all the shots were lined up. As he downed a shot, he grimaced. It was amusing to watch; Max and I thought so anyway.

"Another orange juice?" Max grabbed my empty glass.

"Let's go mad," I replied.

He smiled and headed back to the basement stairs. As he passed Ethan, Verity, and her friends in their drunken state, they pulled Max in for a group hug. I didn't have time to see much else as Mark joined me on the sofa. He's in my literature class. I'd say he's five foot ten or eleven. He has short light brown hair and green eyes. We never talk at college. I don't have an explanation as for why. I do know that he played rugby at a high level when he was younger before he suffered a bad injury.

"Hey, August, enjoying the party?"

"Yes I am, thank you."

"Your boyfriend is having fun." He focused his vision on Ethan.

"Oh, he's not my boyfriend, we've been best friends for a long time."

He smiled. "Really? That's good."

Even in the darkness, it wasn't hard to notice how green his eyes were. You lost yourself in them. But I wanted to know what he meant by *that's good*.

I frowned at him. "How so?"

I glanced over at Ethan again. Verity and he were giggling like a pair of kids. Mark's eyes flicked back between Ethan and me again.

"Well, if I found out you and Ethan weren't together. I was going to ask if maybe, possibly, you'd like to go out with me sometime, get something to eat?" He was embarrassed and shy, but it was kinda cute.

"Yeah, that would be nice." I was a little bashful myself. "I'm free tomorrow, if that's any good, or is it too soon seeing as you asked me ten seconds ago?"

"No, no. Tomorrow would be great. How about the restaurant down from college?"

I nodded. "Yeah, would 3:30 be good for you?"

I was worried I was being too forward and that I might frighten him off.

Max returned, coughing. "Sorry, am I interrupting?"

"No, no. We were just chatting." Mark stood and allowed Max to reclaim his seat. "I'll see you tomorrow, August. 3:30."

"What did he want?" Max asked, passing me my glass.

"We have a date tomorrow," I replied in embarrassment. Max stared at me.

"What are you looking at?" I asked. I'm not sure whether he implied Mark was out of my league, or vice versa.

"Nothing. I always presumed if you would ever date anyone, it would be, you know...Ethan."

I looked down at the floor. In the back of my mind maybe I'd strangely always thought that, too. I opened my mouth to reply but before any words escaped, Max stood. He was looking over at Ethan, who had lain on the floor. He'd survived about an hour before his flop. Max walked over to Ethan and knelt down beside him, followed by me. We lifted him upright.

"How you doing, Ethan?" Max asked.

"I'm great, the room started spinning, so I thought I'd lie down. I'm such a lightweight!"

Ethan smiled up at me and shut his eyes. We struggled to get him to his feet and carried him to the sofa. We didn't place him on the sofa, more of a...catapult. I wasn't expecting Ethan to be so heavy; saying that, I'm not exactly the strongest. He exhaled as he slumped on the sofa.

"Guys, I don't know about you, but I can't drive home." Max and I couldn't help but laugh as we sat on either side of him. Ethan then thought it would be more comfortable to sprawl himself across our legs. "I love you guys, you guys are the best." He kept repeating it over and over. Until it faded into a murmur and then he fell asleep. Verity occupied the sofa opposite us; her makeup had stained the pillows of the cream sofa, a terrible choice of colour evidentially. Her emerald eye shadow however, remained on point. On the downside, she had a bit of drool running out of the corner of her mouth.

It's 10:50 p.m, we've been here around an hour and thirty-five minutes, and it's already time to leave. Nevertheless, I had a wonderful time, even after spending most of the night babysitting. Max and I decided it was time to take Ethan home. We woke him up and helped him to his feet. He managed to stand on his own, so it would only be bundling up the stairs instead of horrendous bundling up the stairs. I said good-bye to Verity's friends while Max helped Ethan upstairs. I asked them to tell Verity we had a good time, but had to leave to take Ethan home. "Bye, Breakfast!" they all shouted over my shoulder as Max and Ethan stumbled up the stairs. I found it hard to grasp how many admirers Ethan had. They seemed to increase by the day. Max and Ethan had made it to the top of the staircase as I left Verity's friends. I think Ethan tried to make conversation, but all that came out was moans and groans, and the occasional random giggle. Max opened the back door to the truck while I held Ethan. I could barely hold myself when I'm sober, never mind trying to help a drunk Ethan remain standing. We stuck him in the backseat, promoting me to front passenger. I didn't fancy sitting in the back with Ethan in case he threw up, which would have also made me throw up. Max decided Ethan should stay at his house. It wouldn't be fair to dump him at home on his own. The truck was silent throughout the first couple of minutes of our journey back home. I kept looking back and checking if the sleeping Ethan was ok. "August?" Max said, holding the steering wheel with one arm as if he was in a rap video.

"Yes?" I replied.

"What are your plans for when this is all over?"

"You mean college or tonight?" I said with a puzzled face.

He nodded, keeping his focus on the road. I hate when people do that. You ask them a question with an optional answer and they reply with *yes*. How on Earth am I supposed to figure out what you meant? I'm not telepathic.

"Well I suppose, if we don't go to university or whatever, you will pursue your journalism career, and I'll pursue my big break in my acting career. If that doesn't work out, I'd like to open a florist. As for tonight I'm going straight to sleep when I get home."

He had a concerned look upon his face as he stared into the rearview mirror. "What do you think he'll do?"

I turned around to check on Ethan. "I'm sure he'll pursue his magic career. He mentioned that he would like to open up his own bar when he retired. He may have to fetch it forward a decade or two if it doesn't work out."

Ethan must've heard our discussion coming from the front since a new lease on life came about him. "Hey, guys, how are we, I love you, you know that right? Can we get pizza? I want a pizza."

I turned around to him and put my hand on his knee and smiled. He tried to force one in return, but struggled. "Do you want me to tell you how I did the apple trick, August?" He closed his eyes and put his head back.

My response was like lightning. "You already did."

"Remember when I said you need two identical apples to perform the trick? Well, you need three...and a little varnish. The first apple I took a bite out of, varnished it so it wouldn't go off. It was in your lunch container before you even got to first period. The second you took a bite out of. The third was a simple whole unbitten apple to replace the second. Clever, huh?"

It did amaze me. First, he explained it drunk. Second, he pulled the trick off without me noticing. Ethan slipped back off into sleep. We then pulled up at a set of red lights. Max stuck on the handbrake. "I'm so tired, I cannot wait to climb in to bed." His tiredness must've been contagious because I yawned straight after. The traffic lights switched to green. Max removed the handbrake and pressed the accelerator. At that moment, a huge bright light on my side of the truck came out of nowhere, blinding us. The light got closer, and closer, and closer until something slammed straight into us. There was a deafening sound of metal scraping on metal, the truck jolted, I couldn't tell if we had flipped over or spun. There wasn't time to say anything or protect myself. I had my eyes closed and kept them closed, hoping we'd be ok. It lasted no longer than a few seconds, but it felt like an eternity. Everything seemed to pass by in slow motion; the thudding beat of my heart echoed throughout my body as I was tugged and thrown in all directions. My life flashed before my eyes: I saw Madeline and Ethan making their friendship bracelets again. I saw my parents cuddling on the sofa while I plaited Madeline's hair in front of the television. I saw myself spitting the black currant juice all over Ethan at his seventh birthday party. Then everything came to a halt. I tried to compose myself and gather my bearings. My vision blurred, my head shaken and numb. I got a tiny glimpse of Max turning around and saying, "Oh my God, is everyone ok?" Then everything went black.

MAY 24ᵀᴴ

My ears woke up before my eyes. There was a strange beeping noise I couldn't comprehend. My eyes took a few forced blinks to respond. I tried to sit up, but a huge stinging pain shot through my head. I placed my hand on it, hoping the pain would decrease. Then I realised I was lying in a hospital bed. I had no idea how I got here. I was just happy to be alive. I couldn't see any other patients as I was hidden behind a large white curtain. The unmistakable smell of hand sanitiser filled my nostrils. My arm had a small plastic tube running from it into a little clear bag, held up by a thin metal rod. A middle-aged black woman wearing a long white coat approached my bed after appearing from behind a curtain.

"Hi, August. Good to see you coming around. How are you?"

My mouth felt so dry I could barely speak. I glanced to my side to see a bottle of water on the shelf. She must have noticed me looking at it as she grabbed it and poured me some into a small cup. Never had water tasted so good.

"My name's Angela. I'm a doctor here at Samuel's Hospital. You were involved in a car crash last night. You hit your head pretty hard. You suffered a mild concussion and a little cut to your head, which, luckily for you, didn't need stitches. We kept you sedated until the morning to be on the safe side of things. How do you feel, dear?"

It's a lot to take in after waking up from a car crash, but as soon as she said *dear* I immediately thought of Ethan.

"I'm fine, my head hurts. How are my friends? Are they ok? Where are they? Are they dead?"

I needed to know they're ok. I began to panic, and breathing became a struggle. Angela crouched alongside my bed. "Relax, deep breaths in and out. Do you remember what happened last night?" I nodded as I followed her instructions. She held my hand as I maintained my breathing. "One of your friends is in the waiting room with your parents. Do you want me to send them in?" I nodded and wiped my eyes. She gave me a comforting smile before disappearing behind the curtain. My parents worried if I'm a minute late home, especially my mum. I remember when I was younger I had an ear infection. One night they had to take me to the kids' hospital because the pain had become unbearable. I was only a kid so I may have overemphasised it a little. My mum was crying because I was crying. After a little medicine I was as good as new. But I'll never forget how worried my mum was. It was like the world was ending…over an ear infection. I can't even begin to imagine what my parents were currently going through. Mum wouldn't have eaten, drank, or slept since hearing the news. I just wanted them to hug me, and tell me everything would be ok.

Mum appeared from behind the curtain first; she'd been crying.

"Oh August, we've been so worried, are you ok, my baby?"

She crouched beside my bed and stroked my head. Her eyes filled with tears. I hated to see my mum cry. There's nothing worse, it's the most stomach-churning feeling in the world.

"I'm fine. My head hurts a little, but it's nothing to worry about."

Dad and Max then appeared from behind the curtain. I smiled at them and waited for Ethan to follow. Then I remembered Angela saying, *one of your friends is in the waiting room with your parents.* It kept repeating in my head over and over—one, one, one, one, one, one, one. I started to cry. My dad crouched alongside my mum and grabbed my hand. "We're here, August, don't worry."

I wiped my eyes. "Where's Ethan? Is he ok? Please tell me he's ok."

I changed my focus to Max, who stood at the end of my bed. He had a small black brace on his right wrist and a plaster above his right eyebrow. He rubbed his nose before sticking his head out of the curtain. I assumed he called Ethan; he must've held back, waiting to see how I was. I calmed down, wiped my eyes again, and sniffled my nose. I smiled over at my teary-eyed parents.

"Is Madeline ok?" I asked.

"She's fine. She stayed over at her friend's last night. When we got the call we thought she would be better staying there instead of sitting in the hospital. It's not always the nicest place for little girls. We didn't want her to get upset."

I glanced over at Max. "Are you ok, Max?"

He kept his eyes to the floor. "I'm good, August."

Angela then returned from behind the curtain. When she reappeared, my tears continued. "Where's Ethan? Is he dead? Please tell me he's ok." I couldn't catch my breath. I could slowly feel my world around me closing in on me.

"No, no," Mum hushed. She looked over at Angela for help. She held a clipboard by her side with Ethan's name written at the top of it. "Ethan, is still sedated—don't worry he'll be fine. He'd been hit pretty hard. A fractured radius and ulna in his lower left arm and a fractured collarbone.

These fractures thankfully weren't compound fractures, meaning the bone didn't penetrate the skin. And a few bruised ribs, but that will be the least of his worries." She paused for a second, flicking onto the next page of her clipboard. "As Mr. Knight sat in the front passenger seat, his side of the vehicle took the full force of the impact."

Angela's voice trailed off. My sight immediately switched to Max as Angela paused to write something on her report. His eyes didn't shift from the floor. I remember little about the crash. But if there's one thing I can remember, it's that Ethan wasn't sitting in the passenger seat next to Max. He was most definitely in the back because I put him there. Didn't I? What am I saying, of course I did. *What is going on*?

"If the impact would have been stronger, it could have possibly killed him. Thankfully, the reinforced sides of the truck absorbed most of the impact. August, you'll feel as good as new in the next two to three hours. Your parents can sign you out then. If you want to see Ethan before you go, I'm around until five. I'd be more than willing to take you to visit him."

I smiled, which she did in return. My parents thanked her for taking care of me, and once again, Angela vanished behind the curtain. Everyone gave sighs of relief, but there was only one thing on my mind.

"Can I have a minute alone with Max, please?"

"Of course," my dad said. "Victoria, let's go to the café we saw earlier. You need a coffee and something to eat, my love." He put his hand on Mum's shoulder. They both looked so tired and run down. Mum put my hand on her cheek and kissed it. Dad leaned over and kissed my forehead. Max walked over and sat on the edge of my bed as they left.

"Hey, rough night huh?"

I wasn't in the mood for laughing about our situation at the moment.

"What happened?" I asked. I needed to get straight to the point.

"Well, two idiotic guys had broken into the local jeweller's. They'd stolen over four hundred thousand pounds worth of money, diamonds, and jewellery. The police were supposed to be right behind their 4x4. Although I don't recall seeing any flashing lights. Anyway, they took a shortcut through the car park of a grocery store. Hit a curb and lost control—which led to them smashing into us. But on the bright side, we stopped a burglary last night."

We sat silently for a second while I processed everything he said. Only one thing replayed in my mind. The one thing I needed to speak to Max about.

"Max." I couldn't have said his name any more seriously.

"Please tell me you remember that I sat in the passenger seat, not Ethan."

It took a moment for him to open his mouth. "I know, August, I know. I can't get my head around it. I don't know how he did it. No one here will believe us when we tell them. What can I say? He loves you, August. I hope you understand that. He didn't want you to be in the condition he is in now, and that's why he did it, I have no doubt."

My mind went blank. Mainly because 1) switching seats in a matter of nanoseconds is impossible. 2) He was severely drunk and shouldn't have been capable of completing the so-called impossible.

"Are you ok?" I decided to change the subject. Overthinking the current situation wouldn't help.

"Yeah, I'm fine. Only a sprained wrist, nothing serious. I asked the hospital for a brace to wear for a week in case I catch my wrist on anything."

My head became heavy to hold as I listened to Max. I felt so weak. I tucked my fist under my chin to keep my head upright.

"I hope he's ok," I murmured.

"Me too," Max replied. "Me too."

My parents signed me out at 2;15 p.m. after being awake for around four hours. Max and I searched for Dr. Angela on the ward. The whole place smelt of cleanliness and rubber gloves. Sanitation filled the air. We found Angela standing at one of the reception desks filling out paperwork.

"Hi, guys. How are you both?" she asked.

"We'll be better once we've seen him. To settle our nerves," Max said.

"I understand. Follow me, I'll take you to him."

She leant over the desk, swapped her paperwork for a clipboard, and walked down the hospital corridor. Max and I shortly followed. Either side of the corridor had a few rooms containing five or six patients in each. We passed each room too quickly to take in any further detail. We walked by a further three or four more rooms before they became smaller with single patients occupying them. "What's the difference between the conditions of the patients in the large rooms compared to patients on their own in the smaller rooms?" I asked.

Angela stopped at the third or fourth room we came across, on our left. She opened the door to the room. "In today's case, nothing. These rooms are supposed to be used for patients with life-threatening conditions. All our other rooms are full, so these patients, including Ethan, have been given upgrades." I liked how she tried to give it a positive appeal. "After you," she said, holding the door open for us. Max and I both thanked her as we walked into Ethan's room. I heard his heart monitor beeping as I stepped inside. I didn't know how to react when I saw him. The first thing that caught my eye was the bright yellow cast on his arm. Other than waking to find himself in a hospital with multiple injuries, he wouldn't be too appreciative of the colour cast he'd been given. Yellow is his least favourite colour. White would've been the better choice. It broke my heart seeing him this way. I could see the end of his wound along his collarbone underneath his hospital clothing. His hair looked lifeless and dull, and his lips were almost blue. It seemed he had an endless amount of wires and tubes running in and out of him. I knelt down beside his bed, held his hand, and stroked it with my thumb. "Based upon my evaluation of his condition, Ethan can be signed out in the next ten to twelve days. We've put several metal pins into his collarbone, which are permanent. The cast can be taken off after around nine weeks. Everyone's bones heal at different rates, so it could be sooner or later. He'll be brought out of sedation tomorrow. We've tried calling Ethan's father many times, but we've been unable to get a hold of him. I'll excuse myself and leave you three alone. There's a button on the side of Ethan's bed if you need emergency assistance," Dr. Angela finished before she left Ethan, Max, and I to get reacquainted. The door closed, leaving a disturbing atmosphere of heavy breathing and beeping machines. I remained kneeling as Max took a seat in the old leather chair in the corner of the room.

"Is this the first time you've seen him?" I asked.

He nodded his head while biting at his thumbnail. I looked back at Ethan. My eyes welled up. I couldn't imagine the pain and discomfort he would wake up to. He really is my guardian angel. It should've been me lying there in his condition. He could have died switching places with me. I know it's not my fault, but I couldn't help an overwhelming feeling of guilt take over.

"How did you do it?" I whispered to him, stroking his hair.

He'll be thankful that he didn't have any severe cuts or bruises to his face. He wouldn't want his good looks to be ruined. A tear revealed itself from the corner of my eye when I glanced down, noticing Madeline's friendship bracelet on Ethan's wrist. I twiddled the letters so MADDIE rotated into position.

"Shall we come back tomorrow? He'll be awake then," Max said.

"Ok, sure, I need some sleep, I'm exhausted and I feel like crap," I replied.

Max smirked. "Come on, let's go find the doctor and tell her we'll be back tomorrow." I turned back to Ethan and kissed his forehead before leaving.

It felt so good to be back home. I'd never been so happy to see it again. I had just closed my bedroom door and slumped onto my bed, recalling everything that took place last night. As I tested my memory I remembered my arranged date with Mark. "*Crap*," I said aloud. It's not that I didn't want to go. After suffering a concussion from a car crash the night before, I wasn't in the right mind to go on a date. I checked my homemade clock that Ethan gave me: 3:05 p.m. I had twenty-five minutes to get to the restaurant.

I should explain this clock of mine. Ethan gave it to me for my thirteenth birthday. Ethan explained that my gift would be a month late because it's taking him longer than expected to prepare it. At first it confused me, but I went along with it. I was excited to see what he had gotten for me; the anticipation of having to wait for another month was killing me. So on September the sixteenth I popped round to Ethan's house to open it. When I unwrapped my gift to find a small, wooden clock, I wasn't sure how to react. Giving a thirteen-year-old a clock isn't the most thrilling of gifts.

"You don't like it?" Ethan asked, squinting.

"No, no I like it! Why a clock of all gifts?"

He smiled at me. "I wanted to give you a gift made by me, and I wanted it to mean something... you know, it'll last longer than perfume."

The clock was excellently crafted...not like one of those hideous ones you'd make at school. It was perfectly symmetrical, smooth, and well varnished. I'm no expert on clocks, but this was a damn good clock. I'd say it was a mahogany colour. Brown would be easier to use for its description, but brown is boring, and mahogany sounds so much cooler. It had a pearl white face, and was marked in black Roman numerals.

"Where's the key for the back?" I asked, examining the lock at the back of the clock.

"Oh, I dropped it somewhere. When I find it, I'll fetch it round to your place one day."

Some may think it's a dull gift, but I appreciated it, and it's been on my bedside table every day since. Like Ethan said, it means something and will last longer than perfume. So, returning to my situation with Mark. "Mum!" I shouted as I opened my bedroom door.

"August, what's wrong, sweetie, are you ok?" She sprinted upstairs within seconds of me calling.

"Mum, I'm fine. I need a lift to the restaurant. I can never remember what it's called. The one down the road. Will you take me please? I said I would meet someone there."

She panted as she turned the corner at the top of the stairs. "Sure, sweetie, you had me worried for a moment there. Are you sure you're ok to go?" she asked with a concerned frown.

I nodded. "Mum, I'm fine."

She examined me with a glare. "Ok, ok. So is this a date or are you meeting a friend?"

I rolled my eyes at her. "A guy named Mark from college asked me on a date last night. I didn't want to be rude."

She grinned. "I don't know why you and Ethan haven't admitted you're perfect for each other, but ok, sweetie, I'll wait for you downstairs."

MAY 25ᵀᴴ

As you can guess, my date was a complete success. I'm joking. It was a total, utter disaster. First, I turned up looking like a homeless person. Second, I had to explain why I looked like a homeless person. He was surprisingly understanding and reassuring. I don't think he even recognised me when I approached him, that's how bad I looked.

"Have a little something to eat. It sounds like you could do with some food. Then you can go home and get some rest," he said as he passed me a menu.

We both had a bowl of tomato soup each while we waited for our mains. Mark had ravioli, and I had a kid's lasagna since I wasn't too hungry. We didn't discuss much, just college life, and then we'd occasionally smile at one another. Mum was already waiting for me in the car as we stepped outside. I rolled my eyes in front of Mark, but he didn't see. Mark kissed my cheek and wished me well. He waved to Mum before walking away. She seemed to scowl at him in an evil way. I don't know why.

"Have you been outside waiting for me this whole time?" I asked as I opened the passenger door.

"Maybe. I assumed you'd probably say something embarrassing and need to abort, so I kept the car running outside just in case," Mum replied.

I stared at her for a few seconds, blank faced. "Wow, thanks, Mum. If you could say those kind, reassuring words at my wedding, I'd really appreciate it."

She took my comment seriously. "Just don't marry that guy, I don't like him," she said. Mark was still visible but he'd become a tiny dot along the path in the distance now.

"What's wrong with Mark?" I asked with glaring eyes.

"He's not hot enough."

I shook my head at her and laughed. But never mind. I've put it behind me. I doubt Mark will want to see me again.

Since Max's truck was going to take around three weeks to fix, my parents gave us a lift to the hospital. I needed to be there when Ethan woke up. I didn't want him to be alone and confused, without a familiar face around to explain everything.

I sat myself in the chair in the corner of the room. Max was getting snacks and drinks from the downstairs café with my parents. They thought it would be a tad overwhelming for Ethan to wake up to everyone gathered around his bed, so they stayed downstairs. I stared at Ethan for a while, watching his chest rise and fall.

"Good news, I found you a Hallway magazine downstairs. That's the girly gossip one, isn't it? And I got you a bottle of water," Max said as he entered Ethan's room.

"Thanks. Did they not have any tea?" I asked.

"Oh blast, I forgot." He quickly placed two bottles of water onto the small coffee table with the magazine and then rushed back out without another word. I reached over to the table grabbing the magazine. Another huge photo of Eleanor Walden printed on the cover. Inside was a special interview about her latest movie *Hard Luck,* which was being released in the next month or two. That familiar feeling of jealousy started to build up inside me. Until I dominate

Britain and then the globe, knocking her off her perch. My big break will come soon. I need it to. I have to fund my expensive taste somehow.

I read until the final paragraph of the interview and Max still hadn't returned. I didn't know what could be taking him so long. I folded up my magazine and dropped it onto the floor beside me. Then out of nowhere I heard, "So this is heaven." I glanced over at Ethan. His eyes were still shut but he had the tiniest smirk on his face. I couldn't help but grin; I knew exactly what he was doing. "Oh shut up! How long have you laid there waiting to say that?" I said, standing and pacing over to his bedside and knelt beside him.

"Not that long actually. About three minutes if we're being precise."

Even after all he's been through in the past seventy-two hours he still hadn't lost his sense of humour. "It's good to see you awake. I've missed you. How do you feel?" The question I least looked forward to asking him. His beautiful brown eyes opened. I've missed them.

"Oh I feel fantastic, dear. Can't feel a thing! Which is a complete lie. I feel dreadful."

I groaned and rested my head on his bed. He placed his hand on top of it, brushing his fingers through my hair, and laughed. My eyes welled up as I raised my head. He pushed my cheeks together and sulked childishly.

"Why did you do it, Ethan?" I mumbled through my compressed cheeks.

It was the only thing on my mind from the second I found out. Ethan wiped a tear that strolled down my cheek, dropped his hand, and looked away. He let out a sigh. "I..." he said before the door flung open. Max stepped inside with the happiest look on his face, holding two cups in his hands. *Perfect timing, Max,* I thought.

"How are we feeling, bud?" Max asked as he popped the

cups on the table and sat on the end of Ethan's bed, grasping his ankle.

"Better now that everyone is here, Maximus my man."

I had zoned out daydreaming once those two reunited their bromance. I thought over what Ethan had just said, *better now that everyone is here.* Everyone. We're everyone to Ethan. He'd lost everything. Everyone. Other than his dad, who's never around. Who doesn't even know Ethan is in hospital. Max and I were his only family. Madeline is pretty much his sister.

"Ethan, I'm gonna come visit you every day, ok?" I interrupted without noticing if the conversation had finished or not. He stopped mid-conversation with Max, rolled his head back towards me, and said, "Ok, August," and winked at me.

MAY 26ᵀᴴ

Madeline shouted for me this morning, saying there was a lady on the phone for me. I rushed over and grabbed the phone in case it was Dr. Angela calling me regarding Ethan. "Hello?" I said, expecting to hear the doctor's voice.

"Good morning, August. It's Ms. Andrews, your performing arts teacher."

I let out a huge sigh of relief and slumped against the fridge. "Hello?"

"Yes, sorry, hi, Miss. Are you feeling better?" I asked.

"Better? Oh yes I was off ill, I do apologise! Yes I'm much better! Your little sister is so adorable, she's very well spoken for a seven-year-old."

Madeline was sat at the kitchen table watching me on the phone. I stuck my tongue out at her to which she returned. At that moment she grabbed a kitchen chair and placed it beside the fridge, standing on top of it and opening the freezer at the top. Madeline is addicted to ice cream; it's her favourite thing in the entire world. Bubblegum is strangely her favourite flavour, but it always has to be Ron's ice cream; that's her favourite brand. It also contains the least sugar so she doesn't turn into a hyperactive lunatic. She eats so much of it that my parents have had to limit her to how much she can eat.

"She's a little angel, isn't she? So what can I do for you, Miss?" I asked as I stretched over and closed the freezer, trapping in Madeline's ice cream. She sulked at me and vanished into the living room.

"Well, if you could come to my office this morning instead of going to your first period, that would be marvellous. I've spoken to your teacher already so they know you will be running a bit late. I just have something to discuss with you if that's ok." I hope she didn't need to see me for a bad reason. That wouldn't be the best start to the day. I thought I was doing well in performing arts, very well in fact.

"Ok, I'll see you soon," I said, as if a million things weren't running through my mind.

I walked to college, alone, worrying about my best friend, and what horrible news waited for me in Ms. Andrews's office. Ms. Andrews is a no-questions-asked, smoking hot woman. I have no idea why she isn't married or even in a relationship. She is forty-four or forty-five, I can never remember. But she looks ten or fifteen years younger than her age. If I look even half as good as her at her age, I will be one very happy lady. My hand hovered over the handle to her office as I reassured myself outside. I took a deep breath and squeezed the handle but paused. I knocked, then twisted the handle to open the door.

"August!" Ms. Andrews said with delight. "Please take a seat," she added.

She returned to the paperwork she was reading as I shut the door behind me and sat. I watched her eyes flick along the final lines of the pages. My heartbeat began to thud. I really hope it wasn't bad news. Bad news was the last thing I needed.

"So, I have some good news for you, August."

I dropped my shoulders and grinned.

"You look surprised," she said with a frown.

"I was expecting bad news, that's all, Miss," I replied, fixing my posture.

"Oh no! I feel I should begin with a small lie I may have told. I wasn't ill Friday. I was having a meeting with a friend about a new job offer."

I felt like this was confidential information that I shouldn't be informed of. I didn't want her to leave the college; why was she leaving? She's my favourite teacher! "Ok," I said, waiting for more detail.

"You've heard of Stanley Tennant, haven't you?" she asked, interlocking her hands and twiddling her thumbs.

"Of course I have, you mean the director, right?" I raised my eyebrows in case I had made a colossal error.

She laughed. "Yes, him. Well, Stanley and I have been very good friends since we were, oh, fourteen, maybe fifteen years old... He's asked me to be the casting director on his new film because I was on a previous one of his over a decade ago before I went into teaching."

My eyes lit up when I heard such news. "I never knew that, Miss, I'm surprised you haven't told me before."

She wafted her hands. "I try to keep it a secret, you know, don't want people nagging me to get his autograph and things."

I acknowledged her with a sincere nod.

"Right, this is the important part. After our final assessment at the end of this week, my new job will be Stanley's casting director. It took him a long time to persuade me, but as always, he persuaded me. I'm heading into London tonight to cast the lead role, Rachel. He's given me strict instructions to find him a star. Someone who takes the world by storm and everyone will know Stanley Tennant gave that person her opportunity to be known. And that was when I mentioned you."

She extended her hand towards me. I laughed, a lot. Her brightened face dropped into a dark stare. "Oh, you're not kidding," I said, tucking my hair behind my ears and looking down.

"It's not really a subject to kid about, August."

I sat upright and opened my mouth to speak, but couldn't find any words. She raised an eyebrow at me, expecting a reply. "I have fifteen girls from top colleges and universities coming to London tonight to audition for the role. If we can get your parents to sign a document, allowing you to join me, I would very much like it if you would be my number sixteen."

I almost began to laugh again, but then I realised I had to take her seriously. This was something I'd been dreaming to achieve since being a little girl, and now was my chance to prove myself.

"Sixteen is my best friend's lucky number so I think it's a sign, Miss."

"Excellent. Listen, I don't want you to get intimidated or worry about all these other girls auditioning because you kick ass in my class. And you have just as much potential, if not more, as everyone else auditioning. So, if you want to call one of your parents and ask them to sign a letter of consent, we can arrange you to join me on a train to London later."

I nodded, and without another word being said, I exited to call my parents. I rested my head against the wall as I shut her office door. I felt like sprinting down the corridor and sliding on my knees and cheering as loudly as I physically could. Instead, I told myself, *this is my time to shine*, and walked outside of college and called my mum. It seemed before I hung up the phone she was already stepping out of the car to rush into college.

"I came as quick as I could!" she shouted, jogging past

in her high heels and up the college stairs, leaving me standing on the path outside questioning if she was actually a superhero. It seemed before I could even open the college door to discuss things with her she was already sprinting back towards her car to go back to work. "I gotta go, sweetie, otherwise they'll fire me for leaving without telling them where I was going! I love you so much! I'll see you at home later before you leave!" My mum is the best, that's all I can say about that matter.

Ms. Andrews and I were on a train to London. After a very flustered day at college and rushing home to make myself presentable, and millions of kisses and best wishes from my parents and Madeline, I made it to the train station in time. We're only going to be on the train for an hour, so I needed to absorb as much advice as possible. "Here's the script you're going to need," Ms. Andrews said, passing me a few pages from her satchel. On the front it had the title *TABLES OF TURNING* printed on it.

"I know your performance capability, but Stanley doesn't. So just be yourself, don't be nervous, and you will be fine."

"Wait, Stanley is going to be there?" I asked.

She flicked her eyes up from the paperwork she was reading. "Yes, now be looking over the script if you don't mind."

The thought had never even crossed my mind. *I'm going to be auditioning in front of Stanley Tennant tonight.* I gazed upon the script Ms. Andrews had given me and turned the first page. A girl called Rachel is sitting in an interrogation room after witnessing a murder. She ran straight to the police station and she's in her chair, shaken, in shock, and very upset. This shouldn't be a problem for me to reproduce since they have been my exact emotions over the past few days. The only difference between her and me is that I haven't witnessed a murder. A policeman begins to interview her, asking her about what she saw, who she saw, where she saw it take place. As the scene continues Rachel becomes more and more upset. It finished with the policeman stepping out of the room to answer a phone call. The scene shouldn't last any longer than two or three minutes. I'm excellent at remembering my lines. If someone asked me what my strongest attribute was, I would say it's my capability to remember my lines. Sometimes I can't remember the name of someone I met five minutes ago, but if you gave me a ten-page script and five minutes, I could recite it to you backwards. It's a gift I suppose. Mum's superpower is to appear out of nowhere all of a sudden. Mine is the capability to remember scripts.

It's 6:14 p.m.; we still had another twenty minutes to go until we arrived in London. I thought Ms. Andrews and I must be the only ones on the train because I haven't seen anyone since we got on. Not even a ticket officer.

"Shall we run through your lines a couple of times?" Ms. Andrews asked.

"Yes please, if you don't mind," I replied.

I'm glad I didn't wear mascara; otherwise, my face would look a mess after all the fake crying I'll need to do.

After the third time of running through the script, Ms. Andrews smirked at me. "Perfect, just perfect. I have no doubt that Stanley will adore you, August."

It was rather humbling to hear, and I think a real tear began to run down my cheek. "What's Stanley like in person, Miss?" I asked, avoiding sounding like an emphatic fan.

"Oh, he's lovely. He may come across as mean and rude, but I assure you, he's really a gentle sweetheart."

The auditions were being held in a small theatre in the centre of London. I didn't know its name because we came through the back entrance. Ms. Andrews explained my audition would be the last to take place, since mine was the last to be arranged. I could also watch all the auditions take place and make mental notes of the approach each actress made towards the character. She and a few other members of the casting team all sat in the third row of the theatre. Stanley would soon be on stage, acting as the role of the interviewing policeman. I was in the eighth row, minding my own business. Preparing myself for my audition, sweating and panicking. Ms. Andrews's advice to not be nervous only increased my nerves. My body was shaking and I couldn't do anything to stop it. Ms. Andrews and the other casting members sitting beside her dropped into silence. Stanley Tennant had walked onto the stage. He was wearing a very smart tweed suit. Stanley was bald and wears glasses. He's very tall and well built. When I searched him online, it said he was forty-five, but like Ms. Andrews, Stanley appeared ten or fifteen years younger than his actual age.

"Good evening. How are we all?" Stanley asked, centre stage.

"Very well, thank you," Ms. Andrews replied on behalf of the casting crew.

"Good," Stanley replied, wandering around the stage.

This man was worth millions and millions, and I'm watching him dawdle along a stage in London. Today had been weird. Two men appeared from stage right. One holding a table, the other holding two chairs. The table was positioned front and center, and the chairs placed either side of the table. I'm guessing this is the interrogation room setup. Stanley sat down at one of the chairs. "Don't judge my performance, ok? I'm a director, not an actor!"

He laughed as he finished his sentence. Ms. Andrews and the other members laughed, too.

"Right, let's do this!" Stanley said, wafting his hand.

A girl walked on from stage left, holding a rolled-up script. Her audition was short and snappy. She was good, but she made it too obvious that she was acting; it didn't seem to come naturally to her. Maybe it's because she was nervous. Which was understandable. Before they began they asked about her. Her hobbies, things like that. I supposed they were trying to get a better perspective of who they had auditioning for them. After each audition Stanley said one or two words about the girl he had just run through the scene with.

"Too tall." Or "Too scary." At the end of one audition he just said, "No." That was after the tenth audition. This wasn't helping my nerves at all. Stanley hadn't said one positive thing about any of the girls yet, which was good for me, but also bad for me. My chances are increasing, but he may hate me the most. What would he say about me? Stanley's phone went off in his pocket as the eleventh girl sat down to audition. Stanley barked into the phone and said to get it rearranged, then hung up.

"I'm terribly sorry about that. Shall we begin?" he said as he returned to his seat with the eleventh girl.

It's 8:30 p.m., and my time was edging closer and closer. The eleventh girl walked off the stage after shaking hands with Stanley. "Perfect," Stanley said, brushing his glasses back and rubbing his eyes. "Perfect," he said again.

This made me angry. She wasn't even that good. You couldn't even hear her, she was almost whispering. I almost booed her off the stage. The only mental note I had made for myself was that Stanley didn't seem to like when the girls over-cry, a moaning cry, like a child who has been denied something at the supermarket. And he didn't' seem to like it when they didn't cry and just read the script in a sad voice. So I have prepared myself to cry, but only tears-running-down-my-cheeks cry. Nothing over the top. It's easy to turn on and off; I do it to my dad sometimes when he won't give me the TV remote. Ms. Andrews walked to my row and sat beside me as the fifteenth audition took place.

"If you perform exactly as you did on the train, you will be splendid."

As the fifteenth girl left the stage Stanley shouted, "Not bad."

Ms. Andrews patted my knee, my cue to take my place on stage.

"You really think I can do it?" I asked.

She gave me a sincere nod and a smile.

I stood, rushed down to the front of the stage, jogged up the stairs, and slowly sat in the seat facing Stanley. The beaming stage lights almost blinded me, and the heat they produced was overwhelming. I thought I might pass out as I sat in the chair. Stanley's very intimidating up close. This man could make or break my dream and career within a matter of minutes.

"You're in a bit of a hurry, aren't you?" Stanley said, leaning forward.

"Well, she runs to the station. I figured that would make her rather flustered, so I thought I'd see if it'd help to run from the eighth row," I replied, out of breath.

Stanley sulked and then raised his eyebrows, realising my actions kind of made sense. "Did it help?" he asked with a blank face.

"Not really, I just feel a little sweaty now," I answered with honesty.

He smirked and rotated to Ms. Andrews and then back to me.

"So you came with Jasmine, did you?"

I didn't know who Jasmine was, but then it clicked that must have been Ms. Andrews's first name. "Oh yes, we got the train together."

"Interesting. Whenever you're ready," Stanley said, offering his hand out, as if he dismissed my knowing of Ms. Andrews. I closed my eyes and took a deep breath. My heart was pounding double time, and the butterflies in my stomach felt as though they were about to erupt. But as soon as I opened my eyes, all those nerves had vanished. It was like I was on autopilot. I was being controlled by a remote. When I regained control of myself, I had tears rolling down my cheeks, and I was scowling deep into Stanley's eyes. He scowled right back at me. I wiped my eyes and sat upright, unsure whether I had just produced the worst audition ever. Stanley leant back on his chair. His dark eyes faded innocently.

"Where on earth did you find this girl?" he asked.

"I taught her PA at the job you stole me from, Stan."

Stanley smirked and returned his focus to me.

"Incredible," he said. "Incredible...thank you, August." He stood and shook my hand before standing and making his way towards the exit.

I opened my mouth, but there was so many things flowing through my mind, that I just didn't say anything. My jaw just moved up and down, as I couldn't select a sentence.

"Steve is waiting for me outside. We're having dinner. I'll call you tomorrow, Jazz," Stanley said over his shoulder.

And just like that, he was gone. I didn't know whether to consider him cool or rude. I remained poised at my chair, baffled by what had taken place. I took a deep breath out and dropped my shoulders.

"How did I do?" I asked nervously.

"Like he said, you were incredible."

MAY 27TH

By the time I climbed into bed last night and rolled over to check Ethan's clock, it was 12:36 a.m. What a long, bewildering, and exhausting day yesterday had been. I finished college early today. Which meant I could visit Ethan earlier since I broke my promise of visiting him every day. I felt awful for breaking my promise. I wanted to see him so badly. To tell him about Stanley and the audition, and to reassure myself that he's ok. We needed to talk. I'd force it out of him somehow. This wasn't a show anymore. He would tell me how he switched seats or I'd be very mad. Even though I can't really be mad at him.

I spent several minutes wandering down the maze-like hospital corridors in a fluster. I just couldn't remember where Ethan was. Luckily, I stumbled upon Angela, who pointed me in the right direction. As I opened the door and stepped inside Ethan's room, I found Verity and her friends gathered around Ethan. I stared at them in silence. Verity walked over and hugged me, squeezing me for a few seconds before I put my arms around her, giving her a comforting pat on the back. I flicked my eyes over at Ethan. His face had regained so much colour in these past few days. He smiled at me and gave me the thumbs-up, settling my nerves.

"Hi, guys," I said.

Scattered replies of, "Hey August," came from Verity's friends. Five of them including her.

"We didn't see you at college yesterday, August. We wanted to check how you were doing," Verity said as she released me.

"Oh yeah, Ms. Andrews planned this last-minute audition for me."

"The girls and I thought we'd pop by and see him. We were all shocked when we heard the news."

"That's very thoughtful of you, thank you."

I appreciated them coming to visit Ethan, but I desperately wanted to be left alone with him Verity must have psychic powers because she walked back over to Ethan. "I promise we'll come and visit you again soon." She rubbed his un-bandaged arm and kissed his forehead. I watched in discomfort. I felt a concerning jealousy come over me, like only I can kiss Ethan's head.

Ethan briefly smiled at Verity, then her friends. "Thank you, ladies. It was nice to see you all." His voice was croaky as he began his sentence, but it smoothened.

"See you later, Breakfast. Bye, Breakfast," they shouted as they left the room. I shut the door behind them, resting my head on it.

"You look nice," Ethan said.

"Thanks. How you feeling?"

I walked over and sat on the edge of his bed.

"Well, I'm being held together by metal. Other than that I'm fine!"

Ethan winced as he shuffled over, patting the space beside him with his unharmed right hand. He raised his arm, implying for me to sit beside him so he could put his arm around me. I rolled my eyes, then sat down alongside him. I didn't want to sit on any important wires or knock him, a typical thing for me to do. He put his arm around me and squeezed my shoulder. "Now we're alone. Tell me what's on your mind. I know you're bottling everything up."

I rested my head on him and sighed. "Yesterday was a really, really good day. I'm so sorry I didn't come to see you. I was with Ms. Andrews, you know, my performing arts teacher. It turns out her best friend is Stanley Tennant, the well-known director, who hired her to be his casting director. She got me an audition, and I think it went pretty well. Stanley seemed to like me."

He squeezed my shoulder. "Don't worry. They'd be stupid not to choose you."

I knew Ethan was in a lot of pain. I knew he's trying not to show it, but it's so good to see him acting like his usual self. I've missed him.

"Ethan, you need to tell me what happened. It's driving me insane, you can't keep this from me and expect me to be ok with it. You're in hospital, Ethan. You could've died. That's what I'm thinking about, it's what I'm always thinking about."

I nestled my head in farther onto his chest. Ethan exhaled heavily.

"August, sometimes…these things, are best kept a secret. Believe me. I couldn't have allowed you to be in the position I am. I spoke to the doctor. She explained if you were sitting in the passenger seat with your seat belt on, you would have most likely died. If not instantly, shortly after attempted treatment in hospital because you're a little dwarf and your positioning would have been different. Tell me, what should I have done with those odds? So I switched with you. If anything ever happened to you, I don't know what I'd do. You're all I have, August. I don't want to lose you, not now, not ever."

His voice stuttered throughout his demanded explanation.

I've never seen Ethan cry. Even now he wouldn't break. I delayed my reply, unsure of what to say. "I'm sorry, I am a dwarf, aren't I?" I replied with a groan.

"Yes, yes you are. But you're my little dwarf. Listen, I'll make you a deal. You have until Saturday to choose one of my tricks for me to reveal. All those years and you get to choose one. You'll need to test your memory. Apart from how we switched seats. That's the deal. Any mention of seat switching, the deal's off. You already know the one I told you in the truck about the apple. That's a bonus one. Then when you come in Saturday, we'll sit and I'll reveal the trick of your choice."

"Ok," I said and closed my eyes.

Arriving home late last night must have tired me out because my eyes opened to Angela nudging me. "Sorry to disturb you, August, your mum is here to take you home." I rubbed my eyes as I sat up. Ethan had fallen asleep, too. I stood and grabbed my things. I didn't want to wake Ethan, so I stroked the hair off his forehead and kissed it. I dawdled out of the room, still rubbing my eyes.

"There you are," Mum said, walking up to me and patting my head as I exited Ethan's room. "Come on, let's go."

MAY 31ˢᵀ

As soon as I woke Saturday, I rushed to the hospital to see Ethan. He was still asleep when I entered his room. He was snoring, which I thought was funny and somehow cute. I sat down on the chair. I tried to budge it closer to his bed so we could talk better, but it screeched as I tried to drag it. So I decided to leave it.

"Either my pretending-to-be-asleep skills are getting better or your spotting-my-pretending-to-be-asleep skills are getting worse," Ethan said with a smile as he sat up. I flapped my arms and raised my eyebrows at him.

"Drag the chair up, my dear, not a moment to waste."

I frowned at the chair and dragged it again. My face grimaced as the wooden legs screeched along the floor. I focused my sight back onto Ethan, who had a straight face. "Finished?" I sat down in the chair and wriggled in it to make the legs screech one last time, just to annoy him more. My face was smug as I looked at him; he just shook his head.

"Good morning by the way."

"Good morning."

"Can we eat before I begin?" he asked. I sighed in annoyance. I'd just sat down. Nevertheless, I returned to my feet and headed over to the café to grab some sandwiches.

The sandwich selection was limited. Luckily there were three ham and cheese sandwiches left. I bought all three because I was sure the third would be eaten at some point. I gently threw the sandwich and a bottle of water onto Ethan's lap as I retook my seat.

"So, have you decided which trick I am revealing today?"

I nodded as I was still chewing on my sandwich. "Yeah," I said, spitting a tiny bit of food out. I tried to catch it, failing miserably. Ethan burst into an uncontrollable laughter. I laughed too because his laugh always made me laugh. "Stop, it's embarrassing!" I managed to say with a mouth full of food.

"Ok, I'm sorry!" Ethan wiped his face with his hands and sighed.

He then grabbed his sandwich, taking a huge bite before looking back in my direction. I paused for a second before I told him the trick I had chosen.

"I've chosen the frozen bottle one you did at Verity's party. The situation makes it difficult to pull it off, you know; first, you've got the crowd, so that means lots of people can spot anything suspicious. Then you have the possibility of whoever fetched you the two bottles over, fetching over the incorrect bottles." I stopped rambling and looked over at Ethan, who was gazing at me.

"Sorry, what? I phased out for a second there," Ethan replied in a clueless manner.

"Nothing, I was rambling," I replied, tucking my hair behind my ear.

He watched me for a second. "So, the bottle trick eh? Are you sure that's your final choice?"

I nodded a few times. "One hundred percent final choice."

I've seen all of Ethan's tricks. Most of them have been card tricks. To pick one out of all those card tricks would be very difficult. Finding out one will make me want to find out another and that'll send me crazy. The explanation might not even be as good as I was hoping, too.

"Excellent choice, my dear. So let's recap what happened before: Verity opened the door and dragged me away from you guys straight away. So when you were upstairs she kept nagging me to do a card trick for her. I told her I would later after she asked for the fifth time." I smirked and nodded as he continued. "But Verity had a big role in this trick without even knowing. I asked her to put a few bottles of beer in the freezer a couple of hours before we arrived as I mentioned I like beer ice cold. It requires about three hours of cooling for this to work. Otherwise after time they expand and shatter. I grabbed one and began drinking it for two reasons. One, because that's what they were intended for. Two, I had to check they hadn't frozen already. Beer takes a long time to freeze, so I didn't need to worry about it too much. Then when you and Max joined everyone downstairs and witnessed me performing the card trick to Verity, which you so marvellously assisted me with." He extended his hand towards me and I gave him the thumbs-up. "The beers were sitting neatly in the freezer, cooling, waiting. So when I struck them together, the energy generated causes the liquid on the edge of freezing point to instantly freeze. It's all to do with science. I dunno, just thought it was cool. Basically when you hit cold beers together, they freeze instantly." He handed me his bottle of water to open as he finished. I visualised the whole event. Picturing every stage and figuring how much had to go right for the trick to work

"So, it could have all gone wrong? Had you practised it before?"

"Yes. It didn't go too well though. The bottles smashed in my hands, I'm surprised they didn't slice my hands open. Sometimes magic is all about luck. I took a shot, and it paid off; everyone would've been too drunk to notice a difference either way."

I was too shy to tell Ethan how grateful I was for him opening up to me like this so I said, "Thank you, Ethan," placing my hand on his. I meant it. I truly meant it.

JUNE 3RD

Three more days until Ethan is released from hospital. I'm happy and terrified. It'll be nice to have my best friend back. Max spends his time in the library, and Mark and I don't speak much. I want to prevent the news about Mark and me from reaching Ethan because I want to tell him myself. I'm not sure how he'll react. That's why I'm afraid to tell him. I don't mean he will freak out. I mean he may think our friendship will be affected and we'll soon see less and less of each other. Who knows what will happen. Honestly, spending much more time with Mark isn't something I intend on doing. He's a nice guy, but relationships are about finding that someone you want to spend the rest of your life with. I certainly can't see myself getting married or having kids with him. That is how you're supposed to feel about someone. Isn't it? I'm telling myself that's why I've not told Ethan yet. Mark and I went for a walk the day after Ethan told me the secret to his bottle trick. There's nothing I can say about it really. It was nice, but there's no spark between us. When I picture myself next to the person I want to spend the rest of my life with, I always see Ethan sitting right next to me. Maybe it's because he's been sitting there for the past twelve years.

I'm furious with his dad for not visiting him. After he wandered off to Italy to play poker, he turned off his phone so no one can contact him to prevent distractions. The hospital has tried calling him countless times, and so have I. What can kind of father does that? I know he's been doing well and fetching good money home. Still, his son is in hospital and he doesn't even know. His son could have died and he wouldn't have known. Two weeks. Two weeks, not one call, not one text to check on his son, the last of his family. Ethan deserves so much better. It's not that I don't like Ethan's dad, he's a great guy, or was.

JUNE 9ᵀᴴ

Monday, the day before Ethan returned to college. I've missed him. I visited him Thursday, the day before he was due to be released from hospital. He asked me to give him until Tuesday. That he had things to sort out. I offered to help, although his stubborn self refused.

Mark walked over during lunch today and we ate together. The awkwardness of it all didn't allow me to enjoy it as much as I should've done. He kept saying, "So." Like a weird amount of times. At least ten times. Then he asked me to go out with him this evening, which I stupidly accepted. I should've cut it off with him there and then, but I didn't have the courage. I decided I'd tell him later at dinner. I'm rehearsing in my head what I'm going to say to him to stop our dating. We're meeting at the restaurant we had our first date in. I've never done this before, never. I at least wanted to give him the decency of telling him in person; surely that is the right thing to do. I've heard people end it over the phone and it doesn't end well. My palms were sweating as I grabbed the handle to the restaurant door. *"Deep breaths, deep breaths."* I'm sure Mark will be fine. He won't be too heartbroken losing little old me. I recognised the back of his head as I entered the restaurant.

"Hi," I said as I slid into my seat.

"Hi," he replied.

"How are you?" I asked, the only thing in my head was, *how long do I leave it until I tell him? Do I tell him now or leave it until later?*

"I'm dreadful, what about you?" he replied.

"What's wrong?" I asked.

He sighed. "Turns out my mum has been cheating on my dad with our neighbour for the past three weeks. They're getting divorced; it's like a war zone at home right now."

I glanced down at his hands. He held a glass of scotch in his hand. His eyes were watery. A mixture of tears and alcohol. *How could I break the news to him now?* The last thing he needed was more bad news. Maybe I was being too considerate.

"I'm so sorry to hear that, Mark, but I really need to talk to you." I sucked in all my courage and decided to tell him I think we should stop seeing each other. It would give him time to process. "With everything that's going off right now, I'm not ready for a relationship. There are too many things happening in my life and the time isn't there for you. I'm so sorry to tell you this now, it's the last thing you need, but I didn't want to mislead you." I felt so bad telling him this now although I knew if I didn't tell him now I'd feel ten times worse later. It'd only mislead him more.

"Oh no, it's fine. I'm seeing somebody else anyway. At least let's have something to eat and let me walk you home."

To be honest I'm surprised I didn't throw my drink in his face. He's seeing someone else and just dismissed it as if it wasn't a big deal. I wanted to stand up and leave. Instead I stupidly stayed, and as time passed Mark continued to drink more scotch. He attracted more and more attention to our table so I called the waiter over to pay for our bill. I tried calling Mark a taxi although he insisted on walking me home. He was managing to walk rather sensibly so I let him walk with me to save causing a scene. I called him a taxi once we arrived at my front door.

"Well, you take care, Mark," I said as I placed the key into the door.

"I will do, August." He slurred his words to the point they were almost unrecognizable.

I nervously laughed. The taxi couldn't arrive soon enough. I knew Mark was going through a tough time at home, but it's no excuse to be an asshole. I'm going through a tough time too, but I don't solve my problems with alcohol or see other people. I guess people solve their problems differently. I stayed with him to make sure he got into the taxi ok. I didn't like the idea of him hanging outside my house drunk. I leant myself against the door and closed my eyes for a moment. I opened them to find Mark's face attached to mine. He was kissing me. I immediately tasted the scotch and felt like throwing up. I pushed him away as hard as my arms allowed me.

"What do you think you're doing?" A few alterations may have been made to what I said.

"Come on, babe, don't be frigid. Let's go inside." Mark grabbed me by my waist, pulling me in to him, kissing me once again, and groping my behind.

I used all my strength to try to release myself from his grasp, but I wasn't strong enough. I shifted my head away from his. The only part of me capable to force away from him.

"Mark, get off me! No!" I yelled.

I nearly called for help before I remembered a program I'd watched on TV about self-defense. There wasn't an alternative. I readied my knee and jolted it between his legs. His grasp instantly released. He stumbled backwards, holding himself. As I turned to open the door, he swung me back and smacked me across the face, causing me to fall and hit my cheek on the side of the door handle. The pain shot through me like a bullet. I quickly returned to my feet in a panic. My hands struggled to turn the key as I fiddled with the lock. The door finally opened. Madeline stood there wide-eyed with shock implanted on her face. I pushed her back and slammed the door behind us, forcing my back against it.

"Lock the door, lock it," I shouted.

She lifted the handle and turned the key. I dropped to the floor with my head in my hands. "Thanks, sis, you're a real lifesaver. Me and my friends were playing a game, and I was trying to hide from them." I could sense her looking down at me silently. I parted my fingers and glanced up at her.

"Tag?" she asked with a blank expression poised upon her innocent face.

"Yes, yes, tag, I'm the winner!" I murmured through my hand.

I turned and peeked through the keyhole to check if Mark had gone. The pain running through the corner of my left caused me to squint. I caught the back of the taxi speeding away. I sighed and returned my face back into my hands.

"Madeline, why don't you go upstairs? Are Mum and Dad home?"

"They went out for food. I'm getting ice cream, don't tell Mum or Dad and I won't tell them about you and your friends playing tag," Madeline said. She's exceptional at making arrangements.

"Deal," I shouted. I peeked through my fingers to see her skipping towards the kitchen. I stumbled to my feet and ran upstairs. The pain on the side of my face gradually increased with each step I took. I closed my bedroom door and raced over to the mirror. The whole side of my eye had gone red. No cutting or bruising surrounded my eye, just redness. Tears had filled my eyes, blurring my sight. I walked back downstairs. My face required something frozen to help numb the pain. Madeline had stood on a kitchen chair, reaching into the freezer for her beloved ice cream. I leant past her, grabbing a bag of frozen vegetables, gently placing it against my tender skin. I returned to my bedroom, closing the door behind me, and sat on my bed and cried. As the tears rolled down my face, reality sank in. I was so disappointed and disgusted. I genuinely believed Mark was a nice guy. The thought of seeing him at college tomorrow terrified me. It's Ethan's first day back tomorrow as well. I rolled over, sinking my head into my pillow. What would he say if he found out? I hadn't even told him about seeing Mark. I felt like crawling into a hole and never coming out. I tucked myself into a ball, resting my hand under my face to keep the frozen vegetables in place, and shut my eyes.

JUNE 10TH

As far as worst days go, yesterday topped the list by far. I felt awful. I stared down at my socks before raising my head to check my reflection. The bruising wasn't as bad as I expected. A mark still revealed itself beside my left eye, but nothing noticeable from a distance. I considered not going to college for the rest of the week. I'm capable of pretending to be sick for the rest of the week, although my parents could see through mine and Madeline's attempts most of the time. I glanced over at Ethan's clock: ten minutes behind my usual schedule.

I left the house still planning how I'd proceed with the day. I couldn't meet Ethan by our tree. He'd be furious when he saw my face, too. I'd need to enter college from the back entrance. I'd catch him at lunch. By then I'd have a plan to explain the marking on my face.

During the first two lessons of PA I sat at the back, out of the way of everyone. I felt like throwing up.

The next two lessons I had free periods. I walked out the back entrance of college towards the wall at the edge of the path. Max must have seen me exit because he jogged after me. He stared at me when I turned to look at him.

"Who did this to you, August?" He kept his distance.

"Max, I'm not in the mood for a chat. Don't worry, I'm fine. Have you seen Ethan?" I snapped.

Max sighed. "He's here, he's looking for you. He will be furious when he finds you. Take it easy on him; he's having a tough time at the moment, readjusting to his life with his injuries."

I nodded and walked away, leaving him behind. I sat myself on the short wall surrounding college, feeling sorry for myself.

After five short minutes of watching the world pass me by, a shadow hovered over me. I knew who it was when I saw the position of his arms in his shadow. I can't explain how much I wished to avoid this.

"Why have you been avoiding me?" Ethan asked.

"Ethan, I'm..." Before I finished my reply he'd knelt down in front of me. It's the first time I'd seen him at college without a tie since the first day. I placed my head into my hands.

"What's wrong? Will you look at me please?"

"No," I replied. I began to cry because I knew what came next.

"August." He softly grabbed my hands and lowered them, raised my chin, and tucked my hair behind my ears. I lifted my head, delaying what I wished he didn't have to see. I began to cry even more. I glanced up to see Ethan crying. The first time I'd ever seen him cry. I saw the disappointment in his eyes. He reached up, wiping my tears away with his thumb, and gently stroked the marking beside my eye. Ethan removed his hand and held it up. It was shaking. He clenched his fist and wiped away his tears. His eyes suddenly filled with rage. He stood, kissed the top of my head, and before I could say anything, already walked back towards the college doors. I figured he was mad at me, then I realised where he was going. I immediately got to my feet and chased after him.

"Ethan, wait. Ethan, come back!" He ran up the stairs to the college doors, swinging one open. It hit the stopper so hard the top glass panel shattered. I jumped back in case any of it flew my way. A few students noticed the door smashing, too. Everyone else had stood farther along the college corridors, deep in gossip. Everyone's attention switched to Ethan entering through the shattered door. Ethan walked towards the main entrance of college where Mark and his friends were standing. I don't know what worried me more, Ethan knowing I had been seeing Mark or that he was making his way over to him now. I sprinted down the corridor. After a few seconds I gave up because I knew I wouldn't be able to catch him. Everyone had fallen into silence. All eyes focused on Ethan. One of Mark's friends must have alerted him that Ethan was on his way over because he had turned around.

He held up his hands in front of him. "Ethan, listen—" Mark started to say before Ethan punched him, his right fist connecting with the side of Mark's jaw. The sound echoed throughout the corridor. Mark stumbled to the floor, hitting his head hard against the ground. He coughed and groaned as he sprawled out on his side on the floor. Ethan knelt down, grabbed him by the scuff of his shirt, and dragged him to his feet. "If you ever, ever, touch her, if you ever speak to her, if you ever go near her again, I swear to God, I will fucking kill you."

Ethan threw Mark into his friends then stormed out the college doors. He hurried down the stairs before stopping. He turned and jogged back up the stairs, reopened the door, and walked through the crowds to me. He smiled and put his arm around me and walked me towards the college doors we originally came from. I was so exhausted from everything that I really didn't care about what happened. I just wished I'd never agreed to see Mark. One day, Ethan had been back one day. Not even one day, a few hours, and he's already going to be kicked out of college, with less than a week to go.

"Hi," I said to Ethan as he stood at his sink. I realised my choice of words could've been better due to the circumstances. We didn't talk as we walked to his house.

"Will you give me a hand here please?" He held up his hand, revealing his badly bruised knuckles.

I took ahold of his hand in my own, analysing it. It was still shaking.

"Sit down and I'll get you some ice."

He'd already gotten a bag of ice scattered on the side. Obviously he's struggling to adapt with his arm in a cast. I grabbed two sandwich bags from the draw, placing one inside the other for strength, filled them with ice and cold water then tied a knot at the top. Ethan had sat on a stool at the centerpiece of the kitchen. I walked over and pulled up a stool. They're big stools, so I always have to climb onto them without looking like a toddler. I hopped onto mine and faced Ethan, our knees almost touching. I lifted his hand onto the side, placing the bag of ice onto his damaged knuckles.

"Better?" I asked.

He nodded faintly in reply. He looked terrible, like he hadn't been sleeping well. His face had lost its colour again. Surely what happened back at college didn't cause all this?

I opened my mouth but Ethan beat me to it.

"Why didn't you tell me?" he asked, staring at his hand.

"I don't know. I didn't know how to tell you."

Ethan continued to stare at the ice on his hand. "There's something...there's something I need to tell you."

"What's wrong?" I immediately replied.

I heard in his voice that this was a serious matter.

"My dad died, last Thursday. I got a call after you left the hospital. He drank himself to death. They brought him back a couple of times in the ambulance and in hospital. He kept slipping out of their hands until they eventually had to give up on him."

I dropped my head and gazed at my lap. It felt like someone had punched me in the stomach.

"It's my fault," Ethan added.

"Don't be ridiculous," I snapped.

I couldn't believe he thought that, there was no saving his dad.

"There's something…else I need to tell you. I've been keeping it from everyone, but I told my dad before he left." The concern that rushed over me when he mentioned *something else*, how could his situation get any worse?

"What is it?"

Ethan flopped the ice off his hand, rose from his stool, and walked out of the kitchen. I heard a door creak open and slam shut. He reappeared holding a black travel bag. He dropped it onto the floor beside my stool. I hopped off my stool, crouching down alongside the bag. I anxiously dragged the zip across to find it was filled with money. I glanced back up at Ethan, speechless. He focused on the bag with disgust.

"Is this your dad's winnings?" I returned to my feet. "Ethan," I said louder, as I didn't receive an answer.

He took a deep breath in. "No, they're actually…my winnings. You see, my dad hasn't been doing well at all these past few months… I have. He's been doing terrible in fact. He'd go out to all these casinos and return empty-handed. If he earned anything, he'd have it lost soon after. He'd come home, leave his bag at the bottom of the staircase, and fall asleep on the sofa. Every morning when I came downstairs I'd check his bag. Empty. Always empty. I'd had enough. I wouldn't allow him to send us bankrupt. So the next time he went out, I myself went out. I've lost count how many times I've done it now. Each time I'd come back with a larger amount. When my dad got back, I'd put some of the money I'd won into his bag. I thought he'd maybe consider stopping for a while, but he'd run on out again to return with an empty bag. That was the disappointing part; he wouldn't even consider saving some. Still, I kept doing it because I had no other choice. I didn't know what else to do. Before he left for Italy, I cracked, and told him it was me putting the money in his bag, not him. He was furious, and sober for once." He paused and rubbed his eye. "I told him he needed to stop, but he refused to accept it and stormed out. I mean, I didn't even get to say good-bye."

I walked over to Ethan and hugged him. There's nothing I could say or do to help during this time. I just wanted him to know that I'm there for him. That I'm always there for him, no matter what. I raised my head and suddenly his lips appeared desirable. A sudden urge came over me to kiss them. Before I could take action he rested his chin on the top of my head.

"Are you ok?" he asked.

"Yeah, I'm fine," I replied, resting my head against his chest.

"Is there anything I can do? Is there anything you need?"

We drew away from each other. Ethan shook his head. "Let's sit down, ok?"

He nodded and made his way into the sitting room. I ran my hands through my hair, joining them at the back of my head as I stared back down upon the bag full of money. The craziest past couple of weeks had now gotten even crazier. What was he to do with all this money? There was enough here to last him for most of his life.

I picked up the bag and placed it along the side of the sofa. I avoided putting it in front of Ethan. Right now I'm sure he hated the sight of it, regardless to the amount. I sat beside him on the sofa. I then noticed how much our lives were going to change. If I got the part for Stanley's film and had to leave for a while to film, who would Ethan have left?

Who knew how long I would be gone? I don't want him to turn into his dad.

"What are you thinking about, Ethan?"

"Do you want to stay here for a while?" he quickly replied.

I opened my mouth to reply, but the answer I was searching for wasn't there. With everything going on lately this seemed like a rushed decision. Ethan did have a big empty house and I supposed I eventually had to move out of my small bedroom in my parents' house.

"I'll talk to my parents and see what they say. I don't have the…" I was about to ask about money, but it occurred to me Ethan would insist that wouldn't be a problem. "Never mind."

"Everything will get better with time, Ethan, I promise. How about when you've had your cast taken off, we take a break and go on holiday? I've always wanted to go to France, let's go there."

He smirked. "Sounds nice."

"I better go home and speak to my parents. I need to be brave and tell them about Mark. They'll be back from work soon. Then I'll come back here and stay with you tonight. Ok?"

Ethan sniffled and got to his feet. "Excellent plan, my dear. I'm gonna head to the bank and sort out this money then come back and take a shower. You have a key anyway so let yourself in." He forced a smile.

I grabbed hold of him again and gave him another hug before leaving for home.

Talking to my parents about recent events was one of the hardest things I've ever had to do. They freaked out about the state of my face and that charges should be pressed against Mark. I explained Ethan punched him very hard and they seemed to calm down after that. Telling them about Ethan's dad was difficult. It upset them more than I had expected; the only time they ever spoke was either at mine or Ethan's birthday parties as kids. Finally I told them Ethan asked me to stay with him. I said I'd stay tonight, but permanently was a big deal.

"How are you going to pay for everything if you do move in?" Mum asked.

"Uhhhhhh," I stalled. "Ethan's dad left plenty of money. Ethan insisted we use that. Until I make my own money, then I can chip in."

My parents looked at each other and shrugged. "See how tonight goes. If you still want to move there tomorrow, I'm sure we'll agree you're fine to stay there until Ethan has returned to full health. We'll call it a trial run."

Madeline then entered the room and jumped onto the sofa beside me. She rested her head on my lap and fell asleep without saying a word. I sat and stroked her forehead for five minutes before slipping a cushion underneath her.

"Be careful, please," Mum said as we pulled up outside Ethan's. She gave me her serious frown. I waved good-bye as I placed my key in Ethan's front door.

"August, is that you?" Ethan shouted as I shut the front door.

"Yep, it's me."

"I'm in need of your assistance, dear."

I rushed to his aid in case he'd hurt himself. I opened his bedroom door to find him sitting on his bed with his shirt half off. It'd gotten stuck midway between his arm and head, blocking his sight. He appeared to be a tad frustrated.

"As you can see, I can't get my shirt off."

I knelt down in front of him and unhooked his shirt from his elbow and raised it over his head, exposing the large scar along his collarbone. I flicked my eyes up to Ethan's. He quickly rose and maneuvered past me, exiting the room without saying another word. I threw my things onto the floor in the spare bedroom. After everything that had happened, I figured Ethan wouldn't have been eating properly. Over the weekend I bet he hardly ate anything.

I emptied a full bag of pasta into a pan of boiling water, allowing it to simmer on the stove whilst I ran back upstairs. Ethan was still in the shower so I entered his room again, to observe his enormous collection of movies along his shelf. Since I'm a dwarf, I had to pull the chair from his desk to analyse the shelf. I quickly hopped off the chair and shuffled it a few feet to my right. I had stumbled upon my choice. No other film can cheer you up more than your favourite: *The Usual Suspects.* Ethan lives for the ending. I think I like it because of how much he likes it.

"Come on, eat up," I said, forcing pasta down him as we sat and watched our film in his bed. We took it in turns to eat; I'd have a mouthful of pasta then I'd feed him a mouthful.

"I can feed myself, August," Ethan growled.

"This is cute though," I said, making baby faces, feeding him more pasta.

We fell asleep after I'd finished feeding him. In the middle of the night I was suddenly jolted upright and awoken. Ethan had flicked me up with his arm.

"Why'd you do that?" I asked angrily.

He grabbed me and hugged me. "Sorry, I was having a nightmare."

I put my arms around him. "Do you want to talk about it?"

Ethan looked like he'd just seen a ghost and it worried me. "No, I'm fine."

June 13TH

My parents sat Ethan and me on the sofa as if we were two six-year-old kids who had misbehaved.

"Your college called and asked us to stop by for a chat," my dad began.

"We met a principal or whatever you call them to discuss recent events. We should have been shown the footage from the surveillance cameras. However, somehow they misplaced the footage, or they weren't working at the time of the incident." He stopped, allowing a disturbing silence amongst us. Both my parents peered over at Ethan, who was analysing his bruised knuckles. I cautiously joined them. Was there something they knew that I didn't?

My dad took a deep breath in. "So, the kid who hit my daughter has a broken jaw. Some mysteriously lost camera footage, and that's it, I think. I covered everything, didn't I?" He stopped and turned to my mum, who nodded. "Right, so all I have to say about the matter is, Ethan, good work. August, you're banned from dating for life."

He walked into the kitchen without saying another word. My mum shook her head sarcastically and followed him. Later on my parents sat and talked to Ethan alone. Probably about his dad. As I sat on the sofa, watching them talking at the kitchen table, my phone buzzed in my pocket, alerting me that I had a new voicemail. Which was strange because I didn't hear or feel my phone ringing in my pocket. It had been playing up recently. Maybe it's time for a new phone. I did still have the first flip-up phone my parents ever bought me. A bedazzled one at that too. I clicked play and placed the phone against my ear.

"Hello, August. It's Ms. Andrews. I suppose Jasmine would be more appropriate now. I've heard about recent activities taking place at college. I hope you're ok. So, first off, I've graded your final assessment based on what I have already seen, because let's face it, I've seen your performance a million times already. So overall you got an A, congratulations, highest in the class, might I add. Now, this news may be of a little more interest to you. Stanley adored your audition. So basically the part is yours if you want it, my love. I insisted on you doing a callback audition, but Stanley said he knows a star when he sees one. Stanley and I would love to stop by your house for tea sometime this week; we can meet your parents and fetch along the contract you will need to sign. Call me back when you can please! Good-bye!"

I dropped the phone and jumped into the air, screaming. I sprinted into the kitchen. "I got it, I got the part!" I yelled. My parents' and Ethan's faces looked as if they were about to burst. Suddenly I was trapped in a giant screaming group hug.

"My little baby is gonna be famous!" Mum cried.

Madeline came rushing into the kitchen, and clinched my leg and started screaming along with everyone else. Within a matter of seconds she was then climbing into the freezer as she saw her opportunity to have a bowl of her beloved ice cream. "Madeline, no!" Dad barked.

We all sat at the kitchen table and took a moment to compose ourselves.

"So what happens now?" Ethan asked, sitting Madeline on his knee.

"Well, they want to pop round for tea and meet you guys!"

"Hurry and arrange it then, sweetie! I want to meet him!"

Ethan, Madeline, and I went for a walk while I called Ms. Andrews back.

"August!" she answered in an ecstatic fashion.

"Hello," I replied, remaining calm.

"Are you excited?" she asked.

"Very!" I screamed. My calmness didn't last long. "I can't believe it!" I yelled. "Thank you so so so so much."

"It was all your own work, August. You should be extremely proud of yourself! We're running on a small time frame because we don't have long until filming begins, Stanley has arranged this film like no other and the turnaround time will be phenomenal. Every tiny detail has been arranged. Is tomorrow too soon for Stanley and I to come around for tea?"

I nodded and then realised words were required. "Tomorrow afternoon would be perfect!"

"Shall we say four thirty? Will everyone be home then?"

I paused and went over my parents' work schedules. "Yes, that gives everyone plenty of time to be ready." I placed my hand on my forehead and ran it through my hair. This was really happening. My dream was coming true, and I was going to be famous! "We will see you then, August."

She hung up, leaving me staring at Ethan in bewilderment.

"Everything ok?" he asked.

"Yes, everything's fine. It's just been such a crazy week," I replied.

He gave me a hug and kissed my cheek. "Ouch! Watch my ribs!"

"I'm so sorry, why am I so clumsy!"

He grinned and pointed at me. "I got you!"

I sulked at him and felt like punching him, but maybe that would actually hurt him. "I hate you," I mouthed.

He nodded sarcastically. "Of course you do."

JUNE 14ᵀᴴ

"How do I look?" Mum asked, walking into the living room, wearing a rather revealing summer dress.

"Mum!" I shouted, covering Ethan's eyes as we sat on the sofa.

"Too much?" she asked, hunching over and fiddling with her boobs.

I placed an extra hand over Ethan's. "Go and change, please!"

"But Stanley is coming! I want him to know you have a hot mum!"

"Why can't I see your mum's cleavage?" Ethan asked.

"Be quiet you," I whispered.

Dad appeared from the kitchen. "Victoria, it isn't my birthday until February." Ethan laughed. I frowned. Mum took it as a compliment.

"Is this really what we're talking about? This is the biggest moment of my life and we're talking about Mum's boobs!" I protested, dropping my hands from Ethan's eyes.

"Woah!" Ethan shouted.

I placed my hands straight back over his eyes.

"In my opinion you look very hot, Mrs. Bishop," Ethan added.

"Thank you, Ethan, I'm keeping the dress on anyway."

Madeline appeared from upstairs. "Do you like my dress, Madeline?"

Madeline didn't reply. She stood with her mouth ajar, then vanished back upstairs. Mum gave us all one quick look. "Ok, I'll get changed."

I waited until she had gone upstairs to give Ethan his sight back.

"Not bad," Ethan said, producing a slight smirk.

Madeline reappeared from the staircase and spread herself across our laps as we continued to watch Patrick Miller's show.

"I'll go see if your mum needs a hand with anything," Dad said, venturing off upstairs. I placed my head in my hands and laughed. My family is so weird. When I reemerged from my hands, Ethan was being a little too adventurous with his eyes at a certain department of mine that my mum may have mentioned.

"Really?" I said with a scowl.

He raised his eyebrows and returned his sight to the television.

A knock came at the door five minutes later. I glanced around at everyone.

"Please don't scare them away!" I instructed.

I took a deep breath before opening the door.

"There's my superstar!" Stanley stated, and then hugged me.

"Hi," I said from over his shoulder. He was wearing a black bowler hat and a long black scarf and coat. Very fashionable attire to come to my house for tea. I stood aside and allowed them to come in. Ms. Andrews and I share a smile as she entered and made her way into the living room. Stanley and Ms. Andrews were already hugging and kissing everyone as I locked the front door.

"It's a pleasure to meet you. You have a lovely home, it's so welcoming."

"I was in charge of choosing the TV, everything else Victoria was in charge of," Dad replied.

Stanley and Ms. Andrews found him amusing and laughed more than I expected. Mum, Dad, Stanley, Ms. Andrews, and I sat at the kitchen table to discuss me. Ethan was keeping Madeline entertained in the living room.

As Mum poured Stanley a cup of tea, he began to explain the movie.

"We're shooting the film in Philadelphia, USA. You're a new girl in town, you've come over from the UK to study at their university or college, whatever they call it. You become friends with your roommate. Who you'll meet over there, she's lovely, I'm sure you two will get along. So let me explain this as quick as I can. Your first night there as you're walking home, you witness a murder, you run to the police station because it isn't far away. The interrogation room scene we did at your audition is our next step, you're being questioned by a police officer. Your roommate from college comes to support you. Then a load of bad guys pull up outside because a cop on the inside informs them that they've been caught. So all hell breaks loose, everyone is getting shot or killed. You and your friend are hiding in the room, and to escape, you can't be afraid to get your hands dirty. You get a gun, shoot a few people, have a few fights, get thrown through some glass, but in the end, you and your friend are the last two left and walk off into the sunset."

Stanley took a sip of his tea. "It will be a lot better than how I just explained it, trust me." We laughed at his comment and everyone looked at me.

"Sounds great," I said with a grin.

"Perfect," Stanley replied. "Normally this movie would take about a year before it is released. But I intend to have it ready for the middle of November. The hopeful plan is to have you in Philadelphia by next weekend, spend a couple of weeks doing script reads, dress rehearsals, stunt practices, little things so we're ready for the first day of filming. Following so far?" he asked, pausing for a moment. We all nodded, allowing him to continue.

"The movie will take around two months to film, maybe a little less. This is because most of the film is going to be shot in the same building, and we don't have that many changes to make. I've also arranged to have the editors on set with me, so at the end of each day, the filming we have done that day can be given to them to work on. If everything goes to plan, the film should be ready well in advance. But like I said, we're aiming to have the premiere for the middle of November. It's costing us a fortune so it better."

Madeline appeared from the living room as Stanley finished.

"Mum, can I have some ice cream?"

I smirked at her because she knew this was a situation where Mum couldn't say no. Mum scowled at her, realising this.

"Of course, sweetie, help yourself."

Stanley and Ms. Andrews found her adorable. "Would you like some ice cream?" Madeline said, looking up at Stanley.

Stanley frowned. "What flavours do you have?"

"We have bubblegum or chocolate."

Stanley frowned again. "I've never had bubblegum-flavoured ice cream before. Have you, Jasmine?"

Ms. Andrews shook her head. "No, I don't think I have."

Madeline watched them, unamused.

"We'll have two bubblegum ice creams if you don't mind, little one."

Dad stood and grabbed the ice cream from the freezer. As she prepared their ice cream Stanley pulled some paperwork out of his bag.

"This is your contract. We've made it as simple as possible to avoid complications and save time. It basically says you agree to be in the film and play this character. And you'll be well looked after and how much you will be paid, and what is required of you and when."

He passed it over to me. I laid it out in front of my parents, so we could read it together. Madeline placed two bowls of ice cream in front of Stanley and Jasmine and disappeared into the living room once again. They ate their ice cream as we read through the contract. The only thing that caught my eye was how much I would be paid. Two hundred and fifty thousand dollars. I nearly fell off my chair. Dad's eyes nearly popped out more than when he saw Mum in her dress.

"I'll get a pen," Mum said, rushing over to her bag.

"This isn't bad you know," Stanley said, referring to the ice cream.

"Not bad at all," Jasmine added.

"Are you happy with everything?" Dad asked.

I nodded. Mum passed me the pen. I glanced down at the contract for a moment before signing it and returning it to Stanley.

"You're going to break a lot of hearts, August," he said with a grin.

They didn't stay much longer as they had to attend to other business.

Mum wouldn't let go of Stanley when he gave her a hug. "Thank you so much," she said, squeezing him.

"We'll be in touch about flight details," Ms. Andrews said as we waited for Mum to release her grasp.

After I closed the door, I rushed over to my parents and hugged them. "Thank you," I said. They had dedicated their lives to me for the past nineteen years and it had finally paid off.

"We're so proud of you, August," Mum said, bursting into tears.

"I want a new TV," Dad said.

Mum nudged him and then went upstairs to stop her crying. Dad followed her. I slumped onto the sofa beside Ethan, resting my head on his shoulder. "Congratulations," he said, kissing the top of my head.

"I'm going to be famous," I laughed. "Who would have thought it?"

"I did," Ethan answered. "I always have."

JUNE 20TH

I'd just arrived in my hotel suite in Philadelphia. My transport here alone made me feel like a rock star. Ms. Andrews insisted that I call her Jasmine from now on since we'd be working together on a daily basis. Jasmine and Stanley arranged for us to travel first class from London to here. Everything was so glamorous and luxurious. My seat moved backwards and forwards, and I had my own TV and my own little fridge beside me. I honestly felt like royalty. I must have taken a thousand photos throughout the flight. My favourite photo was the one the flight assistant took of Jasmine, Stanley, and I holding champagne glasses. I sent the photo to Mum once we landed so she knew we were doing well. I had to leave two days before Madeline's eighth birthday. I hated having to miss it. I wrote her a letter during the flight since it would be eight hours before we landed. I thought she'd appreciate it more coming from the USA. Also, if I sent a text it could be deleted or forgotten within a day. Letters can be kept and reread over time, as long as they're not burnt.

Madeline,

Happy birthday, sis. I'm so sorry I can't be there to celebrate with you. You won't be disappointed when you're joining me on the red carpet and meeting all the hot male celebs! I can't believe you're eight now, you're making me feel old! I didn't buy you a present at home because you already have everything, you little spoilt thing! So I'm going to get you something over here and post it back to you soon. I know Mum and Dad can be frustrating but be patient with them, chick. It won't be long until you're heading out here to visit me! Once you've finished the next couple of weeks of school, we'll arrange for you all to come visit. Take care Madeline, look after Ethan for me please. I know he will be missing me (even though he won't admit it). I'm sure he'll visit you at some point and wish you Happy Birthday.

All my love, August.

JUNE 21ST

I haven't been introduced to anyone yet. I was told to settle into my accommodation last night, and I would be introduced to everyone today. My hotel suite is like something you would see out of movie! I have two floors! Downstairs I have a kitchen and living room. Upstairs I have my bedroom. Everything is so beautiful and modern. There's a window in my bedroom, but I'm too small to reach it. So I don't have much of a view, but that doesn't bother me. My favourite piece of furniture is the chair hanging from a wire on the ceiling. It's almost like a floating bird's nest. I have to hop into it since I'm quite small, but once you're inside you feel like an astronaut. It's perfect for taking naps in or watching TV. It still isn't home, so I've fetched a couple of family photo frames from home and also Ethan's clock. There isn't a clock upstairs or beside my bed so it's helpful that I fetched it. Breakfast, lunch, and dinner are brought to my room by butlers, so I don't have to cook! For breakfast they fetch up various cereals and fruits for me to choose from. While I'm having breakfast they leave you a little card to tick for your choice of lunch and dinner. Half of the things on the card don't make much sense. It just needs to say *pizza* or *spaghetti*. Not *leek and watercress, served with caviar and spinach*. I made that up, but the menu is very similar to that. This must be costing whoever pays for all this a fortune to provide if I will be staying here for two months. I'm extremely anxious to meet everyone. I hope they like me. This won't be fun if no one likes me or we don't get along. I'm determined to make the right impression with everyone though.

At around 11:30 a.m., Jasmine was at my door to escort me down to meet everyone.

"Nervous?" she asked.

"A little," I replied, tying up my hair.

"Don't be. They'll love you."

We took the stairs down so it gave me time to compose myself and prepare myself for meeting everyone. We stopped at a lounge door.

"How many people are in there?" I asked.

She winced. "Thirty, maybe forty people. Today we're introducing everyone, and talking about schedules, how we plan on making the movie. We start reading through the script tomorrow."

I nodded. "Ok...ready when you are."

She grinned and opened the door to the lounge. When it said lounge, I was expecting a big sitting room and everyone to be standing or squeezing onto a sofa. This was like a giant ballroom with a load of desks joined together to make a giant square. Everyone was sitting, chatting. As soon as I entered silence fell over the room and all eyes turned to me. My eyes nearly popped out of my head. It was far more startling and overwhelming than I'd expected. And there were nearly twice the amount of people Jasmine said there was. Someone guided me to a chair and I sat down between Stanley and a young girl.

"Hello. How are we?" Stanley asked.

"Very well, thank you, yourself?" I replied.

"A little stressed but that's very normal for a first gathering. We're just waiting on one of the producers to join us and then we will begin."

I nodded and allowed him to read the paperwork in front of him.

"Hi," the girl whispered beside me. "I'm Eleanor."

I turned and holy moly there she was. Eleanor Walden. The hottest, most stunning gorgeous actress to ever grace this planet. Her eyelashes were so big and flattering. And her beautiful brown hair was tied up in a messy bun, but it still looked perfect. She wasn't even wearing makeup and she looked like a goddess. I stared into her captivating brown eyes for a concerning amount of time before replying.

"Hi," I replied with a grin. "August...I mean I'm August."

She grabbed me and gave me a warm hug. "It's nice to meet you, we're going to be best friends you and I."

It was so tempting to smell her hair, so tempting. But I needed to act cool and normal around these people. Not like a fan. I wanted to continue our conversation, but Stanley stood up and began an announcement. He signalled with his hand for me to join him. I hopped up out of my chair and awkwardly analysed everyone. Stanley was about a foot taller than me so I must have looked really small beside him. I bet they could barely see me from behind the table.

"This is August," he said, placing his hands on my shoulders.

"Say hello, August," he whispered.

"Hello," I said with a smile.

"She is my star, ladies and gentlemen. We love her lots. You can sit back down now, August."

I smirked and returned to my seat.

Stanley explained how everything would run. It didn't make much sense to me, so I'm incapable of repeating whatever he explained. It was all to do with sets and takes. It was mainly a meeting for the technical people and for everyone to meet. But I can't believe I met Eleanor Walden! I mean we're going to be spending so much time together on and off set! And she likes me! How cool is that? It only seems like yesterday I was reading an article about her in my performing arts class at college. It's weird how much your life can change.

JUNE 22ND

My first read-through. Far fewer people were in the lounge today. Maybe ten or fifteen, Stanley, Jasmine and some producers, Eleanor and I, and a teacher from the university/college we're attending. Today we're running through the start of the movie, moving in and meeting my roommate, attending a couple of lectures. Those kinds of things. Basically we're running up until I witness the murder. Eleanor is very professional for someone so young. She's only one or two years older than me; well, she's sixteen months older than me. I thought I'd pretend like I didn't know, but of course I do. But she's such a good actress. I know I will learn a lot from her. I feel like maybe she should have been the lead role instead of me. But Stanley wanted a star, and here I am, wondering how on earth I got here.

After we finished reading through I was given endless compliments. It started from Eleanor, but after she began I was bombarded with them from the producers. "You were marvellous." All I did was read the script. This still feels like a dream I'm due to snap out of any minute. I suppose this will take time to get used to.

JUNE 25TH

I've been given the day off. Rehearsals have been going very well, and today they're focusing on the bad guys' stunts and speaking roles. I only have to do one major stunt, and they said that could be taken care of on set because it's simple and doesn't need to be rehearsed. Eleanor had to return to New York for a week, too, to discuss another film with her agent. Stanley seemed a bit annoyed that she had to leave, but he said it wouldn't have any effect on our progress. I'm going to miss her. I'll miss the little giggles we have. She'll be back next week though, so I don't have to wait too long for her return. I would tell you more about reading through the script, but it's nothing exciting. The only thing I can say is instead of running through the script in one go we have now cut it into chunks. We'll repeat a scene two or three times, until we feel it is perfect. Sometimes we may repeat it six or seven times; it all depends on if we approve of it or not. I'm proud of myself though. I've kept up with everything and everyone without struggling or complaining.

I decided today would be a good time to shop for Madeline's late birthday present. According to the production team, whoever they are, I need to be escorted by a member of security whenever I want to leave. So I'll be shopping for my sister's eighth birthday present with my own personal bodyguard. I found it rather amusing. My bodyguard is a tall, dark, and fairly handsome man, I'd say in his forties with short hair. He is called Wayne.

"I've taken care of a lot of celebrities; most are very rude. But may I say you're one of the politest I've ever worked with, Miss Bishop," Wayne said as he opened the car door for me.

I smiled. "Thank you. I would ask you to call me August, but Miss Bishop sounds too damn sophisticated."

Wayne chuckled and shut the door behind me. Madeline texted me as Wayne and I were driving. She sent me a photo of her and Ethan pulling funny faces. It put a huge smile on my face. Shortly after I received that photo, I received another. A photo of Ethan asleep on our sofa. I missed him, more than anyone else, I'm afraid to say. It's probably because I'm used to seeing him all day, every day. Shortly after that message my mum sent me a photo of Madeline asleep on top of Ethan; she must have cuddled up to him, bless her.

"I'm looking for a present for my sister's eighth birthday Wayne. What would you recommend?"

Wayne hummed and sulked in deep thought. "I've got a friend not far from here who has an excellent jewellery store. Necklaces and bracelets, those kind of things." As soon as he mentioned bracelets I thought I could get Madeline one to sit alongside the friendship bracelet she had made with Ethan.

"Take me there, please."

Wayne nodded and put on his indicator to change our course.

His suggestion didn't disappoint. His friend had a wonderful store, filled with various types of jewellery. Everything was covered in sparkling white and silver. It was in the middle of this huge shopping mall. We didn't get to meet Wayne's friend because he was on holiday, but his nephew helped me find a lovely silver chain bracelet with a silver plaque on it, which could be personalised. It had a small dolphin charm hanging from it, too. It's nearly as cute as her. The bracelet was adjustable, so Madeline could still wear it in thirty years' time if she chooses.

I bought it and had a small message engraved on it: *Madeline, on your 8th birthday. Love, A x*

JULY 1ST

Today I'm rehearsing shooting people. Eleanor hasn't returned from New York yet, but she isn't required because she isn't going to be shooting that many people. My character grew up on a farm in England, where they did clay pigeon shooting and hunting, so I'm supposed to be rather good with a gun. I'm going to look so badass in this film.

So, we're in the lounge. All the desks have been cleared now. The floor has been laid out like the police station. When I say laid out I mean some white X's have been marked on the floor for people to stand on, and some canvas screens have been propped up to act as a wall to hide behind. So I'm hiding behind a wall, using my hand as a pretend gun. Eleanor's character is supposed to be standing beside me, but that's all she really needs to do so it won't be hard for her to catch up. Three bad guys were hiding. Two behind their own desks, one behind a wall. They're shooting at us and I waited for them to reload and then I stepped out and shot them both in the head. I didn't know there was another guy behind the wall and quickly dropped down behind a desk before popping up and shooting him too. If someone walked into the lounge by mistake, they would have probably thought we were all losing our minds. Having this pretend shootout with our hands. Later on in the film, I get to punch a couple of guys, but we're not rehearsing that because they don't want me to accidentally punch him in the face or damage my wrist. Knowing me, I would have probably done both.

JULY 4ᵀᴴ

Today is the day. The day that filming begins. Weirdly, I had no nerves. I was too excited and pumped about starting. Wayne, Stanley and I drove over to the newly refurbished police station. The whole place was flowing when we pulled into the car park. Trailers and people scattered everywhere. People rushing back and forth with different equipment.

Wayne opened my car door. "Have a great first day on set, Miss Bishop."

I thanked him and followed Stanley towards the station. He appeared to be in a rush, which was understandable since it's the first day and he'll expect everything to be in position. I should mention that movies aren't filmed in order. We don't film one scene inside, then head outside and film there, then head inside again. That's how I thought it was done when I was younger. We're shooting in sections and locations. This movie would be rather easy to film since the majority will be filmed in one building, meaning the equipment and trailers needn't be relocated every other day.

"Can we get our chairs, please?" Stanley shouted as we stepped inside the building. "Two-hundred-million-dollar budget and we don't even have any frickin' chairs set up for us."

I smirked, but stopped in case he wasn't implying sarcasm. The station was not the cleanest place, but it definitely looked the part. Obviously outside was the large car park. You came up the stairs inside and there's a little reception desk at the front. You can't turn right so you turn left down a small corridor. If you keep walking straight, there's the interrogation room on your right and then an emergency exit just past that. If you turn right before the interrogation room, you enter a large floor, filled with desks, running on the outside of the floor are separate offices and then there's two floors above us, but I haven't been up there yet. A woman rushed over with some chairs, and she unfolded one in front of me. It had BISHOP printed on the reverse. It was the coolest thing I had ever seen. I pulled out my phone and took a photo, sending it to everyone at home.

The first few hours of filming were spent filming everyone apart from me; this was after I'd spent an hour in hair and makeup. It got to lunch, and I still hadn't filmed one take. It was fun to watch at first, but I wanted it to hurry and get to where I'd be in front of the lens. While everyone ate lunch, I headed outside and called Ethan. I needed to hear a familiar voice to settle down my frustration.

"Hello, Ethan here."

"Hey, it's me. I'm on set now...well, outside. I've been sitting around for three hours and not filmed one take yet. I just needed to speak to someone to settle me down."

"August, don't worry. How are you going to manage for the next couple of months if you're like this after the first three hours? You're gaining experience from watching remember. Consider this, would you rather be sat watching or would you rather be back at college? I think we both know which the obvious answer is. Appreciate it as much as you can, August, because once it's all over, you'll regret it."

"I know, I know. I'm just panicking, and I'm nervous and anxious at the same time. Thank you, Ethan. How are you? Are you doing ok?"

"I'm fine, don't worry about me. I got my cast off early! They said I could take it off and replace it with a brace. It's a lot more comfortable. I can take it off for showering and things now. And it's black instead of that disgusting yellow colour."

"That yellow was horrible, wasn't it? Well anyway, I just wanted to call you and tell you how it's going."

"August, I need to speak to you about something."

"Oh hold on. They're calling me back in. I'll call you later, Ethan, if I can. Lots of love, take care. Bye."

It's the most exhilarating moment, filming your first take. A lot has to be said before the scene begins. I was sitting waiting a minute for everything to be said before we're actually rolling.

"Going for a take. Quiet, please!"

"Camera running!"

Then in quick succession someone shouted, "Sound," and "Speed."

Meanwhile I was wondering what the hell is going on.

"MARK IT!" a woman yelled at the top of her voice.

A guy came running from out of nowhere and stuck a clapperboard in my face and said, "Tables of Turning scene thirty-seven, take one."

All that was left now was for Stanley to shout action. After all that screaming, shouting, marking, and yelling, I was left there, completely baffled. My first take didn't go well because I was too confused by everything that everyone was saying, but by my second take I was in full flow. I'm afraid I can't say that about the other thirteen takes we had to do because the guy in the background failed to fall over the desk correctly. I had to act all shocked and upset, and after thirteen takes, I sensed I would have a meltdown and cry for real. The guy got it right eventually and we stopped shooting for the day.

July 5TH

We had to be up at 7:00 a.m. sharp, prepared to be on set by 7:30 a.m. It's not a problem for me because I've been getting up for school and college my whole life. Ethan's clock said 6:04 a.m. when I opened my eyes. Still, I got up and strolled downstairs for breakfast. Every time I have breakfast now or hear someone mention it, I think of Ethan. I wished he could join me out here. He'd love to stand and watch everything from behind the scenes. He loved all that kind of stuff.

Wayne was sitting and reading a newspaper at a breakfast table as I entered the lounge. He flattened it and looked up. "Good morning, Miss Bishop, you're up early." I gave him a wave and walked to the buffet area. I was starving. As I sat down Wayne handed me the newspaper. "Take a look at the headline." I budged over my plate and grabbed the newspaper.

Who is Eleanor's new mystery man?

"What about Eleanor?" I asked.

"The one underneath, silly," he replied.

Humble British girl announced to be leading role in upcoming Hollywood movie

I looked back up at Wayne. "Hey, that's me!" I couldn't believe it. I'm in the papers now. In America! I wondered if it had been published over in England. I took a photo and sent it to everyone at home. I had so many messages to respond to, but I barely got any time on my phone. I quickly sent everyone a text saying all was well, and my phone service was rubbish. I called Ethan before we left to see what he had needed to talk about yesterday.

"Hello, Ethan here."

"Hello, Ethan, it's August."

"Who?"

"Your best friend."

"Sorry, I don't know anyone called August. Wait, does she smell quite bad?"

"Very funny, so what did you need to speak to me about?"

"Ummm, it can wait, nothing important."

"Are you sure?"

"Yes, I'm sure. Are you ok, my dear?"

"I'm very well, thank you. Did you get the photo I sent you?"

"The humble British girl article?"

"That's the one."

"Adorable dwarf would've been better."

"They can hardly print that, can they? It's not going to sell me well at all."

"It'd work for me."

"Maybe so, but thousands of people would find it weird."

"I might send them an email and ask them to change it."

"You're such an idiot. Anyway I've got to go now. I…"

I almost said *I love you…* I panicked and kept silent, hoping he hadn't noticed.

"August? You there?"

"Yeah, sorry. I'll speak to you soon."

I hung up before he could say good-bye. I placed my phone over my mouth and stared forward. Did I mean what

I nearly just said? I reassured myself that it was a mistake. Then I admitted something I never thought I would. Yes. Yes I did. I love him, and no longer in the best friend way. In the I-want-to-be-with-you way. Oh my God, I love him. I missed his long hugs and him kissing the top of my head. Being away from him has put everything into perspective. *Does he share my feelings? How can I tell my best friend I love him?*

"Miss Bishop, it's time to go," Wayne said, opening the car door for me.

I toddled over to the open door, collapsing into my seat and placing my head in my hands. If I tell Ethan, it'll either end in us being together or destroying our friendship. I don't want to lose him.

"Everything ok?" Wayne said as he got into the driver's seat.

I returned to a normal upright position. "Yeah, I'm fine."

At this moment in time I couldn't allow my newfound feelings for Ethan to get in the way of my job. I had to push them aside and focus on the movie. I made a deal with myself, that I'd tell him once it's finished.

July 10th

Eleanor and I were like sisters. We have such a laugh on and off set. So many takes have had to be stopped because we're too busy laughing at one another.

"I'm so glad I have you!" she always said.

The past couple of evenings we've eaten together instead of sitting in our giant hotel suites alone. Our hotel suites are next door to each other so we're only two paces away from each other's door. Today we're shooting the scene where Jessica will comfort Rachel in the interrogation room before all hell breaks loose. I'll be honest, every time I hear Tables of Turning, it makes me think that it sounds like a crappy horror movie. I think the movie should be called *Twisted*. It's simple and catchy and explains the plot. I suggested it to Stanley on set this morning. He smirked at me when I mentioned it sounded like a crappy horror movie. I think he appreciated my honesty. Everyone else is scared of saying anything. "Thank you, August. I will consider it," he said.

Eleanor and I sat together, drinking green tea while we had our makeup done. There was the same newspaper Wayne had shown me, which I hadn't gotten a chance to read.

"Are you really reading that?" Eleanor asked.

"What do you mean?" I questioned.

She pointed to the article on the front.

Who is Eleanor's new mystery man?

"Oh no! There's an article underneath about me. It's the first time I've ever been in a newspaper."

Eleanor smirked. "Soon you'll wish they wrote nothing about you."

I thought back to the day I read Madeline's magazine in class. Eleanor's boyfriend cheating on her had been distributed to everyone in the world. Nobody needed to know about her personal life. That's her business. I understood that now. I felt sorry for her, really; she's just a normal girl, like me, behind that picture painted of her.

"So is it true?" I asked. I realised I was being nosey and maybe offending her, but she blushed and went red.

"Yeah. He's such a great guy. We've only been dating a week, but he's so sweet and charming. Not to mention he is super cute! He's coming to visit me soon so you'll be able to meet him then."

We both had huge smiles on our faces, I was genuinely so happy for her. After the previous relationships she's had, she deserved to be treated well.

July 21st

Today was the day we moved onto the shootouts and explosions, all the action-packed stuff. Stanley entered my trailer as I was having my makeup done and asked the entire makeup staff to leave. He wanted to talk alone. I thought he was going to tell me I'm doing a horrible job and he regrets the day he met me.

"August, you're doing wonderful so far. I thought I'd check up on you and see how you were finding things. Are you comfortable? Does anything need changing?"

I let out a huge sigh of relief. "I was expecting you to shout at me! Everything is perfect, Stanley, thank you."

"Great. We've changed the movie name by the way. *Twisted* is officially our new title. Pain in the ass to change, but everyone agreed with you. For the record I didn't come up with the name. If you need to talk about anything, anything at all, let me know."

He had a smug expression on his face as he left my trailer. I smiled at myself in the mirror before the makeup staff flowed in once again.

I shot the coolest scene today. It's the first time I've been filmed shooting someone! Jessica and Rachel, or Eleanor and I, are hiding behind a desk while everyone is shooting at each other. An officer standing next to us is shot and killed. He collapses to the floor and drops his gun and it slides towards us, just out of reaching distance. There is only one guy left in sight. He notices the gun and then notices us. He quickly tries to reload his gun, but me being the brave character I am, slide out and grab the gun and shoot him. He drops to his knees and falls on his face. I'm sure there's more action-packed scenes; although in my opinion, this was the best action scene ever.

July 22ND

This morning Eleanor rushed into my trailer in a giddy fit.

"He's coming today! You're going to love him, August!"

She rushed out again before I could reply. I looked at myself in the mirror and shrugged. I'm excited to meet him; she's told me a lot about him. I want to see if he'll earn my blessing of dating Eleanor. It's so weird speaking like this. Two months ago I read a magazine about Eleanor, envying her. Now two months on, we're new best friends. The makeup staff were still dabbing my face as I exited my trailer. They always go over the top with makeup. It's a nightmare to take off and irritates my skin. I paused in the middle of the car park, allowing them to finish. Then a black car came roaring into the car park. I've no idea what type of car, but it looked expensive and fast. Could it be Eleanor's mystery man? The door opened. But to my surprise, it was Ethan. He'd come to surprise me! He had more of a tan and looked taller, somehow.

"Guys, guys, stop for a second, please," I said to the makeup artists.

I immediately ran over to him. "Hey, you!"

"August, my dear, how are you?" he shouted back as he closed his car door. Where on earth did he get a car? He hadn't even taken any lessons or passed his test before I left. I gently hugged him to avoid covering him in makeup. He was wearing one of the ties I bought him for his fifteenth birthday. A plain black tie that has a small white number sixteen in the bottom corner. Sixteen is Ethan's lucky number, because both our birthdays fall on the sixteenth.

"Why didn't you tell me you were coming?"

He looked down. "August, we need to talk."

I frowned at him. "Why?" He only ever said *we need to talk* before revealing terrible news. Before he opened his mouth to speak, a call of, "Hey babe," came from behind me. It was Eleanor. She walked past me, grabbed ahold of him, and stuck her tongue down his throat. NO, NO, NO. How could this happen? How did they ever meet! What? How? Why? What? WHAT!

I wanted to fall to the floor and cry. I felt like pulling Eleanor off him and punching her. I'm sure that would've been fine. Instead I stood and waited for them to stop kissing, disheartened and broken. Eleanor grinned, clutched Ethan's hand, and rested herself against him. She shrugged. "I didn't know how to tell you, August. You two are close and I thought it would be best to leave it as a surprise."

I forced myself to smile. Thankfully, someone shouted, saying we were needed on set. Perfect timing. Of all the people in the world, she had to meet him. She was right when she'd said I was going to love him, because I am, in fact, in love with him. I needed to call Max. Normally, I'd turn to Ethan to discuss my problems with him, but since the problem is him, I can't talk to him.

The day dragged by. Every second Eleanor wasn't on set, she was kissing Ethan. God I hate her. Funny how tables turn, isn't it?

That evening, Eleanor insisted we go out for dinner. It's my own fault. I've had well over a decade to tell him I love him, and now it's too late. They're going to get engaged, married, have kids. Of course, make me bridesmaid and godmother. Just to rub it in more.

"So tell me, how did you meet?" I asked. I knew I'd regret asking, but I needed to know.

"Well, I was in New York after having my meeting with my agent and I went to grab a coffee. I walked into the first coffee shop I saw and was about to leave before I saw this handsome one at a table by himself. *So* I walked over and sat with him and he fell in love with me instantly and began to drool."

"I didn't!" Ethan said.

"Well, it took you at least four or five attempts to finally say something to me," Eleanor said, nudging him. Ethan blushed in embarrassment. She continued, "We sat and drank coffee together and I asked him out to dinner that evening, since he didn't have the courage to ask me. I think the brace on his arm was too tight and affected his speech." She lightly punched him. I scoffed once. You know the scoff you do instead of laughing. That scoff.

"What were you doing in New York?" I asked.

"Can't tell you, top-secret stuff," Ethan replied.

I frowned at him but accepted his secrecy.

"He didn't even recognise me! It wasn't until someone asked to have a photograph with me that he asked if I was famous! He came into his own when he did a couple of magic tricks for me. I found it so cute. I wasn't expecting him to be as good as he was!"

Eleanor went on for what seemed like an eternity. "Oh, and we went ice skating and we went to movies and round museums and walked around the park!" I swear she listed every activity possible. "And we made love under the stars whilst camping."

That was when I choked on my breadstick and nearly passed out. I just wanted to head back to the hotel and sleep. When I eventually climbed into bed after an exhausting and demoralising night, I could hear Eleanor and Ethan having sex. I glanced over at Ethan's clock: 12:22 a.m. That was definitely my cue to exit my room and find something else to occupy me. I wasn't sitting and listening in. I walked into the reception and called Max.

"Hello."

"Max, it's August."

"Hey! How are you?"

"Have you spoken to Ethan?"

"Not since he left for New York. Why?"

"Why did he go to New York?"

"He went to buy something. I'm not sure. Why are you asking me this?"

"I'm in love with him, Max."

"Well, it's about time!"

"Shut up! He's seeing Eleanor Walden. Well, right now he's seeing a lot of her."

"Holy shit, really? Good on him!"

"Max, how is that helping me?"

"Sorry. You've had forever to tell him, August. How long have you had these feelings? How did he even meet her?"

"It's been like this for a while, but I only admitted it to myself recently. Ethan meeting Eleanor is irrelevant right now."

"Ah, August you should have said something. I can't believe he's banging Eleanor Walden, though. She's my dream girl."

"Inappropriate right now, Max. Thanks for your helpful support anyway."

"How is filming going?"

"Well, it was going great."

"I see. I'm sure they won't last long, and then you'll be able to tell him."

"Yeah, you're right. Thanks, Max."

"You're welcome. I hope you're ok. Bye."

"Bye."

I suppose I couldn't expect much from Max. He's not the best on giving advice. He speaks his mind. I decided the advice he provided wasn't good enough. So I called my mum. Mum always helps in uncomfortable situations. I waited as the phone rang and rang, nervously preparing my confession.

"August, is everything ok?"

"I'm just going to get straight to the point, Mum. I'm in love with Ethan."

"Well, it's about time!"

"Why does everyone keep saying that?"

"Well, we've been waiting God knows how many years for you to admit it, sweetie."

"He's seeing the biggest actress in the world right now."

"Oh great! Wait, is that you?"

"No, it's not me, you fool. Eleanor Walden."

"Fair play to him, he's not done bad there, has he?"

"Mum, how is this helping me?"

"I'm sorry, sweetie."

"Ok, I get it, I should have told him sooner!"

"I'm still half asleep, August. Let's speak about this later, ok?"

"Ok. Bye."

The message was clear from Max and Mum. It's about time I admitted I loved him and too late to finally tell him. Just the news I wanted to hear.

AUGUST 8TH

Ethan only stayed two days. He didn't say where he was going. We barely spoke to one another since he arrived. Luckily for me, they required me on set throughout most of the day. Ethan and I both knew there was awkwardness between us. Maybe we needed time apart, or to be alone and talk. Right now, I want to hurry and finish the movie. That way, I can focus on my personal life. I'm sure these feelings for Ethan will fade. I'm trying to persuade myself that it's only jealousy.

The first month of filming is over and the second is about to undergo. The final day of filming has been set for the twenty-seventh. Three more weeks. How time has flown.

I need to straighten things up with Eleanor. We've lost our sister-like relationship; now we only chat about the film. I don't want her to think I hate her. At this moment in time, I do, I really do. But I can't blame her; she's chosen the right guy who makes her happy, which is what she deserves. I just wish she could've found someone else.

On set today, I'm thrown through a glass window. Well, it wasn't real glass. The glass was replaced with sugar glass. I believe that's its official name. Real glass would hurt, a lot. Sugar glass is a really delicate glass they use for most action films and it breaks really easily. A man picks me up and throws me through the windowpane. They placed this huge beanbag cushion on the other side so I would land safely.

"Action!" Stanley shouted.

Then this guy called John, grabbed the top and bottom of my jacket, picked me up, and threw me through the glass. During this I'm trapped in an uncontrollable laughter.

"I'm so sorry," John kept saying. He felt really bad for throwing me through the glass. He thought he was being too rough.

"Don't be silly, this is fun!" I replied.

It took us many takes to perfect it because we couldn't stop laughing for the first few. When I say we, I mean myself. I hope they place those takes of me laughing in the credits at the end, if there's any. The window replacement people weren't too appreciative of my laughing as you can imagine. They must've hated me. Most of the cast and crew saw the funny side of it. It was good for everyone to have a little laugh and release some stress. Sometimes people forget that you need to have fun.

AUGUST 9TH

Stanley came into my trailer again this morning. I really thought he'd shout at me this time for laughing throughout the whole window scene.

"I've noticed you're behaving a little odd lately, August. You've not been yourself. Is something wrong? If there is, you can tell me."

I shook my head. "I'm fine, Stanley. I'm sorry for laughing yesterday."

Stanley stroked his chin, deep in thought. "Don't worry about that, everyone found it very amusing."

I giggled. "Everything's fine, Stanley, you needn't worry."

"So the fact that your costar is sleeping with your best friend isn't bothering you at all?"

My face dropped. "Why can't you call it dating?" I snapped.

"There's my answer," he said, raising his eyebrows.

I placed my head into my hands and moaned.

"Come on, talk to Stanley. What's wrong, my lovely?" He placed his hands on my shoulders.

"I love himmmmm," I murmured through my hands.

"Are you sure it's not because you don't want to lose your best friend?"

I brought my head from out of my hands and checked

my makeup in the mirror. "I don't knowwww." I sounded like a child.

"Ahhh." He paused. "Well, I have experience in this field, August. I too am stuck in this lagoon of friendship with someone we know."

At first I didn't care if he had been in my position or not. But I realised who he was speaking about. Ms. Andrews, well, Jasmine.

I turned and faced him. "Really? Did you ever tell her?"

He shook his head. "When the time came to tell her, I was too late. She'd already found someone."

I walked over to my trailer door and locked it. I didn't want anyone barging in on our heart-to-heart conversation. Stanley found a seat on the chair I had been sitting on. "I've always been afraid of telling her."

I could see he was disappointed with himself. But I burst into laughter, which probably wasn't the most appropriate thing to do.

"What's so funny?" he asked before joining me in laughter.

"Don't take this the wrong way, but I thought you were gay!"

He stopped laughing and shook his head. "Wow, thanks, August! Great confidence boost right there!"

I stopped laughing. "I'm sorry! You always seem flirty with the male producers! Why don't you tell her? It's never too late, Stanley."

Stanley scrunched up his face. "I can't, August. What if she says no or doesn't feel the same way? Or even worse, thinks I'm flirting with the male producers like you!"

I knelt down beside him after laughing. "You won't know if you don't try, will you? If she doesn't feel the same way, you can play the schoolkid card. I was only joking or my friend dared me to do it."

Stanley smiled and stood. "I'll make you a deal, August. I'll tell Jasmine, but only if you promise to tell Ethan, when he's no longer with Eleanor. Let's face it...she's useless at relationships. I'll admit the last one wasn't her fault."

He offered his hand for me to shake in agreement.

I rolled my eyes at him. "Fine, you've got a deal."

A knock came at the door. "Are you guys finished yet?"

Stanley unlocked the trailer door and opened it. "Do we look finished?"

A huge bundle of apologies came from outside the door. Stanley turned, smiled, and winked at me. "Back to work, August."

He reopened the door and stomped towards the station. He's the best.

AUGUST 16TH

Today is my nineteenth birthday. It's upsetting I can't spend it with my family. They always spoil me on my birthday. Instead, I was thousands of miles away, feeling sorry for myself in my hotel room, staring at Ethan's clock. I'm living the dream, doing what I love. But I can't help feeling empty and alone. Mum woke me at 5:00 a.m., calling me to sing happy birthday. As you can imagine, I wasn't too impressed with her. I growled at her down the phone.

"Oh stop being a grumpy bum."

"It's 5:00 a.m., Mum. I think you can allow my grumpiness."

Then there was a knock at my hotel door. "Mum, someone is at my door, I'll speak to you later, ok?" She then said three thousand things at once.

"Ok, sweetie, happy birthday, call me later, promise I'll come visit soon, I love you, I hope everything is going well, say hello to everyone for me, don't forget to take plenty of photos for me. Bye, bye, bye, bye." Why do mums randomly shout all these things to you at the end of phone calls?

It was too early to be dealing with phone calls and people at my door on my birthday. I rolled off my bed and kept the covers wrapped around me as I stumbled down-stairs and dawdled to the door. I begged it not to be everyone waiting on the other side ready to shout *surprise!* I looked hideous and just wanted to sleep. I pawed at the door with my eyes closed in search of the handle. I swung the door open to find Eleanor with a huge grin on her face and a bouquet of flowers in her arms.

"Good morning, birthday girl, rise and shine."

I wanted to slam the door on her and return to bed, to tell you the truth, and almost did. I squinted at her. My eyes were still half asleep.

"Can we talk? I was hoping we could get breakfast to-gether. Sorry it's so early, I couldn't sleep," she said with a puppy dog expression on her face.

"Sure, let me get ready," I replied, waving my hand at her to come in. She shuffled past me and placed the bouquet on the table, then planted her behind on the edge of the sofa with a grin on her face. "Let me have a shower first and then we can go down," I mumbled. "Ok!"

"Since you found out about me and Ethan, I feel like we've been drifting apart. We always clicked before. We were like sisters. I don't want you to think I will affect your friendship with Ethan," Eleanor said as I poured my tea.

I appreciated her saying this because it was true, every word.

"Ethan's never had a girlfriend before, and I don't know how to react to it and I didn't speak to Ethan at all when he was here."

Eleanor smiled and grabbed my hands. "He adores you, August. We both do. Nothing will change! You and I will see more of each other, that's all."

I accepted everything she said like a grown-up best friend who wasn't in love with her boyfriend would.

"August, can I ask you something?" Eleanor asked with a serious stare.

I thought this was it. The moment she asked if I love him. *What am I supposed to say?* I can't lie to her. "Sure." My bottom lip started to tremble.

"When you last saw Ethan, was he having nightmares?"

I immediately relaxed but was concerned about the question she had asked me. "A week before I left we fell asleep watching a movie, and during the night he jolted me up with his arm. He said he had a nightmare and he didn't want to talk about it." I stared down at my teaspoon. This meant that Ethan had been having the same recurring nightmare for two months. That's a worrying amount of time. Maybe we needed to get him help.

"He did the same with me. Woke me up during the night, but he refused to talk about it, too. Do you think we should get him a psychiatrist?"

It was an odd conversation to be having with Eleanor, but it was nice to finally talk to her about Ethan. There wasn't anyone else I could think of (other than me) that I would rather see Ethan with.

We sat and ate breakfast together. If she and Ethan weren't together, this would've been the perfect start to my birthday. We both agreed that if his nightmares continued after we finished the movie, then we would get him a psychiatrist. As I entered my trailer that morning, there was a small white card on the side of my table. I slid the card off the edge.

Happy birthday, my dearest dwarf. Look outside x

It didn't take a genius to figure out that it was from Ethan. I frowned at the card. I returned to my trailer door and peeked out. Nothing caught my eye. I opened the door fully, still nothing. I shrugged and shut the door. The card definitely instructed to look outside. I shuffled around, still analysing the card. And there he was, sitting in my chair.

"How are things?" Ethan asked, holding a bottle of foundation, looking upon it with mystery.

I rolled my eyes at him. "Can you never use a door?"

I walked over and hugged him around his neck. He was wearing one of his tartan ties. I bought him this one for our seventh Christmas together.

"You know me. I never like to do anything simple."

"What's wrong?" I asked.

"Nothing. Your presents are over there." He pointed at a two bags and a box lying on the sofa.

"Thank you," I said, kissing his cheek and patting his shoulders.

His eyes met mine in the mirror for a second. I was hoping my eyes read *I love you, pick me* so I wouldn't have to say it myself.

"Right, open them before you have to go." He stood and picked up the bags, placing them on the floor and sitting on the sofa. "This one first." He passed me a small bag as I sat beside him. I squeezed it before looking inside; it felt soft and squishy, an item of clothing. It was a pair of socks.

"You always need a boring gift on your birthday don't you? They have a letter *A* on them though. I chose wisely."

"You're so clever," I joked.

Ethan passed me a package. It was a book. They're easy to identify. It was a brochure of an apartment called *The August Sky*. I flicked through the pages to view the most breathtaking property I had ever seen. It was like something you would see a villain use in a spy movie. Everything was so bright and modern and pretty. "I don't understand. What's this?"

"This, my dear, is our new apartment in New York. I bought it the same day I met Eleanor. I named it after you."

I nodded calmly. "Cool." I dropped the book onto the floor and scratched my nose. Then flung myself at him and hugged him. "Thank you, thank you, thank you, this is the best gift *ever!* It's so pretty and *beautiful!*"

I was tempted to ask him how much it cost. I thought it'd be best not to ask that question yet.

"August, you're choking me," he said, wheezing through my grasp. I let go. And he passed me my final gift. This box was only small. I emptied its contents into my hand. It was a key. It appeared to be a key to a car.

"Your final gift is outside, but before we go we need to uphold our tradition." Ethan pulled a Polaroid camera upon a tripod out from behind the sofa. He unfolded the legs and adjusted the height. Then shuffled closer beside me and puffed my cheeks together with his hand, whilst kissing one side. I crossed my eyes and focused on my nose, since smiling wasn't an option. The camera flashed, followed by the photo slowly printing out. I snatched at it and wafted it as the image faded onto the paper. We looked so cute and happy. Well, he did; I just looked like a girl with crossed eyes and a guy kissing her puffy cheeks. I popped the photo onto the table and walked to the door.

"Come on, I want to see this final gift!"

He covered my eyes with his hands as we stepped outside. "No peeking until we get there," he whispered as we awkwardly dawdled forward.

"August, we need you on set in two!" someone shouted.

"Okay, I'll be there!" I shouted in reply.

I couldn't stop laughing because I kept stepping on Ethan's feet. He removed his hands after a minute or so. I blinked a few times as my eyes readjusted to the light. Before me, parked on the road outside the station, was a car identical to the one I saw Ethan driving, but in white. I turned to Ethan speechless. He dangled the keys in front of me like he was taunting a child. I snatched them off him and skipped towards the car, screaming. I unlocked it and slid inside. It was so pretty and the leather interior smelt and felt so good. It was so beautiful and it was mine! I screamed with excitement and stamped my feet. Ethan joined me in the passenger seat. The car had only two seats, but I didn't think I'd need any more if it's only going to be Ethan and me living together.

"We're not going to drive it since you have to go on set now, and the last time we were in a vehicle together it didn't end too well. I will allow you to start it though."

I grinned wildly and started the ignition, and the car roared into life.

"This is really loud," I said to Ethan.

"Yeah it is!" he replied.

I turned the ignition off and the car calmly quieted.

"In the boot are a few pairs of running shoes and running bottoms. I know you don't run, but I know you like to wear them because they're comfortable," he said as we got out of the car. He opened his arms and waited for me to enter them. I walked over to him and hugged him tightly.

"Thank you, Ethan," I said against his chest.

"The address for the apartment is in the brochure. Once you finish up here, you can drive to it and I'll be there, waiting for you. The car is all registered, so you don't need to worry about that. It's ready to go when you are. Oh, I've sorted all our visas and permits and things! Your mum and dad were very helpful with those, I didn't have a clue what to do!"

He rested his chin on top of my head. I took a step back and we smiled at one another. I turned and began to walk back towards the station without another word being said. Nothing else needed to be said. I glanced over my shoulder to check on him. He'd vanished of course. I smiled and picked up my walk to a jog. Stanley was waiting at the bottom of the stairs to the station with his arms folded.

"You two make me sick," he said in a sarcastic tone.

I raised my eyebrows at him. He held the station door open for me as I jogged up the stairs. "Is that a hint of jealousy I am receiving from you, Stanley?"

Stanley shook his head and whispered, "Of course not. Who would wish for their best friend, who they're in love with, to spoil them with cars and apartments? Terrible gifts, just terrible I say. Happy birthday by the way."

I laughed and thanked him as he closed the door behind us.

AUGUST 17TH

As far as birthdays go, yesterday topped the list. The talk with Eleanor, and Ethan visiting, were exactly what I needed. Obviously all the amazing gifts I received from Ethan weren't too bad either; they cheered me up a little. It's good that if I'm ever in need of any help or advice, I can talk to Stanley. Since he's been in my situation longer than me. Jasmine returns in three days. I'm super excited to see if anything happens between them. I hope something does. It'll give me hope that maybe one day Ethan and I will work out. It no longer feels strange when I picture Ethan and me as an item. Is that weird?

Today we filmed Rachel witnessing the murder and running to the station like a madman. We did ten takes, from different angles. I had to stand in the middle of the road and pretend to see someone be murdered, then set off sprinting down the road. A track was set up at the edge of the road for the camera to run along. The best way to describe it is that it looks like a tiny train track. The cameraman was sitting on a seat that was fixed beside the mount holding the camera. As I ran, it ran alongside me. It was very distracting because all I wanted to do was look at it. For a couple of takes the camera ran slightly in front of me for a different shot and then behind me for the same reason. They wouldn't let me put on some comfier shoes while running so my feet were in agony by the time we'd finished. I'm not the quickest or the fittest, but I was proud of myself at the end of it for not complaining about it once or asking for a break. When all the special effects are added and the takes of me laughing are cut out, this movie should actually be very good. I can't wait for the premiere! I'm eager to see how the world reacts to me. I hope they like me. Otherwise what I've been striving for all my life has been a complete waste of time and I'll have to find something else to do.

AUGUST 20TH

Ethan's clock read 5:20 a.m., and another knock came at my hotel door. What did Eleanor want now? Unless she is pregnant, engaged, or snuck out last night to marry Ethan in Las Vegas, I was most definitely not interested in a conversation with her at this time of day again. I rolled off my bed and kept the covers wrapped around me as I dawdled to the door, again. I pawed at the door with my eyes closed in search of the handle, again. After a horrific battle in search of the handle, I eventually opened the door to find Stanley standing there.

"You look terrible," he said.

"What do you want at this hour?" I replied with closed eyes.

"We're picking Jasmine up from the airport in an hour, so move it!"

I sighed. "Ok. I'll get ready." I shut the door and stumbled into the bathroom. I tied my wild hair into a messy bun and grabbed one of Ethan's hoodies I had stolen off him and put up the hood. Somehow I didn't look that bad. I don't wear much makeup anyway so it was no different than my normal look. Maybe my tired eyes had lied to me.

Stanley drove to the airport. I scrunched myself up into a ball in the passenger seat and took a nap. The hood of

Ethan's hoodie acted as a pillow. It still smelt of him as I snuggled into it. Not getting enough sleep is the number one thing I despise. It is for a good purpose though.

I insisted Stanley purchased a bouquet of flowers from a florist in the airport. He obliged and bought a huge bouquet of red roses. So big that it covered most of his face when he held them.

We arrived at Jasmine's gate with fifteen minutes to spare. Stanley bit his nails as he stared at the door from our seats. He didn't move his eyes off the door for a second. There was a crowd of fifty to sixty people waiting for family and friends to depart from the plane. We sat and waited. And waited. And waited. Until the door finally opened. Stanley jolted upright, picking up his bouquet.

"Here I go," he said, glancing back at me.

"Good luck," I whispered.

He slowly strode forward. It was lovely to see members from the flight running over to greet their loved ones. Others wearing suits just paced into the airport. Then the moment Stanley had been waiting for arrived. Jasmine searched amongst the crowd of people, hoping to find a familiar face. Stanley lowered the bouquet so his face was visible. Jasmine's face lit up once she recognised him. They slowly walked towards each other and stopped shoe to shoe. I felt like I was watching a romantic movie live, not behind the scenes. The fairytale was taking place right in front of me. I could feel Stanley's nerves in my stomach. I watched as Jasmine and Stanley were in deep discussion. Suddenly Jasmine placed her hands over her mouth and swung her arms around Stanley. I felt like crying it was the sweetest, cutest, most romantic thing I had ever witnessed in my life, but the only thing I wanted to do now was go back to sleep. They hugged and kissed, and Stanley passed Jasmine her flowers.

"It's about time," I heard her say.

Stanley turned back to me, giving me a thumbs-up, which I feebly returned. They walked over to me, Stanley pulling Jasmine's suitcase as she hid behind her flowers. She poked her head around them, producing a shy smile.

"Can I go back to sleep now?" I asked, shutting my eyes.

They both laughed at me. "Let's get you to the car first," Stanley replied.

AUGUST 27TH

It's the final day. This movie has changed my life forever and it will always be in my heart. I've had so much fun! My first movie ever... I hope it isn't my last. It's not been a bad first film, to say Stanley Tennant was the director and Eleanor Walden was my co-star. I can't wait for it to be released now! Stanley gathered everyone around on set to make an announcement before our final takes.

"It has been an unforgettable time with you all. I may be grumpy sometimes, but that doesn't mean I don't love you guys." He paused while everyone laughed. "So, let's get this over and done with so we can all go home early." The crowd cheered and clapped before dispersing back to their stations.

Today, Eleanor and I filmed the last couple of scenes of us stumbling out of the station. Eleanor's character twists her ankle, so she has to limp and place her arm around my shoulder. The first take we did, we made it down the stairs, then our feet got tangled up and we fell over in a heap. We couldn't do another take for a while because we were too busy laughing at one another. We're the only two left alive after the eventful evening. Then we continue limping off into the distance. Once we'd finished laughing, of course. That's when I'd assume the end credits would feature. Eleanor hugged me firmly after the final take.

"I'm so happy I met you." Her voice squeaked.

My bottom lip started to tremble as everyone started to hug. Was it like this at the end of every movie? I hoped not. I'll be a mess every few months. I flicked my eyes over to Jasmine and Stanley; they were kissing. It made me feel all warm and fuzzy. I just smiled at them. Now I wanted to grab my things and meet Ethan at our new apartment. I've been dying to see it. I want to drive my new car, too. I haven't driven it since Wayne still chauffeurs me everywhere. I was desperate to hop in it and speed away. I didn't want to hang around much longer as I'd become an emotional wreckage. Before I did anything else, I had to say good-bye to Jasmine and Stanley. The three of us embraced after I walked over.

"I'm going to miss you guys," I said to them.

We separated away from each other swiftly and shook hands before we all started weeping.

The car roared into life as I turned on the ignition. The car hadn't moved an inch, and I was already in love with it. Eleanor shuffled herself into the passenger seat as I entered the address into the navigation system.

"Ready to go?" I asked Eleanor.

She nodded with a bright face. Then I remembered Ethan saying there was running items in the boot for me. I slid out of the car and clicked it open. Laid amongst the boot were several pairs of Nike running shoes and bottoms. *He knows me too well,* I said to myself. I returned to the driver's seat.

"Ethan said to be careful," Eleanor said, peering down at her phone.

I'm sure Ethan was saying something super cute like *I love you, baby girl, see you soon.* I wanted to snatch her phone off her and throw it out the car window. I beeped the horn as we departed from alongside the station. As weird as it may sound, I will miss that place. I'd spent so much time there that it had started to feel like home. We popped back to the hotel to collect our things before rushing back to the car. I was in that much of a rush I almost forgot Ethan's clock. I had to sprint back inside and collect it.

As Eleanor and I cruised along in my wonderful new car, I thought to myself, what should I spend my earnings on? Jewellery? Clothes? Invest it? I didn't want anything. Maybe get a house in England, but Ethan has that taken care of, too. I'm not sure what inspired him to purchase an apartment in New York, but I'm glad he did. I've always wanted to visit New York; now I'm going to live there! It'll be a test for me to survive without my family. I've managed three months so far and survived. I really want to see them, though. They said they'd visit during the holidays when Madeline finished school. I miss Madeline so much. I want to squeeze her and plait her hair.

As I gazed out of the window, a suggestion popped into my mind. Why don't I hire Leonard Phillips, the magician Ethan grew up watching. He could help me solve how Ethan switched seats with me in the car. Leonard Phillips wasn't a magician on a kid's television show who'd pull a rabbit from his hat. He performed ridiculous stunts. Like burying himself underground in a coffin or hanging himself upside down from a rope over a tank of sharks and then setting the rope on fire. I know this because Ethan used to make me watch Leonard's shows all the time. Every Saturday at eight o'clock. We never missed one. We were only eleven or twelve. Leonard was the only magician who made Ethan really think about how he did his tricks. He figured them out after a day or two. We'd watch the show Saturday and by Monday afternoon, when he walked me home, he'd explain how they were done. I always found it fascinating listening to his explanations. Leonard must have given his wife a heart attack every time he performed. Her blood pressure must have been off the scales. I'm sure after a discussion, he'd be able to help me. I suppose it wouldn't hurt to ask. I grabbed my phone and texted Stanley while we waited amongst the queue of cars. I figured he would know someone who knew Leonard.

AUGUST 28TH

Today was my first full day in my new apartment. It is
the most luxurious place I've ever set foot in. I pulled
up outside in my car. A man, dressed all smart, took my
keys and parked my car for me. Another man in a suit then
opened the door for me and they called me the elevator.
Out of twenty-four floors, our apartment is the sixteenth.
Coincidental, isn't it? Each apartment takes up a whole
level, so they're big. You walk along a spotless hallway to
your door, opening it with your key. Entering the apartment is like entering another world, filled with beautiful
colours, turquoise and white mainly. To your left, behind
the centre island granite block, is the kitchen. Equipped
with loads of cooking items that I have no idea what they're
called or do. Besides the oven and microwave. The kitchen
will be disappointed when I make scrambled egg on toast.
As you walk forward to the open living room, you will find
an eleven-seated L-shaped black sofa, positioned in front

of a sixty-inch television. You'll encounter a staircase to your left. A wonderful, winding pearl white staircase. After you encountered this staircase, there is a balcony stretching out the full length of the apartment. You go out a door before the staircase on your left, or you can walk straight through the living room to the other door. But I won't be going out there much because I'm afraid of heights. At night I could maybe go out onto it, because at night I can't really see what's below me. But during the day it's a definite no go. Walking up the wonderful, winding staircase, you'll find three bedrooms. Ethan had already called dibs on the biggest room. That's fair since he paid for everything and, dare I say it, he will be having Eleanor over to stay. The apartment is full of furniture, but it lacks things to make it feel like home. Adding Ethan's clock and my photo frames to the mantelpiece helped a little, but I still need to bring things over from home. Maybe now would be a good time to mention we have a gym upstairs. I only poked my head around the corner, but it has plenty of equipment in it. My bed feels like heaven, too. It's so soft.

"Eleanor suggested we have a party here soon, so we can make some new friends," Ethan said as we sat eating our cereal on the sofa. He was wearing the pizza tie I bought him for our fourth Christmas together. It's like his tie is a huge weirdly shaped slice of pizza, topped with pepperoni.

"Do we need to make new friends?" I groaned.

"We can't isolate ourselves from everyone for the rest of our lives, August."

I stared at him. Eleanor is turning into his wife.

"Did Eleanor tell you about the television agency?" he asked.

I raised my eyebrow at him. "What about it?"

He ate a spoonful of cereal. "They want me to do a television programme. Street magic, things like that. Eleanor

told me to show her friend who owns the television company a magic trick or two. Well, I did five, and he liked what
he saw and he said the show would have potential and would
hardly cost anything to make. Meaning good profit for
them."

I was happy for him, but I could already sense him
drifting away. He'll vanish off somewhere, leaving me
behind in the apartment alone.

"Sounds great," I muttered. Our eyes met. I quickly
looked away. I grabbed his empty bowl and walked over to
the kitchen. I placed the bowls in the dishwasher and when
I raised my head from behind the side, he had gone. I
sighed. *What's wrong with me?* Not even I knew the answer.
Ethan must think I'm being a right arse. He's given me
everything, and now I'm showing no interest in what he's
doing. Having his own show is such a big deal, and I made
out that I wasn't interested at all. I called my mum in hope
hearing a familiar voice might enlighten my spirit.

"Hi, sweetie."

"Hey, do you want to come to New York?"

"I thought you'd never ask! Madeline and I have been
waiting for your call!"

"Are you being serious?"

"Yes, I'm being serious. We've been waiting for your call
to let us know that you're settled in, sweetie. Madeline
really wants to come visit!"

"When are you going to come?"

"Well, we can be over within a few days. I'll have to run
it past your father first. Is something wrong?"

"I just need to see a familiar face, that's all."

"What's wrong with Ethan?"

"Nothing. He's going to be with Eleanor, isn't he?"

"Oh honey, I'm sorry. We'll be over as soon as we can,
ok?"

"Ok."

"I love you."

"I love you too."

I called Max straight after.

"What's up, bro?"

"Not much, you?"

"Other than sitting in my room, reading all day, absolutely nothing. I'm on my seventh book at this moment in time."

"Max, that's pretty concerning. You should consider going outside."

"I would, but the skin might melt off my body if I do so."

"If you say so. Listen, the reason I am calling you is I'll need an assistant type person soon with all this publicity coming in, aren't I?"

"Right..."

"Do you want to do it?"

"Me?"

"Yes, you."

"Why not find a proper one?"

"Because I don't know any or anyone. You're my friend and you're fairly intelligent. I'm guessing all you need to do is answer emails and arrange interviews and stuff for me. I doubt you will be busy for a while. I'll find a proper one after Christmas because no one will know who I am until November."

"Interesting proposal you're offering me here. Where will I stay?"

"Well my mum and sister are visiting within the next week. After they leave you can stay with us until you find somewhere. It depends if you get a visa sorted or not."

"Have you spoken with Ethan about this?"

"I'm sure he'll be fine with it."

"This is the worst job offer I've ever been given. I'll take it."

"Excellent. Arrange yourself a flight in two or three weeks' time. I'll pay for your flight if you let me know how much it is."

"I'm already searching for them and applying for my visa."

"Perfect. Bye, bro."

"Bye, dude, speak to you soon."

SEPTEMBER 1ST

NEW EMAIL FROM MARY CADDICK
Miss Bishop,
I've been passed your details from Stanley Tennant. He informed me that you wished to discuss something with Mr. Phillips. Leonard is currently away on holiday, but if you'd like to send me what it is you're after, I can forward the message to him. These past few years he's not interested in television or films, but I was assured this was a personal matter.
Kindest Regards, Mary.

NEW EMAIL FROM AUGUST BISHOP
Hi, Mary,
Thank you for emailing me! My friend Ethan is a magician. You won't have heard of him, but he will have his own TV show soon! A few months back we were involved in a car crash. I was sitting in the front passenger seat. Ethan was sitting in the backseat of my friend's truck. A 4x4 appeared out of nowhere and slammed into my side of the vehicle. When I woke in hospital, my friend and I realised Ethan somehow managed to switch seats with me, and suffered the injuries I should have suffered. We both didn't see him do it. This event has

been playing on my mind for a while now. I'm sure you can understand why. Ethan refuses to tell me how he did it. I want Leonard to help me solve how he did it. Ethan and I grew up watching him and we admire him profoundly, I couldn't think of anyone else to help me solve this matter. If you could forward this email to him, I would deeply appreciate it.

Thanks, August.

I felt like a spy secretly doing undercover business as I typed out the email. I most definitely didn't want Ethan to find out. Otherwise my job as a spy could be flushed down the toilet.

September 2ND

NEW MESSAGE FROM MUM
We're boarding the plane now. See u soon. Love u.
xxxxx

NEW MESSAGE FROM MADELINE
C U SOON SMELLY!!!

I'm so excited for my mum and Madeline's arrival. It's a shame Dad has to work. Ethan drove over to the airport to pick them up. I think he's excited to be reunited with them, too. I logged into my email while I waited. *No new emails.* It's too early to conclude that Leonard Phillips wasn't interested. He is on holiday. He doesn't want to be disturbed, I'm sure.

When I heard the key in the door, I jumped up. Madeline looked like she was entering Disney Land for the first time. Her jaw was massively ajar. She sprinted off to view the apartment before even saying hello. My mum clambered through the door with a bundle of bags and suitcases.

"Mum!" I shouted as I ran over and hugged her.

"August, at least let me get through the door first," she said as she dropped her bags. "Ooo, this is nice, isn't it? I wouldn't mind leaving your father and moving in here."

She wandered through the apartment as if she was a lost child in a playground.

I looked at Ethan. He smiled. He's wearing his golden star tie I bought him for his eighteenth birthday. He picked up the bags my mum had dropped on the floor and carried them upstairs. Madeline shortly followed behind him, skipping up each step. My mum watched them as they disappeared up the staircase and then ventured out onto the balcony

"Mum, Mum. There's an ice cream place not far from here. Can he take me, *please?*" Madeline asked, running back downstairs. Mum returned from the balcony and flicked her eyes at me before returning to Madeline.

"Don't have too much, ok?"

Madeline frowned at our mother. "Fine."

Ethan jogged downstairs.

"Mum says we can go!" Madeline shouted to him.

He smiled and grabbed his keys and wallet off the side. "Let's go, Maddie!"

Madeline rushed around and hugged me, allowing me to kiss her cheek before sprinting away. She struggled to open the heavy door to the apartment. Ethan assisted her, allowing her to run along the corridor to the elevator. Ethan smiled at Mum and me, and closed the door behind him. Silence flowed through the apartment, but Madeline's singing could be heard from along the corridor.

"How the hell did he afford all this?" Mum asked, as she stood and examined the mantelpiece. She picked up the framed Polaroid picture Ethan and I took on my birthday. I wanted to tell her about Ethan and his money, but I knew it wouldn't be a good idea. Ethan would be furious with me also.

"I have no idea. What's new with you?" I asked.

"Oh nothing. My daughter is in L-O-V-E."

I blushed and buried my head into my hands. "Oh please don't," I cried.

She leapt back onto the sofa beside me. "Why! Let's talk about it. We never have a gossip anymore!"

I removed my head from my hands to her sarcastic sulking face staring at me. "I love him, he doesn't love me. There's nothing else to talk about."

"What an absurd statement. He loves you. You've both been too stubborn and stupid to admit it." She reached for her handbag and pulled out an envelope.

"What's that?"

"These are all the photos from yours and Ethan's birthdays since you were ten. I didn't bring the earlier ones and Christmas ones because I was tired of taking them out of the big frame."

She laid them out on the table in front of us. Twenty photos, including the framed one from the mantelpiece. "Look at the photos and tell me what you see, please," Mum said in a teacher-like attitude.

"Why?" I asked.

She rolled her eyes at me. You can tell where I get it from. "Just do it."

I did as instructed and scanned through the photos. I haven't seen them in a while. We looked so cute, bless us. In the first one my face is so freckly, and my teeth were still a little crooked. Ethan was missing one of his front teeth because I pulled it out when he kept complaining about it being wobbly. It was odd looking at the photos from when we were ten to the one we had taken a few weeks back.

"What do you notice?" Mum asked. I shrugged.

"They're all photos of me and Ethan?" I guessed weakly.

"No, you moron, look again!"

Annoyed, I scanned through the photos again. Nothing stood out.

"I really don't know, Mum... Can you tell me?"

She snatched at some photos and picked them up, fanning them out in her hands and holding them up.

"Right. I'll explain this to you slowly. Here I hold six photos of you two, aged ten to twelve. On these photos you and Ethan are sitting or standing beside each other looking forward and smiling for the photo, right?" She said this as if I couldn't speak English, but I went along with it.

"*Right*," I elongated.

She placed those photos back on the table and picked up the rest. She held them up and flicked through them one by one, holding them up again. "From thirteen to nineteen. Now he's looking at you, see? You're looking at the camera. He is looking at you. O-K?"

I still didn't understand what difference that made.

"So? Just because he is looking at me, it doesn't mean anything."

"Ok, ok. Bear that thought in mind though, the fact he's looking at you."

She rummaged in her bag and pulled out another envelope. "Now, these are photos of me and your father from when we were younger. This photo was when we were celebrating being together nine months. Here your dad is looking at me, like Ethan was looking at you."

She flicked along to the next photo. "This photo was the night your father proposed; here he is looking at me, like Ethan was looking at you."

She flicked onto the next photo. "This photo was on our wedding day. Here your father is looking at me, like Ethan was looking at you."

She viciously swept away her wedding photo, revealing the last image. "This photo, our honeymoon, again your father is looking at me like Ethan was looking at you. Don't you see what the common connection is?"

I sighed because I had absolutely no idea what she was talking about.

"I don't know, Mum. Guys look at girls weirdly in photos after they reach a certain age?"

She threw the photos in the air and ran her hands through her hair.

"No. You bloody idiot. Ethan is or was in love with you. Like your father was in love with me. It's very fucking clear in the bloody presentation I put a lot of hard work into. Pardon my French, but I thought you were a lot more intelligent than this, August."

She picked up the photos and stacked them on the table. I sat silently, staring at her.

"I need a wee," she said in a fluster.

I laughed and pointed towards the downstairs toilet. She smiled and rushed towards it. It shocked me a little that she swore. Mum very rarely swears.

I returned to the photos on the table and picked them up. I compared the photo of Ethan and me at his seventeenth birthday to the photo of Mum and Dad on the night he proposed. Mum was right. They were both looking at us in the same unmistakable way. I can't believe I hadn't noticed this. Saying that, if I couldn't see it when Mum explained it as clear as daylight, I wouldn't figure it out by myself, would I? Does this mean Ethan loved me? Why didn't he say something? Does he still love me? Did he ever love me?

SEPTEMBER 12TH

We visited the Empire State Building today. Since it's Mum's and Madeline's final day, we decided to treat them to a little sightseeing. I would tell you how magnificent the view is from the top of the Empire State Building; however, as we all remember, I am scared of heights. I had my eyes shut the entire time. Even before we got in the elevator. I clung to Ethan like my life depended on it. The only reason I agreed to go up was because it was something to cross off my list. I could actually say I reached the top.

"You're such a loser!" Ethan laughed.

I squeezed his arm and scrunched my face while shushing him.

"She's always been like this for some reason," Mum mumbled.

The elevator wobbled as it came to a halt. The doors beeped as they opened. I heard Madeline's stomping footsteps sprint out of the elevator and onto the roof.

"Be careful!" I yelled to her. A whiteness flooded my eyelids as we stepped out. The sun's heat followed. It was warm, but the wind dimmed it.

"It's so beautiful," Ethan whispered, escorting me out.

"I don't care what you say, I am not opening my eyes," I muttered.

"What if I told you Hugh Jackman stood no farther than ten feet away from us?" Ethan said, squeezing my arm.

"Ethan, Hugh Jackman isn't here, that isn't going to work, you fool."

"Mr. Jackman, we're such huge fans. It's so nice to meet you," Ethan said in a brightened voice.

For a second I genuinely thought Hugh Jackman really was standing in front of me, and I considered opening my eyes for a moment.

"Why thank you. Beautiful up here, isn't it?" I heard in an Australian voice.

"Ethan, that is the worst Australian accent I have ever heard," I said, turning my head with an unimpressed look.

"I thought it was quite good."

I shook my head. "No, it really wasn't."

We continued wandering around in silence. Mum and Madeline had left us behind. I couldn't even hear Madeline's voice or her feet stamping around.

"Aren't you that magician?" Ethan started in his pathetic voice again.

"Yes I am!" he replied to himself.

"I'm such a huge fan! I'm sure you are a fan of Wolverine?"

"Who isn't, Hugh? I can't believe you're a fan of mine, this is so humbling!"

Ethan's one-man show between him and a fake Hugh Jackman was equally as annoying as it was funny. I had a smirk on my face, but tried to hide it.

"You're such an idiot!" I managed to say through my laughter.

"I'm just trying to keep you distracted!" Ethan said, joining me.

I squeezed his arm and rested my head against his shoulder.

"It's so weird walking around with your eyes closed," I whispered.

Ethan hummed as we continued to walk. A gust of wind would often lift my hair and chill the back of my neck. Madeline's voice started to become louder and clearer.

Ethan let go of my arm. "Maddie, no! Get down from there!"

"Madeline!" I yelled. "Whatever you're doing, stop it!"

My eyes remain closed as I helplessly stood still.

"Maddie, just climb back over the fence, please, I don't want you to fall," I heard Ethan say.

"Fence?" I yelled. "I thought the fence was huge?"

"Well she's on the other side of it. Don't worry, I'll get her," Ethan replied.

"Madeline, climb back over it immediately!" I screamed.

My heart began to race uncontrollably and my legs started to shake. I tried to force open my eyes, but it was as if they were glued shut. I tried to follow Ethan's voice, hoping to get closer to them.

"August," Ethan said calmly.

"What?" I replied, distraught.

"We're standing right in front of you, dear."

I felt Madeline's tiny hand grab mine to prove his statement. My body filled with rage. This was a cruel, cruel joke that shouldn't be played on anyone. They started to giggle as I felt my anger rise throughout my face.

"You mean bastards!" I screamed.

Everyone must have stopped to look at me in disgust. I took a deep breath and dropped my head. Suddenly I was extremely embarrassed.

"Do you really think Madeline could climb that?" Ethan asked. I could sense the sarcasm on his face.

"I don't know! I was just following what you were saying. Oh my God, I feel sick, can we please go?"

They both continued to laugh as they took hold of my hands.

"Don't you ever do that again!" I commanded.

"The joys of having kids," Mum said from behind me. "Constant heart attacks," She added.

I took a deep breath and composed myself. I desperately wanted to open my eyes after this dramatic ordeal, but I knew I would freak out and faint afterwards. They escorted me back to the elevator and placed my hand onto the railing. I opened my eyes, expecting the elevator doors to have already closed, and as they readjusted to the light, I caught a glimpse of the skyline of the beautiful city I now called home.

September 13ᵀᴴ

I've had the best time with my mum and Madeline. I wished they could've stayed for longer; ten days wasn't enough. It's a shame Madeline has school.

"Thank you," I whispered to Mum as I hugged her good-bye.

Ethan enjoyed having them over, too. He disappeared most nights with Eleanor so we didn't see him much during the evenings. When he wasn't with Eleanor, he was taking Madeline to the ice cream parlour. It's her new favourite place in the entire world. Ethan hated admitting it, but he was tired of eating ice cream. Apparently, Madeline spent so much time in there that they named an ice cream flavour after her. I'm sure they called it *obsessed* or *lunatic for ice cream*. I bet she thought it was the coolest thing ever, having her own ice cream. I wish I had an ice cream flavour named after me, but then again, I have an apartment in New York named after me. So as far as getting things named after you, I was kicking her ass. "Bye, Madeline," I said, covering her in kisses. She giggled and clung to my neck.

"Ready to go?" Ethan asked, opening the apartment door. He wasn't wearing a tie today, which was unusual. Very unusual. He insisted on driving them back to the airport.

A date has officially been set to start filming his new show in Los Angeles for two weeks. Not only is he going to be gone for two weeks, but he'll be on the other side of the country. He's leaving on the twentieth and returns on the fifth of October. He's only doing five episodes as a trial run. It's going to be like a handheld camera view. I'm guessing it's a really good quality one if it's going on TV. But you will almost feel like a member of the crowd watching him. That's how he described it. Ethan being gone gives me time to bring Max over here and spend time with him. Ethan asked if I wouldn't mind Eleanor staying with me while he's away. Which will be... great.

I'm glad Ethan's been given this opportunity. He deserved his dream more than anyone. He dedicated his life to magic, literally. I don't want him to be gone for too long, and suddenly he moves to LA and leaves me alone. Our careers forcing us to go our separate ways. That's what scares me the most, losing him.

SEPTEMBER 19TH

Ethan had another nightmare in the early hours of this morning. I was downstairs raiding the fridge when I heard him shout my name. I dropped my milk shake and sprinted upstairs to his room. I burst in to find him sitting upright with his head in his hands.

"Are you ok?" I asked, flustered and out of breath.

"This nightmare is driving me insane!"

I closed the door and turned on his bedside lamp. I snuggled alongside him in bed and put my arm around him.

"Ethan, what's going on? What aren't you telling me? You know what happened last time you kept things from me," I said, rubbing his shoulder with my thumb.

He kept his head in his hands and sighed. "I'm back in Max's truck. I'm sitting in the passenger seat. The 4x4 is heading straight for me and smashes into the car. And then I wake up."

As I gazed into his eyes they appeared possessed. He was so shaken by it, and he was covered in sweat.

I rested my head on his shoulder. "I'm here."

We lay back and he rested his head on my stomach. I ran my fingers through his hair until he fell asleep.

Since I was trapped underneath Ethan, I stayed with him. I didn't want to disrupt his sleep. It was a slight shock to be woken up by Eleanor. Her eyes beamed down upon me with rage, maybe because we were sharing a bed and he was still asleep on me. I slid out from underneath him and stood up.

"Morning," I whispered to her.

"What were you doing?" she whispered back.

"He had a nightmare during the night, so I stayed with him."

She nodded suspiciously and then sat alongside him in bed, nudging him awake. "Baby, wake up, baby," she said.

I felt like screaming, *Just call him Ethan, you idiot!* Does she really need to call him baby? Really?

I left them be and walked out of the room. Eleanor had popped over to help Ethan pack since he's leaving tomorrow. Normally that would be my job, but I guess she's beaten me to it since she's now a higher authority in Ethan's life.

NEW EMAIL FROM LEONARD PHILLIPS

Dear Miss Bishop,

My agent, Mary, forwarded your email onto me. Forgive me. It's been a while since anyone has contacted me for business. So this friend of yours, Ethan, switched seats with you in a car crash? And he's been a magician for the majority of his life? This sounds like an interesting act given the time he had to complete it, but I'm always up for a challenge. Since my granddaughter has recently become a fan of yours from all the magazines she reads, I'll do it for free if you send her an autograph or something nice. It would really put a smile on her face. Send me all the details you can about locations and times. I have friends who will track down the CCTV footage. It won't be easy, but I won't know until I have seen the footage.

Best Regards, Leonard.

It was weird receiving that email from Leonard. I watched his show growing up, and now we're going to be doing business together. Even though I was never a *huge* fan of his, it was still cool to receive an email from him! All I need now is a letter from Scooby-Doo and my list would be complete. I sent Leonard an email regarding all the details I knew about the crash. I wasn't much help, but he said he'd make do with it. Max has planned to arrive on the twenty-first. Ethan agreed Max could stay for a month or two. I'm glad he's coming. I'm sure he would be more than happy to help me keep Eleanor entertained due to the fact he adores her. I'm sure he envies Ethan sincerely.

SEPTEMBER 20TH

Eleanor couldn't keep her hands off Ethan as she said good-bye to him this morning. I practically had to drag her off him so I could hug him and say good-bye myself. He was wearing the black tie with his initials in I bought him for his birthday this year. I focused down at his bag; the more I stared at it the more saddened I became. He raised my chin with his finger and his eyes looked into mine. We didn't say anything; we just looked at each other. I forgot Eleanor was standing right next to us, so I gave him a firm hug to avoid her becoming suspicious. He kissed the top of my head as he always does and let go of me. It was sad watching him leave. But he'll be doing the thing he loves, and he'll only be gone for two weeks. I'd be more upset if it were two months. I offered to drive Ethan to the airport, but he preferred driving himself. Then he just left, leaving Eleanor and I staring at the door. We sat in silence for at least five minutes.

"Chinese?" I asked, I was starving, and I'd been craving some.

"You read my mind. I'll order now," Eleanor said, reaching for her phone. Within thirty minutes of me asking, our living room was filled with Chinese food. I insisted we sat and watched Eleanor's film *Hard Luck* to brighten the mood. She made mental notes on herself as she watched.

"My ass looks so small on that shot. I need to squat more, don't I?" Eleanor asked, picking at her nails.

I stared at her behind on the screen, maybe for too long.

"Um... I'm not sure I should comment on that subject. Kinda weird, isn't it?"

She scrunched her face at me and shuffled her bottom on the sofa. "I'm gonna head upstairs and do some squats. Coming?"

I was eating noodles, and I considered carrying on watching the rest of the film. I swallowed them and nodded. I placed the box of noodles onto the table and followed her upstairs. I suppose joining her in the gym would be more beneficial than watching a movie and eating noodles.

SEPTEMBER 21ST

Eleanor and I were having breakfast, finishing the film we'd started last night. Five minutes after it finished a knock came at the door.

"I'll get it," Eleanor shouted, running over to the door like an excited toddler. She swung the door open to reveal Max with his mouth ajar. He stared at her for a good seven to ten seconds before I shouted, "Max, I thought I was picking you up from the airport!" Max said nothing. He remained in his stare.

"Hi," she said enthusiastically. "I'm Eleanor." Max grinned.

"H-h-h-hi-hi," he replied.

"Smooth, Max," I said with a mouthful of cereal. He stepped inside and scanned the apartment in wonder.

"What happened to picking you up from the airport?" I asked.

Max returned his sight to Eleanor. "Can I have a hug?"

"Sure," she said, opening her arms.

Max dropped his bags and wrapped his arms around her. I bet you all the money in the world he smelt her hair. He definitely smelt her hair.

"Max, time to let her go, bud," I said.

"Oh hey, August," he said, walking over and fist bumping me.

"Anyway, I'm gonna get ready," Eleanor said, disappearing upstairs.

Max tilted his head as he watched her go upstairs.

"Could you make it any more obvious, Max?" I punched him in the arm to regain his attention.

"Would it be weird if I asked her to marry me?"

I rolled my eyes at him. "You've been here thirty seconds. Maybe when she knows who you are and wait until she isn't in a relationship with Ethan before doing so?"

He nodded. "Good idea." He began to walk upstairs. I was beginning to regret my remark of complimenting his intelligence. "I'll ask her which room is mine." I laughed because I knew this was either going to be a nightmare or loads of fun.

SEPTEMBER 29TH

Max and Eleanor were inseparable. It's like they're the ones in the relationship. They clicked from the second they met. Obviously, they're not kissing or sleeping together, but they understand each other's humour. They've barely spoken to me over the past few days. It's like I'm invisible. I hope Ethan realises this when he returns: that they make a cute couple, and that August, his smoking hot best friend, is the better choice for him.

NEW EMAIL FROM LEONARD PHILLIPS
Dear Miss Bishop,
I have returned from Italy. I shall begin right away on your demands. The thing that is taking the most time is finding the camera footage from the surrounding shops' surveillance systems, but I'll get ahold of them.
Our investigation is under way basically! Leonard.

I was unsure whether to inform Max of my recent arrangements with Leonard. He'd probably never heard of him. He can't hold his own water, too. Ethan would find out within five minutes of Max finding out. Moving off subject here, but I think Max is in love with Eleanor. He was before even meeting her, but now he has, he really is. I know this because he's acting the same way I was, did, or do with Ethan. She's been away for an audition the past day and a half and I can see that he misses her, even though she's only known of his existence for a week. I saw them out on the balcony before she left. He can't take his eyes off her. There was one moment I saw and I immediately knew. Eleanor was gazing over the city and chatting. I couldn't hear what she was saying; it was a distant and unclear noise. Max turned and looked at her, and he smiled: not a grin, just a slight unmissable and unmistakable smirk. And I knew right then he was in love with her. Eleanor turned and blushed. There may have even been a slight spark between them there, but one cannot be sure. I've arranged to have dinner with Max later to talk about being my personal assistant. Though I'm really planning to speak about Eleanor.

NEW MESSAGE FROM ELEANOR WALDEN
Do you think I should go to LA and surprise Ethan? xoxo

NEW MESSAGE FROM AUGUST BISHOP
It's hard to say. Do you know exactly where he is? I don't want to encourage you to go and then you can't find him! xoxo

NEW MESSAGE FROM ELEANOR WALDEN
Maybe you're right. He'll be back next week, won't he? Max and I were supposed to be grabbing lunch at my friend's restaurant tomorrow as well. I don't want to let him down! xoxo

NEW MESSAGE FROM AUGUST BISHOP
Yeah…maybe if he were gone for longer it would have been a nice surprise! Hey, thanks for inviting me! You

and Max seem to have gotten close over the last week! You're inseparable! xoxo

NEW MESSAGE FROM ELEANOR WALDEN
That's true. Sorry, I discussed it with Max and forgot about you, sorry! I guess we're...lol. I'm beginning to think I chose the wrong friend to date! xoxo

NEW MESSAGE FROM AUGUST BISHOP
Oh it's fine, don't worry about it! & You don't say... xoxo

"How are you finding life in New York, Max?" I asked as we found our seats at our table in the new Italian restaurant we had discovered.

"I love it. I'm so glad you asked me to come out here, August."

I took a sip from my glass of water. "On a scale of one to ten. How in love with Eleanor are you?" I smugly asked. My intentions of sneaking it into the conversation lasted approximately seventeen seconds. Now I understand how Stanley felt when he asked how I was coping with Ethan.

Max looked down at his glass of water. "That obvious, huh?"

You could see it was playing on his mind. I felt like someone was showing me a reflection of myself a month or two ago. In male form of course.

"Max, I know how you feel, and you know I know how you feel. If you want to talk about it, we can, and yes it is obvious."

I wanted to tell him that Eleanor might feel something for him too. But I didn't want to mislead him in case it wasn't true, or she was joking.

"Thanks. It's just I've never had a relationship before and this is all new to me... I just want her to be mine, you know. You must've felt horrible when you found out."

"It honestly felt like someone kicked me in the stomach. Just give yourself false hope and pray they don't get engaged. Maybe talk to her tomorrow when you go for food and see how she feels?"

He frowned at me immediately. "We've only known each other for a week, are you mad? You've had twelve years to tell Ethan. I think you're unable to provide advice on telling or asking them how you, or they feel. But this is Ethan's girlfriend. I couldn't do that to him."

His comment hurt slightly, but it was true, so I couldn't argue otherwise.

"All I'm saying is don't leave it until it's too late, like I did. In my case until it's a bloody long time too late."

OCTOBER 1ST

NEW EMAIL FROM LEONARD PHILLIPS

Dear August,

I've tracked down the case file for your accident. (I told you it wouldn't take long.) I'm going to peruse it now. The camera footage is going to take a while longer to be sent over to me, but that shouldn't be too long. I will update you once I have received the footage or if anything of significance comes to my attention, Leonard.

Only one week until Ethan's return, give or take half a day. He hasn't texted me since he's been away. I don't know if he's busy or isn't interested in talking to me. I hope it isn't the second one. I've been thinking about what Mum presented with the photos. I wished it was easy to ask Ethan about the photos and if it was true. Life would be so much easier if we had the courage to ask the questions we fear the most.

As I sat and ate my morning bowl of cereal alone on the sofa, I noticed Max and Eleanor weren't around. They went out for dinner last night, hadn't they? I wondered if anything happened between them. I headed upstairs and checked Ethan's bedroom: empty. Then I checked Max's room, knocked: no answer. I slowly opened the door. The room was empty. Where on earth were they? I headed back downstairs and called Max.

"Hello."

"Max? Where are you? Did you go out this morning?"

"I'm at Eleanor's. I can't remember a thing from last night, we drank so much."

"Do you want me to pick you up?"

"Please, August, I'm freaking out right now. I don't know what happened..."

"Are you in bed with her?"

"No, we're on the sofa."

"I'll leave now. Give me five minutes."

The apartment stank of booze as Max opened the door. "Morning," I said.

He scowled at me. "Let's go. She's still asleep."

He walked over to her and kissed her head before quietly closing the door behind us. He hid himself under his shirt as I drove back home.

"Do you remember anything?"

"I remember being in the restaurant and we fancied a drink, so Eleanor said let's go back to her place. We had these really strong shots, they burnt your throat they were so strong. Then we kissed and that's it." He remained hidden under his shirt. It was surprising to hear how casual he sounded about the kissing part.

"You kissed?" I shouted, punching his arm.

"Ow! Yeah, she kissed me..."

I couldn't believe it! The cheating bitch! Saying that, Max was hardly going to avoid kissing her.

"Do you think it meant anything? Or was it just a drunken kiss?"

He sighed. "I dunno. God, what have I done?"

Ethan wasn't going to like this. Eleanor was going to be in big trouble, which was perfect. I would be the one to swoop in and be his shoulder to cry on.

Max stumbled upstairs to the bathroom as we got back to my apartment. As I closed the door and locked it, I heard a familiar voice.

"Where were you guys? I've been waiting for you!" It was Ethan.

I stared at the door. *He doesn't know anything. Let Max or Eleanor tell him. Keep your mouth shut.* My conscience told me. I prepared my smile and twisted.

"Hey!" I ran over and hugged him. He was wearing the tie I bought him for his sixteenth birthday. It's a dark navy tie covered in a pattern of small yellow suns. It's not my favourite if I'm honest.

Ethan must've appeared from the balcony when he heard the door open.

"How come you're back so soon?" I asked in a surprised, delighted high-pitched voice.

"We worked longer during the day so we could finish early," he said, hugging me again and swinging me around.

"Patrick Miller wants me to be on his show on Christmas Eve! Can you believe that? I've been dying to tell you!" He stopped and I regained my balance.

"That's so cool! I'm so jealous! I can't believe you beat me to it, I always thought I'd be the first on the show!"

"Well, I'm cooler than you so it's a clear choice."

I opened my mouth in disbelief. "Impossible!"

He grinned and tilted his head. "That is true. Is Max here? I thought I saw him on the staircase."

Max appeared at the stairs. "Hey, dude."

I took a few steps back in case he decided to tell him straight away.

"Maximus," Ethan formally replied. "I'm going over to Eleanor's now. Have you guys seen her recently?"

My eyes felt like they were going to pop out. I shook my head furiously.

"Nope." I glanced up to Max, who was staring at the floor.

"Can we speak when you get back?" he said to Ethan.

Ethan's eyebrows dropped. "Sure, bud. We can go for lunch when I get back."

I had no idea what Eleanor would tell Ethan. I had no idea what Max and she did. Max doesn't remember much. Was Max lying? I couldn't help but feel guilty. My stomach was churning and I felt sick. What was I supposed to say? *Max kissed your girlfriend last night. Good to have you back!*

Max or Eleanor needed to own up to their actions. I hated them for placing me into this uncomfortable situation.

Ethan had been gone an hour and fifteen minutes. I knew he'd be back any moment. Ethan isn't one to argue. His arguments are fairly short and snappy.

Max slumped alongside me on the sofa with his head in his hands.

"Can you remember anything else?"

He sat silently for a moment. "Nothing I can be sure of."

Then the door opened. Max's head shot out of his hands. I was too scared to turn around and look at Ethan entering. I tried to see his reflection in the TV, but I couldn't catch a proper glimpse.

"She's all yours, bud. I was heading over to break up with her anyway," Ethan said as he opened the door to the fridge.

I was debating over in my mind, *How long do I leave it before I rush over and snog him? Five minutes? Five hours? Five days? Five weeks?* Knowing me, I'd leave it five months or five years.

Ethan took a few gulps of something before placing it back into the fridge.

"I think it would be best you go stay with her. I'm not mad. I'm just disappointed, Max. I expected better from you."

Max wiped his eyes as he rose from the sofa, heading straight upstairs. I assumed he was going to pack up his things. Ethan sat beside me on the sofa and patted my knee. I grabbed his arm and put it over my head and onto my shoulder. I tucked my legs up and laid my head on his chest. "I'm so sorry, Ethan."

OCTOBER 5TH

I was awoken to Ethan shouting my name again at 3:00 a.m. It was even more terrifying than the first time. I shot up and burst into his room. I sat beside him and put my arms around him. Ethan has had a roller coaster of a journey over the past few months. He needs a holiday or something to take his mind off things. It must be driving him crazy. I'm not sure if breaking up with Eleanor was part of his plan, but more and more bad things keep popping up for Ethan and he definitely doesn't deserve them to.

NEW EMAIL FROM LEONARD PHILLIPS
Dear August,
I have received the camera footage from your crash. Hopefully I'll be able to piece what I have together and take a proper look at them. From what I've heard and read, it sounds like your friend is extremely lucky to be alive, Leonard.

Ethan's new show was scheduled to start broadcasting on the twentieth of October. It'll be so exciting and weird seeing Ethan have his own show. It seems like only yesterday we were kids watching Leonard Phillips. Now kids would grow up watching Ethan.

OCTOBER 10TH

NEW EMAIL FROM LEONARD PHILLIPS

I've pieced together the camera footage, but somehow it doesn't cover the side of the vehicle where it was hit. Meaning I've watched a lot of footage from the other side. I'm almost guessing. It's like watching the TV from behind someone's head. You weren't kidding when you said he swapped seats with you in a matter of milliseconds. All I can see so far is before the crash you're sitting in one seat; the next second, you're in the back. This may be the best trick I have ever seen. Maybe "trick" is the wrong word to use given the circumstances. "Act" would be more suited to the situation. I'll continue to analyse the footage. I'm using my office at the moment to plan the act how I would myself. Hopefully this will open a new perspective. I haven't been here in years! Leonard.

NEW EMAIL FROM AUGUST BISHOP

Leonard,

Ethan here. Big fan. As humbling as it is to hear you're having trouble solving how I switched seats, I will save you time and effort and tell you, you're wasting your time. I'm sure this won't affect you at all to stop your pursuit, but I ask you to stop your pursuit of emailing August. I also ask you to send her one last email saying the act is unsolvable. I will delete this conversation between us so she won't know of our discussion.

I'm sure we'll meet one day. Until then, Ethan Knight.

"What are you doing on my laptop?" I asked Ethan as I entered the apartment.

"I thought I told you to drop it," Ethan snarled, grabbing his jacket from the hanger.

"What are you talking about?" I knew exactly what he was talking about.

"Don't play stupid, August!" He stormed past me, his eyes filled with rage. Like when he saw the marking on my face after Mark hit me. Surely he was overreacting a little. Max entered the apartment behind me and closed the door. Ethan walked straight past him, too. They still weren't talking.

"Ethan, I'm sorry!" I shouted in despair.

"What did you do?" Max asked.

I sighed. "I hired someone to figure out how Ethan switched seats with me in the truck."

Ethan walked down the corridor and called the elevator.

Max sighed. "He never told you, did he?"

"Told me what?" My concern rocketed. These moments never end with good news.

He looked down, then at Ethan and then looked down again.

My bottom lip started to tremble.

"He died, August... His heart stopped in the impact. They brought him back in the ambulance on the way to the hospital. I stayed with him for as long as I could. I asked them not to say anything because I knew he would want to be the one to tell you."

I turned my head and looked at Ethan with tears rolling down my cheeks. His back facing me and his gaze lowered to the floor. I fell to the floor and cried. Like I've never cried before. I screamed through my tears. I couldn't breathe. I was gasping for air. I really thought my lungs were not functioning properly and I was going to pass out. I wrapped my arms over my head as I curled up on the floor. Darkness engulfed my body. I thought I was going to pass out.

I heard rushing footsteps, Ethan asking Max to leave.

"Don't cry, August, please don't cry," Ethan said as he sat beside me and stroked my back. "Please don't cry."

I couldn't stop. It felt like the world around me had collapsed. My lungs then kick-started, and I coughed as I tried to inhale. He scooped his arms underneath me and lifted me to his chest. I wrapped my arm around him and cried into his neck. We slumped onto the sofa. He tucked my hair behind my ears with his free hand. He hushed me silently as he rocked me in his arms.

"August you're breaking my heart. Please stop crying, please."

He rested his forehead against mine. "I'm sorry I didn't tell you, but I knew this is how you would react and I hate to see you cry. It's my least favourite thing. I hate it more than smoking."

I giggled through my tears.

"It was never me sitting in the passenger seat in my dream. It was you. I'm sitting in the back. You're sitting in the front and the car is heading straight for you. I can't move. My belt is stuck and I'm fighting to unclip it, but it won't budge. The car hits us and I wake up calling out your name."

I opened my eyes and looked up, deep into his distressed eyes. My tears stopped. I desperately wanted to grab him and kiss him.

"I saw it when my heart stopped; it was just like a dream or a vision, and when I woke, there were two defibrillators attached to my chest."

I sat up and tightened my arms around his neck. He was wearing the plain yellow tie I bought him for his seventeenth birthday. It tangled in our arms. Ethan pulled on it, allowing it to fall free, smirking as he did so. This was the moment. The moment I tell him. I couldn't hold it back anymore. I wouldn't.

I took a deep breath, "Ethan, I..." I said nervously. My jaw was still trembling from crying. He shushed me and covered my lips with his thumb.

"It can wait, dear." He wiped my cheek and kissed it.

October 11th

We fell asleep on the sofa, nose-to-nose, and woke up later that evening. I felt awful. My heart was aching. A horrible feeling of guilt built inside of me. My stomach was bubbling. I didn't know if it's hunger, nerves, or the flu. I was too tired to drag myself upstairs and into bed so I insisted I slept on the sofa. Ethan wouldn't have any of it, picking me up and flinging me over his shoulder as he carried me to my room.

"Will you stay with me please? If you have a bad dream, I don't want to force myself up and check on you. I'll be lying here beside you when you wake up."

I know what you're thinking, you're thinking, *Well played, August. I'm sure that's the real reason you asked him to stay with you.* To tell you the truth, I just wanted him to hold me. That's all I wanted.

I nestled my head into his chest as we snuggled into my bed together. He softly played with my hair as I shut my eyes. I snatched at his hand when he stopped. I placed my right arm across his chest, resting my hand on his shoulder. I wanted to feel the beat of his heart against me. If his stopped again, I think mine would, too.

We had breakfast at the ice cream parlour he and Madeline went to. They serve pancakes and waffles. Ethan had a huge smirk on his face as we waited for our food.

I selected his tie today. I chose his cute sunflower one I bought him for his eighth birthday. It's a tie filled with hundreds of sunflower heads, like hundreds placed on top of each other.

"Why are you smirking?" I finally asked.

"It's about time!" He rolled his eyes at me. The roles had been reversed.

I rolled my eyes at him rolling his eyes.

"I have good news for you," he said with a mouth full of pancake.

I scooped pancake into my mouth. "What is it?" I coughed and spat it back onto my plate. Almost choking on it. Ethan coughed because he was choking on his food from laughing at me. I covered my face in embarrassment. He almost fell off his chair from laughing at me. I threw my napkin at him.

Everyone around us must've thought we were a set of lunatics. After he finally composed himself, he said, "Guess who will be joining me on Patrick Miller's chat show in December?"

Puzzled and oblivious, I asked, "Who?"

Ethan frowned at me. "You, you fool!"

The biggest smile came across my face. I was visualising it.

I could see Patrick standing there.

And my next guest, the one the world has been dying to meet... the beautiful, the amazing, the talented, the goddess herself, the next big star... you get the idea ... AUGUST BISHOP!!

Then I would walk onto the stage and smile and wave to the wildly applauding audience. I'd run over to Patrick and we'd kiss on both cheeks.

"August?" Ethan said, leaning forward.

I shook myself and emerged from my daydream. "Sorry. I can't believe it! This is a dream come true!" I'm going to be on the show I grew up watching. It's amazing how much your life can change. I always said to myself I would be on the show although I never thought I actually would!

"Are you excited?" Ethan asked.

"Of course I am! Will you be on the show with me then?" There was no one else I would prefer to sit next to on my first appearance than my best friend.

"Kind of..." he said, scooping more pancake into his mouth.

"What exactly does 'kind of' mean? How can you 'kind of' be on a show? You either are or you aren't."

Ethan chewed his pancake and swallowed. "I will be in a different location, performing a magic trick. It will be broadcasted live on the show. So you'll be on the sofa watching it with Patrick while I'm performing my trick. The production company of my show organised it with his producers because they're predicting this will be huge."

It was disappointing to hear. I was thrilled to be on the show, and I was thrilled for Ethan, but I wanted us to go on the show together. Just go on the show, laugh, talk, have a good time. Just something...simple. I gazed out of the window, considering the possibilities of why he would need to be in another location to perform a magic trick. "What trick are you going to do?" I hated the feelings he created where it gave me such a rush of worry. Why couldn't he tell the bit I'll be worried about first? It would save me a lot of stress.

He coughed and cleared his throat before mumbling.

I frowned. "What?"

He mumbled again.

My frown increased and I leant forward. "What?"

"A building is going to collapse on top of me."

I returned to my upright position, cautiously looking into his confident eyes. "What do you mean, a building is going to collapse on top of you?"

He shushed me and suggested with his hands for me to lower my voice. "I'll explain it to you later. Here isn't the best place to talk about it. I don't want anyone finding out. I'll explain how I will do it so you won't be worried about me, ok?" He tapped the top of my hand twice.

"Ok," I said uneasily.

October 12ᵀᴴ

So, yesterday evening Ethan sat me down on the sofa and explained this fantastic new trick he was to perform on Patrick Miller's show. He'd invested in a whiteboard to help with his explanation.

"Before I begin, I want you to know that I've thought this through a million times. Nothing will go wrong. I want to reassure you of this because I know you will be worried," Ethan said, crouching in front of me with his hands on my knees. He stood and walked over to his board. "I saw this newly closed hotel set to be demolished later this year. This appeared as an opportunity to produce something spectacular. Following so far?"

I nodded.

Ethan drew a vertical rectangle on the board and a few squares inside that rectangle. (He was poorly trying to represent the hotel with windows.)

"Excuse the horrific drawing but I'm a magician, not an artist."

I smirked and allowed him to continue by waving my hand.

"I will be inside the building."

I immediately interrupted, "No you won't."

Ethan sighed. "Can all comments please be reserved

until the end, please? Thank you. As I was saying, I will be inside the building."

I immediately interrupted again, "No you won't."

"Why won't I?" He asked, blank faced.

"You don't have my permission to do so," I replied.

I didn't want him anywhere near that building during its demolition.

"Would you like me to call Patrick Miller and tell him I can't be on his show Christmas Eve because you won't give me your permission to do so?"

I nodded. "Yes, if you could please. I don't want you anywhere near that building when it's being demolished."

"But...but...but that's the trick!"

I pulled a funny face and shrugged. "Tough."

"This is why I am explaining it to you though, so you won't have to be worried. Look."

He drew more detail onto his drawing. He added what looked like a pipe running underneath the hotel. "This is a tunnel. The basement staff used it as an emergency exit or something. I will exit through here and escape with plenty of time to spare before the building collapses, ok?"

He was trying his upmost hardest to seek my approval. Although I wasn't having any of it.

"You're not doing this trick, but please continue," I said bluntly. I bit my fingernails as he hopelessly stared at his board.

"The hotel will be lined with dynamite or C4, whatever they use these days. It will come down floor by floor. I'll be in handcuffs that I'll get out of quicker than anyone can say *August is the greatest person ever*. I'll pop down the tunnel, which is directly beneath where I'll be standing, and escape from demolishment with plenty of time to spare. I might even catch the ending of it."

I stared at him with an unsure look. He stared right back

at me. He soon broke from our stare and sat beside me. "August, I'm going to do this regardless of what you say. I've explained this to you so you won't have anything to worry about. You can sit and watch all relaxed because you know I will be fine. I want to perform something no one has ever seen before. Something that will go down in history, an opportunity I have to grab with both hands."

I rolled my eyes at him. "Ethan, I will beat you up myself if you keep saying you're going to do this."

He laughed. "You're so adorable when you're angry."

He went to grab my cheeks, but I karate chopped his hand away. And glared into his eyes with my mean look and flared nostrils.

"What are you doing, you weirdo?" he asked, moving away from me.

"I'm giving you my super-serious I'll-kick-the-poop-out-of-you look."

He nodded. "I thought it looked familiar. But you just look like you need a poop, August. It's not scary at all."

I tutted in disappointment and stuck two fingers up at him.

NEW EMAIL FROM AUGUST BISHOP
Dear Leonard,
You must keep everything I am about to say to yourself. First off, I apologise for Ethan's rudeness the other day. The crash isn't his fondest memory. I'm sure it's been playing on your mind, so if anything pops up please discreetly let me know. Ethan's street magic shows start on the twentieth. I thought maybe you would like to watch it. I wanted to email you because, of course you've been a magician previously, but if you were going to drop a building on top of yourself, whilst handcuffed, how would you escape?
Thanks, August.

OCTOBER 19TH

NEW MESSAGE FROM STANLEY TENNANT
You'll never guess who got married!

NEW MESSAGE FROM AUGUST BISHOP
I haven't heard anything on the news. Spill it!

NEW MESSAGE FROM STANLEY TENNANT
Me! Jasmine and I had a secret ceremony in Cuba yesterday!

NEW MESSAGE FROM AUGUST BISHOP
No way!! That's so great! I'm so happy for you! Congratulations!

NEW MESSAGE FROM STANLEY TENNANT
Thank you! We would've invited you, but we didn't even invite our families. We felt like being spontaneous as we strolled along the beach one day, so we got our friends who's villa we were staying in to be our witnesses!

NEW MESSAGE FROM AUGUST BISHOP
I'm so thrilled for you both! I bet the ceremony was so cute and romantic!

NEW MESSAGE FROM STANLEY TENNANT
It's so weird being married! But I wanted to thank you, August. Without you I would never have sucked up the courage to tell her. How are things with you and a certain someone? A little birdy told me he is single…

NEW MESSAGE FROM AUGUST BISHOP
Awww, you're welcome! The birdy informed you correctly. I've been dying to speak to him and we've been really close lately…but I don't want to spoil anything. He's gone & going through so much and I want to wait until the right time; eventually it'll be so obvious he'll probably just ask me…

NEW MESSAGE FROM STANLEY TENNANT
Oh August, stop being a wimp & tell him! Promise me you will tell him before the year is out? I wish I'd told Jasmine sooner!

NEW MESSAGE FROM AUGUST BISHOP
Fine, I'll tell him by then. I'll be seeing you for the premiere soon, won't I?

NEW MESSAGE FROM STANLEY TENNANT
Yes, you will. November seventh we're having 5-10 days of premiere & promoting so we'll see you then! This film has cost a fortune to prepare in a ridiculously short time. Let's hope it's paid off!

NEW MESSAGE FROM AUGUST BISHOP
Ok haha! See you then, Stanley, congrats again!

OCTOBER 20TH

"What shall we do for Halloween?" Ethan asked as we brushed our teeth.

I held my hair and spat. Yesterday I spat all into my hair, which sent Ethan into one of his audacious laughters.

"I'm not going trick or treating if that's what you're asking."

Ethan spat. "Of course not. I mean, should we have a costume party?"

I gave him a puzzled scowl in the mirror. "Who are we going to invite?"

He scrunched his face before spitting again. "We could ask Eleanor and Max. It's time I spoke to them again, isn't it?"

I smiled. "Maybe. Why don't you call them?" I wasn't going to allow him to persuade me to call them for him.

He rinsed his mouth and popped his toothbrush back into the holder. "Fine, I'll call them."

I watched him on the phone as he stood on the balcony. He was out there for a long time. Eleanor was probably crying on the phone, begging him to take her back. It would infuriate me if she were. Everything was going rather well between Ethan and I recently, compared to a few weeks ago. If he agreed to take her back, I would probably attack him. She had feelings for Max, too. She can't have both. My poop stare, as Ethan calls it now, increased by the second as I watched him. He strolled back in, tapping the phone in his hands.

"I've made up with Max. Eleanor wants me to visit her so we can talk."

I sighed, because I knew if he went over she'd flash her beautifully long eyelashes at him and he'd be hers. I wanted to tell him he shouldn't, but then he'd ask why and I wouldn't have a valuable explanation. I'm still not ready to tell him. I've set myself a goal of telling him before Christmas, or New Year's Eve. It provides me with the perfect opportunity to kiss him. I want to see how we do over this next month or two with the premiere and the launch of his TV show. Which was due to start in a couple of hours.

"Are you going to see her?" I asked.

Ethan paced around the apartment.

"It wouldn't hurt to pay her a visit. If I leave now I can make it back in time to watch my show with you."

Without consulting me, he vanished out onto the balcony, I assumed to call Eleanor back, and that was the moment my misery restarted. They'd get back together and my life would become a total and utter disaster. Ethan ran in and grabbed his jacket off the stand. "I won't be long," he said, walking over to me and kissing the top of my head. I closed my eyes and preserved it. The door closed behind him before I could say good-bye. My eyes didn't move from the door the whole time he was gone. I kept saying to myself, *He'll be back any minute now,* every minute.

An hour and twenty-four minutes later, the door reopened. Ethan reappeared from behind it, blank-faced.

"How did it go?" I urged.

He slowly walked over and sat back beside me. "We've decided to give it another go. She's been on the set of another film these past few weeks and she's taken time to think about it and wants to be with me. I want to give her one last chance because...I like her."

He knew I didn't like it. Each word he spoke brought me more misery and anger. It felt like turning back the clock a couple of months and seeing them together for the first time. I sighed as he stopped talking and dropped my head, quickly raising it again before he noticed anything suspicious. He had the biggest grin on his face.

"I'm just kidding! God, can you ever be happy for me!"

The fury that rose inside me was indescribable. I gritted my teeth and punched his shoulder. "Stop it with all these jokes!"

"Aww, come here." He opened his arms and I foolishly fell into them. He patted me on the back as I rested on him.

"Stop being so stubborn," he whispered in my ear.

"Eleanor has feelings for Max apparently. She hasn't spoken to him because she has been away filming. We agreed that they have better chemistry."

"Cute." I was still recovering from his cruel joke.

"Right, let's watch how amazing I am, shall we?" he said, grabbing the remote, flicking through the channels to find his show.

OCTOBER 31ST

Ethan's show was nothing short of magnificent. It's called *Deception*. It's nothing like the stunt he is hoping to perform in December. It's simple street magic. Well, according to him it's simple. It involves him walking around performing card tricks to small groups of pedestrians. The more tricks he did, the more the crowds around him grew. He wore the other tie I had bought him for our fifth Christmas together throughout his first show. It was a charcoal grey tie with purple spots dotted on it.

In his second show, aired on the twenty-seventh, he wore the red tie I bought him for his ninth birthday. A normal red tie, that's it, nothing too special about it. In his second show, Ethan was by the beach, continuing his card tricks. He performed his usual slip-the-card-in-your-shoe trick although he was working with flip-flops. I don't know if that made it more difficult for him or not. I'm sure he had figured it all out before performing them.

He met Natasha Thompson along the beach, the tall, wonderfully tanned, and beautiful model. I'd never paid much attention to Natasha. She was stunning, drop-dead stunning. However, modelling isn't something I follow, so I don't know much about her. I've been asked to do some photoshoots for magazines, so I suppose I will be modelling soon, too. As an interest though it isn't something I follow with passion. The producers of Ethan's show thought it would be a good idea for him to perform a trick for her. Ethan somehow forgot to mention this. I find it hard to believe he'd forget to mention such huge news.

"What was she like?"

He shrugged. "She's cool."

It wasn't the exciting explanation of their encounter I was expecting.

They sat in an empty beach bar, drinking coconuts through a straw. If I remember correctly, Natasha was twenty-two or twenty-three. She looked about the same age as Madeline to be honest. The beaming sunlight lit up her face, making her hazel eyes appear even more indulging. Ethan and Natasha shared a smile for a moment before he asked for the ring she was wearing.

"Don't worry, you'll get it back," he said smoothly.

She had a sly grin on her face as she handed the ring over.

Ethan examined it in the sunlight before grabbing an empty clear glass bottle from the bar. He passed the bottle to Natasha, asking her to inspect it and making sure the lid was securely fastened and not capable of leaking.

"It looks good to me, Ethan," she replied, returning it and taking another sip from her drink. She had such a broad English accent. I mean I'm English and I guess mine is *plain-ish*. But hers was very...*posh*, I guess would be the best word to use.

"Now watch closely," Ethan said, holding the ring against the bottle. He moved them apart from one another before snapping them together, transporting the ring inside the bottle. The jolt startled Natasha, but amazement soon followed. "Oh wow!" she said as she snatched the bottle off him, tapping away at it. "How am I supposed to get this out now?" She flirted. She was definitely flirting. The bitch.

I snarled at the TV over her overreaction and perfection. Ethan held the bottle over her hands, and the ring dropped back into them. Just like that. Astounded, Natasha gazed down at her ring. I could have gone into further detail regarding this encounter, but it's annoying me and I was jealous. I also wasn't too fond of the trick Ethan did for the Brazilian girls on the beach. Let's just say their breasts were rather noticeable...well, huge. With these girls, instead of putting the card in their flip-flops, Ethan was slightly more adventurous with the placement of the hidden card. I'm sure you can guess it was placed in one of their bikini tops. I shook my head at Ethan; he didn't notice though. He was too busy giggling at himself. They performed a magic trick of their own by slipping their phone numbers into his pocket.

I'm so pleased for Ethan, his show is doing great. The amount of viewers he received for his second show tripled the viewers from the first. The first two episodes were brilliant. I just get jealous easily when I see him performing another trick for another girl. I'm his magic girl.

He's leaving again in a few days to film the next series ahead of the New Year. They've made a huge profit from it already just with advertising so they want him straight back out there ahead of the New Year. He's also got to plan everything ahead of his special appearance on Patrick Miller's show on Christmas Eve. I'm starting to develop a real dislike for magic.

Tonight we're having a Halloween costume party that Eleanor arranged. Ethan and I spent all day shopping for costumes. Ethan was insistent that he wasn't wearing makeup or face paint. My utmost best to persuade him otherwise failed. He was decisive that he would go as a magician. I went along with his decision and sat on the stool in the store, watching him try on a million top hats.

"I'm getting you one," Ethan said as he tilted the hat on his head.

"No, no you're not!" I joked.

Ethan took the hat off and turned to the assistant beside him. "Can I get two of these, but one in the smallest size, please?"

The assistant bowed their head and took the hat away.

"You're having a hat, August. We need matching suits now."

I rolled my eyes at him. "Do I not get a say in this?"

He shook his head. "Nah."

NEW EMAIL FROM LEONARD PHILLIPS

Hi, August,

Sorry I haven't replied. I've not checked my emails for a while. There is no need to apologise. I've spent a lot of time re-watching the footage of the crash. However, I'm still no closer to solving it. I watched Ethan's show and I must admit it was impressive. He has a certain swagger about him. I think it will take him far in the world of magic. As for bringing a building down on top of myself, I would pre-record it, using special effects. I'd sit and watch myself perform from my trailer without lifting a finger. I hope this helps, Leonard.

"Ethan, isn't there any way you can use special effects to bring the building down on top of you instead of risking your life?" I asked while we were looking through suit colours and materials.

He looked at me with disappointment. "How would that make it the best trick ever, August? Magic is about leaving people on the edge of their seats. The audience wants to feel like this could genuinely kill me, and they're waiting to find out if I'm alive or not. That's the beauty of it. Never knowing how I did it. Everyone has their suspicions, but they'll never be told if they were correct or not. If anything slipped up from one of the special effects people, the entire press would jump on it and call me a joke. Then for the rest of my life I'd be known as the coward who used special effects."

I couldn't argue with him; he was right. "Please come back in one piece."

He grabbed a top hat off a shelf and popped it on my head.

"I will." The hat slipped over my ears and covered my eyes.

"I'm serious, Ethan. We both know what happened last time."

"What's gotten into you lately? You're always worrying. Don't you trust me?"

I removed the hat from my head, examining it in my hands. "Of course I trust you. But bringing a building down on top of yourself has nothing to do with trust. I'm making one rule."

Ethan squinted. "Ok, let's hear it."

I rolled the hat around in my hands. "If you even so much as receive a scratch from this, I'll beat you up and you can go back to putting cards down Brazilian chicks' bikinis."

My eyes didn't blink to make my intentions clear and then I brought out the poop stare. Ethan tucked my hair behind my ears and then pulled a small section forward so my ears poked out. He thinks this makes me look like an elf.

"Ok, my tiny mean elf wife. You're so demanding!"

I karate chopped his hands away and ruffled my hair.

Ethan couldn't choose a suit for us to wear, so he chose

one at random since I was uninterested in doing so. I sulked through the entire fitting as an elderly lady sized us up with her tape measure.

"You're so adorable when you're grumpy," Ethan said with a grin on his face as he sat and watched the elderly lady measure me to his amusement.

"I hate you," I replied. I wanted to dress up as someone hot, like Catwoman or some other sexy character. Not some ridiculous sidekick for Ethan wearing stupid top hats.

Ethan grinned. "You love me."

I remained silent because it was true, but not in the way he implied. The suit Ethan had chosen was green, a hideous green. Like the colour furniture your grandparents would have in their house, green.

"Why New York, Ethan?" I asked as we drove home. We hadn't spoken about the sudden idea of moving to America and buying an expensive apartment.

"I wanted to move somewhere we would enjoy. I figured with your acting career taking off as well, it would be perfect for you."

I raised an eyebrow. "So, you did this all for me?"

Ethan gazed out the window. "Well, yeah. Who else do I have to spoil? If your acting career took off, I decided being in New York meant I would be closer to wherever you would be filming, and we'd be able to see each other more than me being in England."

My stomach fluttered from his cute considerableness. I quickly peeked over at him before returning my attention to the road. Why couldn't he tell me he loved me too? If he ever did. He must do. If what Mum explained was true, that meant all those years growing up together he never mentioned it once. Why?

NOVEMBER 1ˢᵀ

Last night's party was, let's say, eventful. Around fifty or sixty came, thanks to Eleanor's organisation skills. I felt utterly ridiculous having to wear my top hat and suit. Ethan thought we looked cute. I disagreed.

We met some interesting new people. I doubt we'll become friends with any of them. Their egos are too big and they came across as snotty.

I did meet the singer Alex Farrell. His new album had broken nearly every record in music. He's super sweet, not to mention gorgeous. Ethan was standing beside me, though, so I tried my best to keep my cool. The girl he had with him was lovely, too. She was called Wednesday. We clicked because both our names are based on the calendar. When I asked if she was his friend or girlfriend, she smirked and glanced over at Alex.

"We dated before fame interrupted; now we're just friends... It's complicated," she whispered.

"I'm in a complicated situation myself," I hinted over to Ethan discreetly.

Wednesday winked, nodded, and then zipped her lips shut.

I enjoyed talking to her and Alex. It was a shame they had to leave early. Max still hadn't spoken to Eleanor properly since the day Ethan returned. He spent his night on the balcony sulking in his hilarious dragon costume. By far the best costume of the evening, maybe ever. Everyone else had focused on showing cleavage or being a metaphorical emotion.

"Why don't you talk to her, Max?" I said, wearily standing beside him.

"It's pointless, August. She won't be interested in my pathetic speech of how much I love her."

"Max, she's a normal girl. Ethan told me she's been away filming. That's why you haven't heard from her. She deserves someone to love her after the horrible previous relationships she's had. The last one she kinda messed up by herself, with your help of course. She likes you more than you think."

My encouraging words raised his head. Ethan then joined us out on the balcony. "What's wrong with you, grumpy?" He was wearing the tie I bought him for Halloween a few years back; it's black and covered in a pattern of bright orange pumpkins with various scary faces carved into them. Ethan was drunker than I assumed; he appeared high-spirited due to his recent circumstances with Max.

"Nothing, just enjoying the view," Max replied.

"Max, buddy, I will do a magic trick for you. As an apology for my unnecessary behaviour," Ethan slurred.

Max frowned, and so did I.

"Hold your arms out in front of yourself, please, keep them strong."

Max followed as instructed and held out his green and red dragon arms.

"Now, I will count to ten in a moment. When I start, I want you to reverse into the apartment, ok?"

Max closed his eyes and laughed once in amusement.

"Ten-nine-eight-keep those arms strong, Max-six-five."

Ethan grabbed my arm as Max walked back. "Look at the bottle at the door there," he whispered in my ear.

It confused me; still, I did as he instructed. An empty wine bottle lay alone on the floor inside the apartment.

"Three-two-one!" Max stopped. Then a loud cry came from the apartment. Eleanor suddenly came flying out of nowhere and landed straight into Max's arms. Her eyes closed, with a look of shock on her face. Max was equally astounded for another reason. The bottle Ethan had asked me to focus on was behind Eleanor's foot while she stood chatting. She fell over the bottle and straight into Max's arms.

"Thanks, Max! Cool outfit," Eleanor cried out desperately in his arms.

"Dragons are cool, aren't they?" It was a cringeful moment, but cute.

I rolled my eyes at his blabbering comment and turned to Ethan while they got reacquainted.

"It's all about timing sometimes, dear. Let's move before she sees us."

He grabbed my hand and walked around the balcony towards the other door. As we reentered Max and Eleanor were too busy sticking their tongues down each other's throat to notice everyone was staring at them.

"Ethan, if you hadn't had died for me, I'd have to admit that was the best trick you have ever done."

He let go of my hand. I didn't want him to; it was nice.

"They needed a small push," he replied. "I'm going to grab us a drink, I'll be back in a second, ok?"

"Ok, I'll stay here." Ethan swivelled and wandered towards the kitchen. Max and Eleanor were now talking on the balcony and kissing every three seconds. Things then plummeted downhill. A drunk guy walked over after Ethan left; he was one of Eleanor's ex-boyfriends. But they were now friends. I didn't understand how people could do that.

I spoke to him as he swayed beside me. The longer he stood with me, I began to feel more and more uncomfortable. I was having flashbacks of my time with Mark, and I needed to get some air. I excused myself and tried to exit, but he grabbed my wrist.

"Where are you going?" he asked. His breath stank of liquor. I could feel a rush come over myself, like I was about to have a panic attack. My pulse throbbed in my ears as my heartrate rose.

"Let go of me," I quietly and politely said.

"I'd do as she says." Ethan appeared from behind me.

"Sorry, I meant nothing by it!" he replied, holding up his hands.

"Who are you here with? Maybe you should go find them and leave," Ethan said, stepping in front of me.

"Well, I came with your mother, she disappeared a while ago so I'm just waiting on her." Of all the shit comebacks for this fool to say, he had chosen by far the worst possible one. And that's when Ethan knocked him out, and then beat up two of his friends who came rushing over to his aid. Security seemed to have no issues dragging them out of the apartment and escorting them from the building.

I announced to everyone that the party was over and that they should all leave peacefully. Max and Eleanor stayed. Eleanor wasn't pleased with Ethan knocking out three of her guests, including her ex-boyfriend, but she understood. She and Max tidied up the apartment while I gave Ethan some ice for his bruised knuckles.

"I'm sorry," Ethan said, rocking back his head.

I grabbed his cheeks with my hand and pushed them together. "You're being silly. Don't waste another second thinking about it, ok?"

Ethan couldn't say or do anything because I'd squeezed his cheeks together. He looked cute with them squished together. I don't know why I don't do it more often. Max wandered over and hugged Ethan from behind, wrapping his arms around his waist.

"Thank you," Max said, resting his head against Ethan's back in his stupidly brilliant dragon costume.

"Don't mention it," Ethan replied.

"Max, that is the best outfit I have ever seen, ever."

I couldn't stop laughing at him. Max released his grasp from around Ethan and patted him on the back.

"You're not staying here tonight, though, don't push it," Ethan shouted as Max flew away.

Ethan glanced down at me, and then I realised something. He'd pretended to be drunk earlier with Max on the balcony. What if he had pretended to be drunk during the crash? It seemed stupid, but it played on my mind. I stopped what I was doing and ran upstairs.

NEW EMAIL FROM AUGUST BISHOP
Leonard, did I mention that Ethan was drunk during the crash? August.

NEW EMAIL FROM LEONARD PHILLIPS
Impossible!! If he was, I will happily write a newspaper column and announce he is the best magician the world has ever seen!

NEW EMAIL FROM ETHAN KNIGHT
August, Leonard.
I thought we agreed we wouldn't talk about this matter anymore? Leonard, I'll tell you how I did it. Just so I can sit on my balcony enjoying my cereal while reading your article about how I am the greatest magician ever.
August, we need you downstairs, Ethan.

NEW EMAIL FROM LEONARD PHILLIPS
August, if I were you, I'd marry that boy. Leonard.

I don't know what was in that email from Ethan to Leonard, and I never will. That's the magician's code. Ethan remained silent as I returned downstairs; obviously he didn't want to cause a scene in front of Max and Eleanor, even if there was one to cause. Our eyes met, as if an understanding took place between us. Then he tried to re-create my poop stare, but failed horribly.

NOVEMBER 3RD

"Why do you have to go back to LA?" I groaned to Ethan, holding on to his leg as he dragged me along the floor towards the door.

"August, let go of my leg, you weirdo! I'll see you soon, don't worry. I will only be gone a few days. Is it because I can't make it to your premiere?"

I tightened my grip around his ankle. "I will be lonely and alone and by myself. I have no one to be my date for the premiere either. Max is going with Eleanor, obviously."

Ethan bent down and picked me up like a small child and stood me on my feet. "I'm sorry, ok? This is the last time for a few months. Once I get back I'm all yours, ok?"

I sulked and crossed my arms. "Fine." I grabbed hold of his Rubik's cube tie I bought him for our ninth Christmas together as he kissed my forehead. He swivelled and picked up his bags. My head suddenly screamed, *Kiss him, you fool, kiss him!* But by the time I lifted my head, the door had already closed behind him. I stared at the door for a minute or two in hope he would return and sweep me off my feet. Instead, I found myself in his room, wrapping myself in his clothes and duvet.

NEW MESSAGE FROM AUGUST BISHOP
Are you free to discuss work stuff with me?

NEW MESSAGE FROM MAXIMUS PARKER
How long has it been since Ethan left?

NEW MESSAGE FROM AUGUST BISHOP
I think it's been fifteen minutes now.

NEW MESSAGE FROM MAXIMUS PARKER
LOL, I'm on my way.

"I was gonna send you an email with all this information. But I might as well tell you in person now I'm here. I'll email it all over to you anyway, in case you forget. Recently, I've had hundreds of emails, asking for interviews and photo shoots. I'll send you the list of them for you to take a look at," Max said as we sat down to discuss taking my career forward.

"I've had three movie auditions sent in my direction for you. The first is a film directed by your last director, Stanley Tennant. It's another action film. This one, however, has mythical creatures or zombies. Something that isn't real anyway. They want to start filming in January or February. The second, a romantic film. You play a small-town girl who falls in love with a pop star; cheesy I know. Apparently it will be huge. They're willing to push the start date back for it until June if you get the part for the film directed by Stanley. The third: you play an astronaut who's on the moon with your team. You wander off, stumbling into another dimension or something, discovering this whole new planet and aliens and blah blah blah. They're also willing to push the start on that one, too, to November. These guys love you. Everyone does. You're a massive star behind the scenes already with no one really knowing who you are yet! Newspapers have worked in your favour so far! Stanley hasn't stopped talking to everyone about you also. The good thing about all these productions is they're no farther than two hours away from New York. So when you and Ethan finally admit that you're madly in love with each other and can't live without one another, then it's perfect for you. You best get your audition game ready!"

I nodded. "You think he's in love with me?"

Max flapped his arms. "I've just presented three auditions to you, and that's what you ask me?"

I grinned. "I'm kidding! I'll audition for them all, please. I'll read the scripts later, they all sound good, especially the astronaut one. Thanks, Max. Shall we have lunch?"

Max jotted in his notepad. "Right, ok, I'll get back to all of them for you. Yes, lunch sounds great, I'm starving."

And just like that, I casually landed three more major movie auditions.

November 15TH

NEW MESSAGE FROM MUM

I'm so sorry we can't be there, sweetie. Dad has to work, as always, and so do I. Madeline is dying to visit, but we know you're busy so we don't want to just drop her on you. She still has school for another couple of weeks before she finishes for Christmas and New Year. Please come visit soon, August. I hope the premiere goes splendidly. Take plenty of photos for me! I love you lots.

November 16TH

Today was the final day of promotion. Tonight I'll be walking down the red carpet signing autographs as we end with the premiere. The past few days have been spent doing private interviews, radio shows, and press conferences. At first I found them overwhelming, and they scared me. I soon got used to them though. I have to. This is what the rest of my life will be like. I enjoyed doing the radio shows most. They're a lot more fun and relaxed. You just have a laugh and then have a slight discussion about the film. Simple really.

Stanley and Jasmine have organised a dress for me to wear for the premiere as a thank you for everything I've done for them. I don't know why they keep thanking me. I didn't really do much. I just gave Stanley the encouraging push.

I'm hoping my size hasn't changed at all since filming. I've been working out at the apartment, and I've started to develop the cutest little six-pack, so I'm praying it'll fit me. Otherwise I'll forever be known as the wonder girl who's dress didn't fit her. Great start to my career. Way to go, August. I'm a little nervous. Maybe it's because the time had arrived for the world to meet me, and for me to meet the world.

It's been great spending time with Stanley and Jasmine again, and Eleanor. We have rekindled our sister-like relationship now she's sleeping with the friend I'm not in love with. I wish Ethan could make it tonight. My first big event and he's missing it. I know what he's doing is equally important, but I wanted him to be by my side.

We have one final press conference before we need to get ready for tonight. Everyone was only interested in asking me questions during these conferences. Ninety percent me, ten percent Eleanor, Stanley, and the others. It's becoming tiring telling everyone how long I've wanted to be an actress.

Eleanor and I shared a dressing room to prepare ourselves for tonight. We had our own makeup teams at our disposal. I would die for Eleanor's eyelashes. We used the same mascara, but somehow it made her lashes appear miles better than mine. We both hate fake eyelashes, too. Eleanor's hair looks *amazing*, too. The hair stylists told me she is having a straight, centre-parted style, which will come over her shoulders. And I'm having a messy chignon with tousled strands to frame my face. It baffled me, but I still pretended like I understood what they meant and that it was exactly what I wanted.

Jasmine knocked on the door as she entered. "August, I have your dress! It's so beautiful!" She had such a bright, bubbly grin on her face. She trotted over with the dress bag in her arms. Eleanor, Jasmine, and I gathered around it as if we had discovered a treasure chest. Jasmine opened the bag and removed the cover to reveal what can only be described as perfection. The makeup staff gathered around. I swear I saw a tear come out of the corner of one girl's eye. We all admired it as if it were a painting at a gallery. The lights shone upon it and it sparkled beautifully. Not too bright so I looked like a disco ball, but not too dull so I'm dressed for a funeral. It's a mysterious black, and *so* elegant. I was concerned at the length around the chest area, however. I was worried my breasts would be the slightest bit...exposed.

"Oh August, if you've got them, flaunt them," Jasmine said as I slid into the masterpiece behind a curtain.

I took a deep breath before turning and checking myself in the mirror, and I have to say, I looked hot. I mean I was smoking in this dress. I performed a twirl and for a second, I felt like a princess. The gown only dragged behind me a couple of inches, so I wouldn't clumsily trip over it. I was sure I'd somehow find a way. I stepped out, holding my chest, and allowed Jasmine to zip up the back.

"I think I've chosen the wrong gender friend altogether," Eleanor said, scanning my figure. I blushed because she didn't look as though she was joking. The makeup staff once again gathered around and admired. This time there were definite tears shed. The dress felt so smooth and soft. Whoever designed and created this piece of perfection was a genius. My concerns were correct: a lot of my upper torso was on show. I doubted people would complain about that though. I just hoped nothing that shouldn't pop out, popped out. All I could think about was how much this dress must have cost Stanley and Jasmine.

"Stanley has a friend. I wish I'd gotten a wedding dress made by this guy. I might have to get married again just to wear one!" Jasmine replied when Eleanor asked which planet the dress came from.

I was anxiously sitting in my limo on the way to the red carpet. My heartbeat was throbbing in my ears. I poured myself some champagne and gulped it, carefully avoiding smudging my lipstick. The fizzing flowed into my churning stomach and didn't produce a good combination with my nervousness.

"Nervous?" my driver asked as he rolled down the privacy glass.

The throbbing in my ears made the voice sound a lot quieter than it should have been. "Petrified," I replied.

He stuck his head around the privacy glass and smiled; it was Wayne.

"Hey! What are you doing here?" I asked.

"They asked me to drive you! Since we're best friends." He chuckled.

"It's good to see a familiar face. I've been worrying my ass off, I mean look at me, look at my dress!"

He flicked his eyes in the rearview mirror. "The dress looks wonderful, and so do you! What are you worrying about? Is it because you don't have a date tonight?"

"Affirmative. I wanted someone to be here to support me, you know."

Wayne nodded. "I understand."

I poured myself more champagne, taking a sip this time.

"I will not throw up," I told myself.

We came to a halt at some traffic lights.

"We're coming around the final corner now, Miss Bishop, so you'd better prepare yourself. Stanley told me to tell you there is a final gift for you in the compartment behind me here," Wayne said, rolling the privacy glass back up.

"Ok," I softly said as I inhaled and exhaled. I leant forward, clicking a small button. A flap dropped. Inside was a small navy blue velvet box with a small note on top. I opened the box. It contained a sterling silver chain necklace, with a small key attached to it.

Over the past few months I've received so many extraordinary gifts. Some big, some small, and I'm running out of profound adjectives to describe them all. I snatched at the card and read the message:

This will look nice with the dress x

I grinned and held the box close to my chest. I delicately took the key chain necklace from its box. It was so beautiful. It glistened below the dim lights above me. Suddenly a huge burst of flashing lights and screams erupted as we turned the corner. The limo stopped in a queue behind the others as the guests exited their limos and made their way along the red carpet. I was the last to arrive, to increase the anticipation. I quickly struggled to clip the necklace around my neck. The tiny handle on the back was too small for my trembling fingers, but I got there in the end. I'm surprised to meet myself, if that makes any sense. This is the biggest moment of my life. Only two cars waited now, Max and Eleanor's, and mine. Their limo door opened, and the cameras flashed. Max must've been terrified. Eleanor almost had to drag him forward.

"Here we go, good luck!" Wayne shouted.

My heart was beating out of my chest. The throbbing in my ears had returned. Even with my throbbing ears the roar from the crowd was deafening. This was it. The moment we'd all been waiting for. I checked my reflection in the privacy glass, practicing my smile. The last thing I wanted was criticism over my smile.

This is it. I shuffled over to the door as it opened, carefully hoisting my feet out. Maneuverability in this dress was limited. The cold, bitter air struck my face, chilling my cheeks. A hand extended towards me, offering assistance. I reached out and grabbed a hold tightly. I gazed up to thank them.

And there he was, with the biggest smirk on his face, knowing I had been oblivious to his presence. I stood up with a beaming smile on my face. My nerves and unassuring feelings vanished. I had my best friend here with me now. All was well.

"You really thought I'd miss your first premiere?" Ethan said in my ear.

I'd completely forgotten about everyone else. The blinding camera flashes reminded me to remain focused. There were hundreds of cameramen squeezing forward, holding their cameras in the air to capture a glimpse of my arrival.

"I thought you couldn't make it?" I shouted into Ethan's ear.

We were stood no farther than a foot away from each other, but the noise made it hard to hear.

"I planned this from the beginning! I wanted to surprise you! You look as beautiful as ever, my dear, a little too beautiful. It's giving me flashbacks to your mum's dress when we met Stanley." He flicked his eyes down to my cleavage, to which I raised an eyebrow up at him. For the first time in, well, ever, he had a bow tie on instead of a tie. He looked rather handsome and dashing.

"I hate you. I'm bloody freezing!" I shouted to him.

"You love me and this is the best surprise ever, so shush, you. You can have my jacket after we've done all these photos."

I rolled my eyes at him, linked my arm with his, and we took our first steps together down the red carpet. We stopped on the marker positioned in front of the cameramen. All the flashing cameras sent my eyes funny. I turned to Ethan to block some of the beams and regain my sight. I noticed he was already looking at me before rotating his head swiftly away. It made me think of Mum's explanation with the photos. *Could he have been doing the same just then*?

After we passed the cameramen, we entered the next group: fans. Far more overwhelming although there weren't as many flashes now. Eleanor and I wandered off down the crowds signing books, magazines, and photos. One girl asked us to sign her forehead. We laughed, but we signed it. Ethan and Max stood aside and watched in a clueless fashion. Ethan might be used to fame since his shows' release; Max, however, was new to this. He couldn't have chosen a bigger event to make his first major public appearance with Eleanor. I looked over my shoulder to check on them and saw them both posing for a few photos with a group of screaming girls. I smiled at them before posing for a photo myself with a little girl who was wearing the cutest dress.

"You look very pretty," I said with a comforting smile. She was being held in her mother's arms. I think the loud atmosphere scared her.

"Say thank you," her mother said.

"Thanks, my mummy bought it me," she murmured before clinging to her mother, hiding her face. She was so adorable. She eventually came out of her shell and gave me a hug before I had to attend to the other screaming fans.

It made me think of Madeline, and how I wished I could have brought her here. She would be skipping up and down the carpet with great excitement. And striking many poses in front of the cameras.

All the continuous signatures made my wrist ache. I was exhausted after spending twenty or thirty minutes with everyone. Many members of the crowd were so sweet and lovely; they all commented on how beautiful I looked and said how they loved me. It was so humbling to hear. I couldn't have dreamed for a better reception. I wish I could have spent more time with everyone.

We were then escorted to the next department, interviewing. Sweat had gathered at the top of my forehead. I wanted to wipe it away, but knowing me, I'd wipe my entire makeup off and leave a blotch of it on Ethan's jacket. The interviews didn't last too long.

- What's your favourite meal for breakfast?
- What book was your favourite growing up?
- Who is your idol/role model?
- Dogs or cats?
- Who's your favourite *Friends* character?
- Are you in a relationship or do you have a special someone in your life?

My eyes darted over to Ethan after the last question. I snapped them straight back before a connection was made.

"Uh, no," I replied and laughed it off.

Everyone then made their way into a cinema screen. Eleanor and Max, Ethan and I, were all seated together alongside Stanley and Jasmine.

Stanley sat beside me. "Excuse me, August Bishop is supposed to be sitting there. Do you know where she is, because you're clearly not her?"

I smiled and shook my head. "I can't thank you enough, Stanley. I feel so beautiful in this dress."

Stanley slumped into his seat then leant on the armrest. "It's the other way around. The dress feels so beautiful on you."

I blushed. "Thank you for the necklace, too."

"What? Oh the necklace! You're welcome. I figured you'd probably lose a ring," he joked.

The screen then started to flicker.

Everyone's conversations died into silence.

Ethan patted my hand to reassure me. "You can relax now."

I rearranged my posture slightly to not appear so upright and eager. It was hard to change my shape because of the dress.

Stanley leant over his armrest with a look of delight stamped on his face. "Here we go!"

There's something odd about watching myself in a movie that made me nervous. Maybe it's because I'm scared that I might not approve of my performance. I made mental notes in my head throughout the movie:

- Look more upset when you're fake crying.
- Sound more posh.
- Have better eyelashes than Eleanor.
- Become less cool. (Every time I shot someone it was the coolest thing ever.)

And finally:

- Do more squats.

A huge applause erupted from everyone as the end credits ran. Everyone started shaking Stanley's hand, congratulating him on his phenomenal production. "I didn't think it could be done in the time given, Stanley my boy," one man said, kissing Stanley's cheek.

Ethan pretended to be asleep for the final moments of the film; I nudged him and he grinned like a toddler.

We stood in appreciation for everyone's reaction, while Ethan and Max remained seated. It was so humbling. Since walking into my first acting class as a kid, I've worked my ass off my entire life and it's finally paid off. I've made it. My dream had come true.

After being bombarded by everyone waiting to shake my hand, and *even more* photographers, Wayne drove us all home in his limo. Ethan and I were seated at the section nearest Wayne while Max and Eleanor sat across from us. Eleanor had spread herself out and rested her head on Max's lap and fallen asleep. He gently stroked her hair behind her ear in a smooth rhythm.

It was midnight and we were still another hour away. I flicked off my heels and tucked my legs up while spreading myself across Ethan's lap, mirroring Eleanor's position. I watched the dim yellow streetlights flow by in the dark night sky, quickly drifting off to sleep.

When I woke, Ethan's face was hanging over me. We were in the elevator heading up towards our apartment. He was carrying me in his arms like your mum or dad would carry you to bed when you had fallen asleep on the sofa.

"I can walk now, thanks."

"Oh now you can walk, can you?" Ethan joked.

He placed me on my feet as the elevator door opened. I dawdled forward and fiddled with the key in an attempt to open the door. Ethan took the key off me and opened the door.

"Thanks," I whispered. "Will you undo my dress, please?"

I needed to get to bed as soon as possible, but more importantly, I didn't want to ruin this dress. I walked into the apartment and stood still, waiting for him to undo my zip. There was a small pause before he zipped down my dress and unhooked the clip.

"Thanks," I whispered before slithering out of it, and placing it over the back of the sofa. I shivered and then realised I stood in nothing but my underwear. It was the last of my concerns. Sleep was more important, and it was calling me. I flopped onto my bed. Tucking myself underneath the heavy cold covers, I lay on my back and gazed up, suddenly wide awake.

"Ethan," I shouted.

The door creaked open marginally and his head poked from behind it. "Yes?"

"Will you stay with me, please?" I asked, patting the bed beside me with a sulk on my face. I wasn't trying it on, *promise*. I wanted someone to cuddle and warm me up. I always crave that.

"Put some clothes on first," he replied.

"Give me your shirt, I'm too tired to move," I groaned.

"Fine." The door creaked open and shut.

I switched my bedside lamp on so he could see where he was going; there's nothing worse than stubbing your toe on the corner of your bed during the middle of the night. He unbuttoned his shirt and threw it over me. It floated down, landing on my head.

"Thank you," I murmured from under it. I leant forward and flung the shirt over me, buttoning it up. Ethan's shirts are like wearing a small nightgown. It was warm and hugged my body.

Ethan snuggled in beside me. "You're freezing!"

I shushed him and rested my head on his chest as he tucked his arm underneath me. I placed my arm across his chest and rested it on his left shoulder, so I could feel his heart beating against my arm again.

"Thank you for surprising me tonight," I mumbled, since my cheek was squished against him.

"I wasn't going to miss it, was I?" he replied, rubbing my shoulder.

I smiled and drifted off to sleep as he softly played with my hair.

November 20TH

Everywhere I looked I saw my face: newspapers, magazines, news channels, gossip channels. I was becoming tired of seeing myself. The movie was released into cinemas the day after the premiere. Around twelve more movie parts had been sent my way. Over half of them were ones I wouldn't benefit from doing. After reading through the details of the movies, only two tempted my interest. Max emailed them and both productions replied saying they would love me to audition. Meaning I have five auditions lined up. I hate that everything takes a while to sink in with me: I have five movie auditions and I'm casually sat eating a fruit salad like nothing has happened.

Ethan and I are going to visit home before Christmas. Time has just flown by and it's taken a while for me to notice how long it has been since I left home. Mum and Madeline came to visit not long ago, but I haven't seen my dad for six months. Ethan said he had booked us a private plane to take us home next week. Ethan's house had been left unattended for a while, too. We'll need to check on it. I'm not sure what he intends to do it with it. I doubt he'll want to sell it. It's his parents' house, so I'd assume he'd keep it, and then when we're in England we'd have somewhere to stay. The house means more to Ethan than he knows. It means a lot to me, too. I spent as much time in Ethan's house as I did my own.

I've noticed I need to hurry with purchasing my Christmas presents. I have given little thought to what I will get everyone. For Max, I'm thinking of buying him tickets to a concert. Not sure which one; Eleanor will help me. Purchasing anything for Eleanor is going to be difficult. It's hard to think of anything she doesn't already own. I'll speak to Max or Ethan about that one. Maybe we could buy her something from us all. I always say we should do joint gifts so then the blame can't just be pinned on one person if it goes wrong. For my mum and dad, I cannot explain how much I would love to give them a new house. The house they have is too small. Even with me not living there. It may have three bedrooms, but it is still very cramped. All their hard work has paid off, and I want to thank them for it. Ethan is considering giving them his house. That would eliminate my gift. They won't want two houses. Maybe a holiday or a villa abroad is the only other idea I had. They deserve a holiday at least. I don't want to see them waste their lives away working. They still have Madeline to take care of so they can't disappear until she's old enough to be alone, I suppose. This was why I hate shopping, you never know what to get anyone. I'm tempted to insist Ethan and I send gifts from the two of us. It saves messing around with individual presents. Ethan will obviously need a few more ties. Money isn't an issue since being in the film, but I don't want to get him loads of expensive pointless ties. That isn't the tradition. So I'm on the hunt for some funny or patterned ties. I'm considering finding a tie production place and getting a photo of us put onto a tie. I hope they don't make me purchase a thousand of them. That would be such a hilarious present. One thousand ties all with the same photo on. At least they would last him a long time.

Ties are a side gift. I want to get him something extra special for Christmas. The things he has done for me are beyond meaning, and I am so grateful for having him. I don't know what I'd do without him. So my main agenda this Christmas is to purchase Ethan the best, most brilliant, fantastic, amazing, awesome present in the entire world. Max suggested I buy myself some lingerie, to which I replied, "Go away," in a much more offensive way. After he left, I secretly added it to my list. It is a most definite last resort.

NOVEMBER 23RD

"Ready to go?" Ethan asked, picking up our bags and holding the door open with his foot. I planted myself in the middle of our wonderful living room and rotated on the spot, scanning the apartment in one final search of anything we would need for our ten-day trip home to visit our family. I snatched at our passports on the sidetable, placing them inside the handy pocket inside my bag.

A new bag is what I am in need of. I hardly use bags, although when I do, my previous college bag isn't the most glamorous accessory for a rising star. I'm holding out until Christmas because no doubt Ethan will buy me a magnificent one made of a material man wasn't even aware existed. That's not what I want though. I want a satchel, a normal leather satchel. With my initials on it, and inside a cute message from Ethan telling me how much he loves me. If that turns out to be the only gift I get for Christmas, I would be the happiest girl. Anyway, I placed the passports in my bag and shut the door behind us.

Ethan hired a private car to take us to the airport, where his private jet was waiting for us. I glanced over at Ethan. He was wearing his second favourite tie today. He must have been considering today a special occasion. This tie I bought him for his eleventh birthday. It was a white tie covered in a splattered paint design. Red, blue, yellow, green, and black squirted onto a blank white canvas. It's very artistic.

He says when we return to New York he will take me around the site of the hotel. I don't want to go, but I will try to show my support. Ethan handed me a bottle of water as we sat in the plane.

Too early for champagne, I thought to myself.

I fell asleep during takeoff. Ethan and I were listening to some classical music on his MP3 player and I dozed straight off. Somehow I remained in that slumber. We did wake up during the early hours of the morning, so I suppose I hadn't gotten as much sleep as I would normally do. I do love my sleep.

"Why didn't you wake me?" I asked Ethan as the captain called over the speaker that we were coming in to land.

"You looked so cute and peaceful and I didn't want to wake you. I know how grumpy you can be when someone wakes you up. You were snoring, too."

I scowled at him.

We could be the cutest couple ever, I said to him telepathically.

Ethan and I stood waiting outside Madeline's school. We wanted to surprise her by picking her up. I told Mum to let us pick her up so she could go straight home without having to rush over and collect her. Our surprise was almost ruined when crowds of people gathered around us for photos and autographs. We rushed through the crowds; most were mums sneaking a picture kissing Ethan on the cheek. My crowds were kids asking for autographs. A lot of them were so young, their parents shouldn't be letting them watch me shoot people at such a young age!

Madeline appeared from school, scanning the yard for Mum, as she always picks her up. I grinned at her. It took her ten seconds or so to spot us. Her face lit up and she sprinted towards us. I held my arms open and crouched to embrace her. She ran straight past me and wrapped herself around Ethan, squeezing her arms around him. Ethan picked her up and swept her around.

"What's happening, Maddie, you miss me?" He placed her down.

Madeline wobbled in her dizziness. "Where have you been?" she shouted, folding her arms and sulking.

"I've been looking after August! What else would prevent me from seeing you?" he said, matching her sulk. He placed his hands on her shoulders and twizzled her around to face me.

I raised my eyebrows, with my arms still spread. "Don't forget about me!"

Madeline grinned and dawdled into my arms. How I've missed her ginger hair, and her cute freckled cheeks, and her bossy attitude.

She's such a delicate little flower, I didn't want to let her go.

"Did you get married yet?" Madeline whispered.

"To who?" I giggled in her ear.

She released her arms from around me, planting her hands on either side of my face. I stared into her adorable, serious eyes, awaiting her reply. She stared right back at me and then attempted to roll her eyes. She was clearly trying to indicate Ethan; she tilted her head in a further attempt to imply him.

I laughed again. "No, no, why would we get married, Madeline?" I asked with curiosity, holding up my hand to reveal I wasn't wearing a ring.

She squinted at me and raised her head. "I'm just checking cuz I'm supposed to be the bridesmaid."

I bit my lip and peeked up at Ethan; he was smiling down at her as if he were her parent. I imagined that's how he would look at our kids, if we ever had any. Madeline was still wearing the bracelet I had bought her, along with her friendship bracelet from Ethan. They slid down her arm as she raised it to grab a hold of Ethan's hand. They started to walk out of the school gates and towards the car. She squeezed her right hand as they walked away, implying for me to grab hold of it. I lunged forward and linked my hand with hers. She jumped into the air, lifting her feet off the floor, swinging forwards and backwards on our arms, nearly pulling me over. I'm too small and weak to sustain a good frame for swinging. Within the first five seconds of clambering into the saloon car chauffeuring us around, Madeline had pressed every button possible in the car. The electric windows jolted up and down repeatedly to her amusement. She loved when the TV screen unfolded down from the roof. Patrick Miller's show was on. I'd seen it already, but we watched it on our trip home anyway.

My dad was sitting at the kitchen table as we entered through the front door. I crept on my tiptoes as far as I could before sprinting behind him and covering his eyes with my hands.

"August, I saw your reflection in the mirror as soon as you walked in."

I cuddled his neck and kissed his cheek. "Did ya miss me?" I asked, squeezing him.

"August, you're choking me, love. Of course I missed you." He coughed and rose from his chair and hugged me. "I'm tired of seeing you on the bloody television and in all the newspapers, though! Can't catch my breath without seeing you!"

He avoided hugging Ethan. Instead they shook hands in a manly fashion. "Loving the TV show, Victoria and I are hooked! That model you had on was smoking, wasn't she?"

I was unsure as to whether Dad knew of my love for Ethan or not; perhaps Mum hadn't told him. Either way, his comment made me roll my eyes.

"Natasha is very nice, and funny too," Ethan replied.

Suddenly my mum came bolting downstairs, sliding on the wooden flooring in her fluffy socks, and swooped Ethan and me into a group hug.

"Did everything go ok collecting Madeline?" she asked.

"Everything went well, no need to worry, Mrs. Bishop. Parents and children swarmed us as we first set foot on-site, but they soon disappeared. Madeline looked so adorable when she recognised us and sprinted over to us," Ethan replied, patting Mum on the back.

"Oh, I've missed you both so much. Since your faces are everywhere it reminds me you're all grown up and don't need me anymore. Now I have to pretend I like talking to your father."

Madeline raced over and huddled into the middle of our hug.

"August, that dress you wore for your premiere, my word, it was beautiful! You nearly looked as hot as your mum! Where did you get it? Your father can sell the car and buy me one for our anniversary or Christmas, a dress for both occasions perhaps," Mum asked with bulging eyes.

"Stanley, the director of the movie, has a friend who creates masterpieces. We'll sort you one out, don't worry," I replied.

"Who's this model chick you're seeing then, Ethan?" she suddenly turned and asked with a blank face.

Ethan's eyes lit up. "Natasha? Oh no, no, no, no, no, no, no, we're only friends, Mrs. Bishop," he stuttered back to her.

"Smooth," I said, nudging him with my elbow.

Mum winced her eyes at him. "Ok, sweetie."

NOVEMBER 29TH

We stayed at Ethan's house. We didn't want to cramp up my parents' house. Only my bed was available, and my dad made it very clear that Ethan and I wouldn't be sharing it.

Ethan stood and observed the deserted house as we first entered. He paced around the room, stroking his hand across the dusty furniture. I felt so helpless watching him. I just wanted to give him a crushing hug and reassure him that everything would be ok. It saddened me so much knowing he was the last of his family. He has me and my family, and we're a family. The Knights, however, could become extinct unless Ethan decides he wants a family of his own. I can't imagine a world without an Ethan Junior or his little princess of a daughter.

We're cleaning Ethan's house today, throwing anything out that isn't needed, tidying up and packing up anything Ethan wants to take with him to New York. He's finally decided he wants to give my parents his house for Christmas. *Our* home, Ethan calls it *our* home, not *his*. *Our* home is far more spacious, so we agreed they shouldn't turn down the opportunity to live here. The house they live in now could be saved for Madeline when she decides she wants to move out. They can rent it out until then. This is currently the plan we have lined up. We can hardly wrap the house up in wrapping paper, so I suggested we give them the key in a little box with a note.

Ethan was in charge of rearranging everything downstairs while I took care of his parents' bedroom. His parents' bedroom had a depressing ambiance. It was tidy, but there wasn't much to tidy. The wardrobes were already almost empty. Ethan's dad hadn't had many clothes. I removed the clothes from their hangers and stuffed them into a bag. I dragged the bag to the top of the staircase. Ethan said he didn't want me to carry anything downstairs, because he knew I would trip and break my neck.

Then I rummaged through the cupboards. I found more screws and instructions on how to build the wardroabe in the wardroabe than anything else. I sighed as I shut the final door, flopping onto the bed and staring at the ceiling. It was tougher than I had expected.

As I sat up, I realised I hadn't checked the bedside drawers. I shuffled my bottom along the bed and opened the first of three drawers. Nothing. Disappointed, I frowned and shut it, opening the second draw. Nothing. I sighed and opened the final draw to also find... nothing. Angered, I slammed the draw shut. *Who doesn't contain one item in their bedside draw?*

I fiddled with my thumbs then peered over my shoulder. Maybe that wasn't Ethan's dad's drawer. Maybe it was his mum's. I stood and walked over to the other drawer, refusing to part my sight from it. I thought maybe everything would escape if I removed my eyesight from it for more than a second.

I knelt down and took a deep breath to calm myself. Opening the first draw, it contained a pair of earphones and many packets of headache tablets. The next two draws were empty. I gritted my teeth as I closed the final drawer, I thought I would find something, anything.

"Wow, this was boring," I said to myself. I misplaced my foot as I got to my feet and kicked the corner of the drawer. I mumbled many words that shouldn't be repeated, hopping on my uninjured foot and holding my agonised foot in my hands, rubbing my big toe in hope to cease the pain.

Out of the corner of my eye, I noticed an object under the drawer I had just searched. After I rubbed my toe to a bearable pain. I knelt, dropping my head to the floor. It was a small, dusty wooden box, no bigger than an A5 piece of paper. I held it between my fingers, scraping it along the floor. This hadn't been opened in years. The surrounding dust had almost created a cocoon layer of protection around it. I wiped the dust off the lid in disgust. It was a dark mahogany and had a smooth finish once the dust had been removed. I rubbed the rest off with my sleeve. It had ETHAN engraved on the top of it. I ran my fingers over the letters, wiping away the molded dust. "What do we have here?"

I unclipped the latch at the front of the box. The lid hinges squeaked as I folded them back. It contained an envelope and taped on the inside of the lid was a square Polaroid picture. I delicately tore off the tape and blew the thin layer of dust covering the photo. It was a picture of a woman, smiling and holding a baby in her arms in a hospital bed. After a moment or two, I figured out who it was. It was Ethan's mum. I'd never seen a picture of her before, ever. Ethan's dad had removed all the photos from the house after she died and put them into storage. She was a beautiful woman, but you could see by her skin and expression she wasn't well. She had shoulder-length brown hair and such a beautiful smile. Ethan definitely has her eyes and her smile. I forced a smile as my eyes began to fill, trying to convince myself that I was happy, not sad, to finally see an image of her. I carefully stuck the photo back into its original position and grabbed the envelope.

It wasn't sealed, but the back had been folded in to prevent the contents from falling out. I did the same with my envelopes. I hated having to lick them. My hands trembled. I suddenly became angry with myself for not being able to open the envelope. I pinched the letter inside with my thumb and finger and shook the envelope to bring it free. I inhaled and exhaled a few times to compose myself. *August, stop being an idiot.* I unfolded the letter onto the bed. Then I paused. *Should I read this?* If it's meant for Ethan, he should be the first to read it. *Should I give it to him now?* Maybe I should check it first and see if it was something he would need right now. The handwriting was messy. I understood why when I saw *Mum x* signed at the bottom.

My darling Ethan,

You're such a beautiful baby boy. So sweet and beautiful. We've only known each other for two days, although it seems I know you so well already. Your tiny little hand wrapped itself around my finger for the first time today. My heart is aching knowing I won't be there with you to watch you grow up. As you lie on me, I've forced the final strength inside of me to write to you. I didn't want to leave you with nothing to remember me by or think I didn't have anything to say to you. You won't see me when you first learn how to tie your shoes or have your first kiss or at your graduation, but I'll always be there with you, don't forget that. I hope you find love, Ethan, and you live long and happy lives and will have children of your own one day. It should be easier for you if you have my looks and not your father's! You're my greatest achievement, Ethan, and I want you to know I'll always be proud of you. I know you will achieve greatness in whatever profession you choose. Look after your father for me, Ethan. He may be stubborn, but he always gives his everything. He's a first-time parent, so you will have to help him out as best you can. Things may get a little messy! You will forever be with me, and I with you. I don't want to go, Ethan, but it's my time. Tears roll down my face as I say my final good-bye to you. I desperately look forward to the day I will be reunited with my grown-up beautiful baby boy. Until then I wish you a lifetime of love, happiness, and affection.

I love you so much, forever and always, Mum x

I placed the letter onto the bed. I didn't want the stream of tears running down my face to drip down onto the letter. I wiped my eyes and cheeks with the back of my hand. My face uncontrollably winced during my struggle to stop crying. I tucked my head into my knees, allowing my emotions to get the better of me. I honestly wished she were still here. I bet she'd be one of the coolest chicks ever and we'd get along like two peas in a pod. I assumed Ethan had never received this letter, which the cleanliness of the box containing it suggested. Maybe his dad was waiting for the right opportunity to give it to him? Something as precious as this isn't forgettable. After five minutes of rocking myself, I finally calmed down. I wiped my hands on my shirt and carefully folded the letter, returning it into its envelope and neatly placing it back into the box. I'm glad I decided not to wear mascara today, otherwise I would be a total mess. I grabbed a small spare towel from the upstairs cupboard, wrapping the box in it, and hid it in my suitcase, where it would stay hidden until I knew what to do with it. Handing it to Ethan wouldn't be easy; finding the right moment would be difficult. *How will I give it to him? What will I say?*

When I popped downstairs, Ethan was walking around topless. I was maybe staring at him for too long before he saw me standing there.

"You ok?" he asked, turning around with a puzzled look.

I stared at him for another few seconds before snapping out of my gaze. "Oh, I'm finished upstairs."

DECEMBER 1ST

Since we've been back we've seen our family every day. Ethan picks Madeline up from school while I help Mum prepare food, and Dad, well, he's always late home from work. He likes to keep out of the way, anyway. Mum can be aggressive if she's disrupted in the kitchen. He sits and reads the newspaper that either has mine or Ethan's face printed in it somewhere. It's gotten to the stage where Mum has given up on saving all the articles of me because there are too many.

We're leaving tomorrow. I don't want to leave my family again, especially at Christmas. I suppose I've got to return to New York now and prepare myself for Patrick's show. Ethan needs time to sort out his performance for the show as well; that can't be done in a matter of hours. I don't know what preparations he needs to do, but as long as his escape tunnel is there and keeps him safe, then that's fine. Ethan hasn't told my parents about Christmas Eve yet, nor have I. We want it to be a surprise. I'm sure every single advert leading up to Christmas will say don't miss our amazing guest stars, and witness Ethan Knight's exhilarating escape from the plummeting hotel. Max and Eleanor will be joining me on the show now, too. She's coming on so we can do some final promotion work for *Twisted*. I'm glad they're going to be there with me. I'd be a mess otherwise. I wouldn't be able to speak because of the amount of worry running through me. A familiar face by my side would surely help me remain calm. Max will be nervous too, I bet. Now everyone knows who he is, they want him to be in the spotlight more often. Eleanor has gotten Max a job at *Hallway* magazine. He gets to write reviews on movies. So all he has to do is go to premieres or cinemas and watch films, then say how good they were. That's like the best job ever, isn't it? I'm actually seriously jealous of him. I wish I could do that on the side as well as being an actress. But at least now Max has a proper job and he should hopefully get a proper visa and won't have to fly back home. Jasmine says she knows a representative who will be able to replace him.

My parents booked today off work so we could all go for a walk by the coast. Hardly the best time of year to plan such a trip with the cold, but we all went anyway. Madeline ran along the vast beach like a dog chasing a flock of seagulls. She was wearing her cute little yellow wellingtons, accompanied by her lilac raincoat, as she ran, circling around us all. I kept grabbing her and kissing her when she came too close. Mum and Dad held hands while I'd pinned myself to Ethan because I thought I might come down with a case of hyperthermia. Ethan was wearing a ridiculous orange bobble beanie and a rather large padded winter coat. He may have looked a fool, but at least he was warm. I had enough layers on to protect the whole family; somehow it wasn't enough. Ethan and I stayed on the beach while Mum, Dad, and Madeline nipped into the nearest fish and chip shop for lunch.

"August, it's like I'm in the middle of an earthquake with your shivering."

"Sorry," I mumbled.

"Come here," he said, pulling me off his arm.

He unbuttoned his jacket and hugged me, wrapping me in his jacket with him. My cheek pressed against his warm chest, instantly soothing my frozen skin. He was so warm and snuggly, how was this possible? He's literally a walking radiator, and there I was freezing to death with ten times the amount of layers he had on. Ethan rested his chin on the top of my head. I couldn't have wished for anything else more perfect. I only wished the weather were warmer. I nearly drifted off to sleep once I'd stopped shivering.

"Better?" Ethan asked. His voice was soft.

I nodded my head against his chest, wiggling my nose to bring it back to life. Ethan was wearing the autumn leaves tie I bought him for our third Christmas together. It's just an image of a stack of fallen leaves on a tie.

He released his grasp around me momentarily, allowing the cold to chill me once more. He placed his hideous orange hat on my head, pulling it down over my eyes before tightening his grasp back around me, sealing me into his warmth.

"You did that on purpose," I mumbled.

He laughed and placed his chin back on the top of my head before letting out a sigh.

"Is it your collarbone?" I asked.

"The cold makes it feel like I've got an icicle in my collarbone."

Whenever anything pops up regarding the crash, I suddenly feel awful. I still feel responsible somehow.

"Stop it!" he snapped, shaking me.

"*Whaaaaat?*" I groaned.

"Stop overthinking it, why do you do it?" He squeezed me this time.

"You died, Ethan. I will never be fine about it, will I?" I replied, squeezing him weakly.

Our heart-to-heart conversation couldn't be taken seriously by myself due to the fact my sight was blocked by Ethan's gloriously warm, but ridiculous beanie.

"You're so adorable." He kissed my forehead protected by the beanie.

Why does he do this? I wanted to shout, *Just tell me you love me, you moron, and stop being so sweet, and stop smelling so good!*

Before I opened my mouth, my dad shouted from behind us. "Enough of that, thank you!"

Of all the times to be an overprotective father, he had to choose now.

DECEMBER 2ND

Madeline refused to let go of Ethan as we tried to leave our parents' house. We made the correct decision of packing all our bags and putting them into the car before stopping to say good-bye. Madeline was ready to leave for school.

"I don't want you to go!" she shouted and started to cry.

I knew my emotions were not capable of lasting long so I quickly hugged everyone and rushed back to the car. Ethan's emotional side was far stronger than mine. "Are you ok?" he asked, sliding into the car alongside me.

"I'm fine," I replied.

Today Ethan was wearing his piano tie I bought him for our first Christmas. The design of it is very self-explanatory; it was a sideways keyboard printed along the tie. "Is there anything you want for Christmas?" I asked to distract myself. I've decided to give him the letter from his mum on Christmas Day. Any time before then might affect his concentration towards his performance on Christmas Eve.

"I haven't given it much thought, to be honest. Ties are clearly essential, but you only need to buy me one or two. There's no point buying loads because it'll ruin the tradition," Ethan replied, peering out of the window.

"You must want something."

Ethan wiggled his face. "I already have everything."

I scowled at him in sarcasm. "Stop turning into my mum and tell me what you want."

"How about a holiday?" he responded quickly.

I thought for a second. "You already have a plane."

He patted my knee, "Yeah, but the holiday still needs organising, doesn't it? The plane gets us to wherever we're going."

I nodded. "Ok." My mind began to wildly search for the perfect holiday destination. "I'll surprise you," I added.

"Perfect, thanks, August."

DECEMBER 10TH

Better late than never as my dad would always say. So now I was frantically arranging all of my Christmas presents. Today was a productive day. I spent the entirety of my morning working out in the gym. My New Year's resolution was to work out more and stay in shape. I'm trying to make my six-pack appear a little more prominent. I can also wear all the running clothes I own for what they're supposed to be used for.

After my workout, I took a shower and grabbed my laptop and searched online for my Christmas presents. I had written a list of everyone's gifts.

Mum—high heels

Dad—new TV

Madeline—sneakers, tour around ice cream factory

Max—concert tickets

Eleanor—the same gift as Mum's

Ethan—holiday, personalised playing cards, ties

Since Ethan is giving my parents our house from us both, I realised my gifts to them should be more...normal. So I got Mum, Eleanor, Jasmine, and I, four of the same size black high heels; we all have the same size feet. I added Jasmine to the list when I decided to call the genius who designed and created my dress. He also does heels. He explained he would deliver my mum's shoes in person since he's visiting his boyfriend's family for Christmas, and they only live thirty minutes away from my family. So that's very, very, very convenient and cute. He's extremely nice and polite. He's French, and has a very lovely broad accent. He wasn't too happy with the short notice I left him with, but because I looked so good in his dress, he made an exception for me. He said he would surprise us, too. So I'm super excited to see what these shoes look like. If they're as good as my dress, I don't think we'll be taking them off!

I ordered Madeline six pairs of Converse—purple, red, black, white, blue, and pink. I know she'll love them. It's the unwrapping I'm sure she will enjoy the most, having all those boxes piled up for her. Her excitement will be uncontainable. And I called Ron's ice cream and organised a tour around their factory or whatever they call it where they make the ice cream. So she'll be able to see how her beloved bubblegum ice cream is made! It's going to be the best gift *ever!* I can just imagine walking around and turning to find Madeline had vanished, then the next moment I just see her swimming in the bubblegum ice cream mixer.

When I spoke to Eleanor about a gift for Max, she explained that Max would like two tickets for the ballet. Obviously they're for her, but she said to get them for him anyway. I know it doesn't really make sense, but I followed her instructions. Her happiness brings him happiness I guess. Relationships are weird.

As for Ethan's gifts, I've designed him some golden playing cards that have his own cool design on the back with his initials inscribed on them. Every card is the same, apart from the queen of hearts; on that one it has a photo of me with a cheesy childish grin and two thumbs up. I thought it'd be funny. They come in a lovely wooden box. I hope he likes them because I spent *forever* designing them!

As for a holiday I booked a trip to the Maldives. The main reason I booked this holiday was because it's beautiful and sunny and we'll be marooned on a small island for ten days. Meaning we'll be able to spend lots and lots and lots of time *alone*.

And of course, ties. I had a long search through a huge collection of ties, although none appealed to me. The perfect one inevitably showed itself. Nothing else came close to this tie. It was a sky blue tie with falling snowflakes draping on it. It even came in a unique crafted box; how cool is that? Out of all of his ties, this one would be my favourite.

I shut my laptop after ordering everything, letting out a huge sigh of relief. Ethan was doing press-ups in the gym when I emerged from my bedroom. I rushed in and lay across his back as he continued, wrapping my arms around his chest. We're by far the cutest couple, not to be a couple, ever.

DECEMBER 16TH

It's almost midnight. Ethan and I were in bed watching an episode of Patrick Miller's show. I wasn't watching it to tell you the truth. I was drifting off to sleep. Something had been on my mind all day though, the source of where all this came from. Ethan paid for it all, but the money in that bag I saw a while ago hadn't paid for everything.

"Ethan?" I whispered, rolling over and onto his chest.

"Yes, dear?" he replied, flicking his eyes off the television.

"How did you pay for everything? Honestly."

I closed my eyes in hope he'd think I was adorable, so he wouldn't get mad at me for asking.

He inhaled and exhaled deeply. "My dad didn't drink himself to death. He was…shot, because he owed a casino owner in Italy a severe amount of money. When the owner found out he didn't have the money he was owed, he shot my dad. I went over to Italy as soon as I left the hospital, saw my dad one final time before having him sent back home to be buried next to my mum. The casino owner had twelve casinos scattered around Europe. They all closed that same weekend. Each one mysteriously emptied of its sixty or seventy million banks… I walked away with seven hundred and seventy three million by the end of the weekend. I bought myself a private plane with the money from the first winnings, to fly me to every other casino. Then I went to Switzerland, to open a bank account where the money remains now... Not bad to say I'd just come out of hospital, huh? I think we can both agree that I'm pretty good at roulette."

I remained silent. A tear ran down my cheek as I winced my eyes. I knew why he had kept this a secret: it's not easy telling someone your dad was murdered. And then so many questions would have to be asked. I felt nothing needed to be said, so I cuddled up to him and squeezed him, snuggling my head into his chest more. He already knows that I'm sorry and I'll always be there for him. Our emotional moment was interrupted when I burped out of nowhere. Ethan laughed so hard he had to roll out of bed to compose himself.

"Way to brighten the mood, August!" he joked.

Embarrassed, I laughed with my head underneath the pillow, desperately wishing that hadn't just happened.

DECEMBER 17TH

Horrible cramps struck me at lunchtime, resorting me to my bed, feeling sorry for myself. Ethan, being the annoying person he is, brought me a hot water bottle, a basket of assorted muffins, a large tub of Ron's cherry ice cream, a huge bunch of flowers, and last but not least a massive teddy bear bigger than me. He stumbled into my room, dropping the bear beside my bed as he scanned my room to find a suitable place to put it. He was wearing the love heart-patterned tie I bought him for our eighth Christmas together.

"Sorry I didn't come to your aid earlier, I was busy searching for things I thought would help."

I snatched the hot water bottle off him, settling it on my stomach.

"Come here," Ethan said, sliding into bed and cuddling me.

"I want my bear," I murmured into his chest.

Next thing I knew, there was a teddy bear's face smothering us both.

"Where on earth did you get this?" I asked.

He laughed. "Teddy bear shop." He kissed my forehead and squeezed me.

"No kissing," I growled.

"Ok, sorry." He released his grasp and rolled the teddy bear off us. A muffin then appeared in front of my eyes. The muffin was quickly inhaled.

"You're so adorable," he whispered.

I reached over him and grabbed a couple of muffins, stuffing one into my mouth and one into his. We spent the whole day lying in bed and watching movies. If I weren't in so much pain, this would have been a wonderful day.

We shared the ice cream while watching *When Harry Met Sally*. Not the most convenient film to watch regarding my situation in all honesty. So I fell asleep. Later on at 11:42 p.m., I woke up, still in Ethan's arms. I slipped out of bed and wandered to the bathroom.

When I came back, Ethan was still asleep. I sat beside him and watched him sleep peacefully for a minute or two before kissing his forehead and whispering, "I love you," making sure I avoided waking him.

DECEMBER 19TH

As I strolled downstairs this morning, the biggest bare Christmas tree I had ever seen in my entire life was planted in the corner of our living room.

"How the hell did that get in here?" I asked as I descended the stairs.

"That's for me to know, and you to find out," Ethan replied.

I shook my head in disbelief and wandered into the kitchen after gazing upon its magnificence. There's no way that tree could have fit into the elevator. It must've been fifteen feet high.

"We'll decorate it later; we need to get decorations first. I figured you'd want to go shopping with me to buy them." Ethan said as I sat on the sofa, observing the tree while eating our breakfast. He was wearing his lovely bird tie today. A dark navy tie, with a pattern of white birds on it. However, they're not proper birds. Can you remember drawing at school, instead of drawing a seagull or a bird, you'd draw a funny-styled tick? Like the tick you would use to mark someone's question correctly on a paper? The tie had those ticks on it anyway, showing them as birds. I bought Ethan this tie for our tenth Christmas together.

Later on, Max and Eleanor and Ethan and I all went shopping for Christmas tree decorations. Since Eleanor has lived here longer than us, she knew all the handy places to get all the required essentials from. We bought several boxes of lights, and a cute little star to go on top of the tree. We found loads of boxes of nutcrackers and snow-flakes, the typical Christmas tree decorations. We didn't have a colour scheme; we just chose the coolest-looking decorations. My favourite was the small snow globe you can hang on your tree. Inside, Santa and his reindeer are flying over a village. So cute! I kept it aside and left it until every other decoration had been hung up since it was easily breakable. Ethan bought some funny-styled Christmas jumpers to wear while we decorated our tree. Ethan's had a big snowman on the front with googley eyes, and mine had a Christmas tree on the front with little tiny bells hanging from it. Ethan thought it would be funny to buy me a jumper that's six sizes too big for me. So the jumper pretty much covered my knees and the arms almost touched the floor. Ethan threw me onto his shoulders to try to place the star on top of the tree. But we failed because we were too busy laughing at one another. We hadn't thought it through. I was still a few feet away from reaching it, too. So the star, unfortunately, didn't make it to the top of the tree. We placed it on the mantelpiece instead.

DECEMBER 20TH

As I lay in bed this morning the floor below me started to vibrate. Like a booming noise, shaking the whole room in a repeated pattern. I threw my dressing gown on and rushed downstairs. Ethan had discovered the surround sound button for the music system but didn't know how to turn it off. He was wincing with his fingers in his ears. "Sorry!" He was wearing his coffee beans tie I bought him for his twelfth birthday. I rolled my eyes at him, snatched the remote off him, and turned the music down.

"I didn't know we had that," he said, removing his fingers from his ears. He examined the remote with great wonder and skipped through the songs, stopping on a song, Elvis Presley's "Can't Help Falling in Love"—one of Ethan's favourite songs. I rolled my eyes at him when he grabbed my hands and began to sway. He raised my right hand, placing it onto his shoulder. Linking his right hand with my left, he lowered his left hand onto the small of my back, smirking in amusement as I tripped over his feet. He lifted me off the ground and slotted my feet on top of his. "That's better," he whispered as we gracefully swayed around the living room. I blushed as he moved his arms around my waist, to which I joined my hands at the back of his neck.

"You have bad morning breath," he said as we gazed into each other's eyes.

"Oh shut up! Where did you learn to dance?"

"I took dance lessons for prom."

I looked into his eyes as he looked beyond me, focusing on his steps. I was a second away from grabbing him and kissing him. "Ethan, that is the sweetest thing I have ever heard," I replied, tightening my hands around his neck.

"Being August Bishop's prom date was a big deal. I didn't want to disappoint you."

This was possibly the most romantic gesture I had ever heard. I don't know what came over me. I was leaning in to kiss him. I really was.

Then a knock came at the door, breaking our trance. Whoever it was on the other side I may attack. Ethan walked over to reveal Max.

"I was walking by and I remembered I left my rubber duck radio in your shower, so I thought I'd collect it," Max said.

Ethan laughed and turned to me to see if I found it as funny as him. I forced a fake smile, but quickly returned to my poop stare at Max.

Ethan ventured upstairs to retrieve Max's stupid radio duck. Meanwhile I wandered over to Max and punched his arm.

"Ouch! What was that for?"

"I was about to kiss him, you moron! And you bloody interrupted for a radio duck. Are you kidding me?" Some swear words may have been replaced with non-swear words in that sentence, but I can neither confirm nor deny I said such things.

"I won't disturb you with my radio duck issues anymore." Max smirked.

"Better not," I snarled with glaring eyes.

Ethan returned and handed Max his stupid radio duck. And I slammed the door on him before he could say another word.

DECEMBER 21ST

Of all times for Ethan to plan a last-minute trip to Miami to meet Natasha, he had to choose today. Of course I'm jealous; it's a natural thing for me to feel. It's his relationship with Eleanor all over again. I tried to not let it bother me; still, it constantly toyed with my mind. The TV even appeared to be against me, repeating all of Ethan's shows ahead of Christmas Eve. Then the next channel was repeating episodes of Patrick Miller's show. So I popped over to Max and Eleanor's. I hadn't discussed my schedule recently with Max, and was hoping a few more movie roles had come along to attract my interest.

"My first article will be in next week's magazine," Max said as he passed me my cup of tea.

"Great work, Max, congratulations!"

"Can I speak to August alone for a moment, Max?" Eleanor asked, raising her eyebrows.

It concerned me because I was certain I'd done something wrong although I wasn't sure what, and I'd only been here two minutes.

"Oh, ok. I'll go...and buy you some flowers from across the road," he replied, swiftly leaving the apartment.

Eleanor sat beside me on the sofa, almost knee to knee. "August, I know."

"Know what?" I replied, my voice shaking.

She squinted. "About Ethan and the crash."

I dropped my sight to the floor. "I thought he would've told you when you saw his scars." It surprised me that he hadn't told Eleanor about the crash; his scars are hardly discreet.

Max obviously broke the news to Eleanor; I still was unsure how much she knew. Did she know his heart had stopped?

"What else do you know about the crash?" I asked.

Her eyes suddenly darted at me with a look of sorrow.

"Oh." Her response wasn't required.

"I know it's a hard subject, but I wanted to speak to you and see how you were doing. Does it still bother you?"

I took a sip from my tea. It was too hot, so I placed it straight back down.

"It plays on my mind now and again," I replied.

She hugged me and rubbed my back. "Do you want to talk about it?"

I shook my head on her shoulder.

"Are you sure?"

I nodded my head on her shoulder.

"Why do I feel so guilty?" I asked in a weirdly exhausted voice.

"I don't know, August. It's one of those things you can't change and you have to accept that."

We separated. "I know," I replied. "I know." I stared at my tea and sighed.

"You love him, don't you?" she asked.

Without thinking I nodded. After a few seconds I realised what I had admitted and I glanced up sharply. Eleanor smiled, not a happy or sad one. Just an understanding one.

"He loves you too," she said.

"How do you know?" I breathed, trying to not let it show that my heart was dancing.

"It's the way he looks at you. Every girl dreams of being looked at the way he looks at you. Even me when I was with him. You just never catch him when he does."

DECEMBER 22ND

Max messaged this morning saying there was an interesting article in the newspaper about Ethan. So I bought a newspaper, expecting to see a photo of him with Natasha, kissing and holding hands along the beach.

ETHAN KNIGHT, GENTLEMAN.
My work is built around phone calls. Phoning up the latest celebrities and interviewing them because everyone wants to know what he or she are doing. This month's hot topic for me was Ethan Knight, the magician everyone is talking about. Strangely on this occasion, a phone call wouldn't help me. Ethan Knight was unreachable; maybe because he's a magician, or maybe he doesn't like to be disturbed. Either way, this required me to find him and speak to him in person. Verging me on the cliff of becoming more like a paparazzi than a writer. Nevertheless, I set off in pursuit of him after hearing he was in Miami. He wasn't hard to find. I encountered him helping an elderly woman carry her shopping home. A sincere gesture of goodwill, regardless of his stature. I walked beside him and introduced myself. He knew who I was and we walked and talked about his upcoming appearance on Patrick Miller's

chat show, and his successful TV series. The elderly woman's name was Jean, a very polite and lovely lady. After five minutes, Ethan stopped, and placed down the shopping in his hands. He asked me how much I made a year and if I had a family. Surprised, I answered his query and asked why he wanted to know. He reached into his jacket pocket and wrote me a check for two years' wages. "Go and be with your family, take a break, go on holiday. Before you know it, you'll be paying for their tuitions, and they'll be gone. Spending time with your family is far more important than walking beside me helping this lady carry her shopping home. I'd give anything to spend Christmas with my family," he said. He slipped the check into my pocket and continued on his way with Jean and her shopping. This kid is nineteen years old, nineteen, and wrote me a check for two years' wages. Bearing in mind he has never met me before. But he couldn't have been more right: Family is the most important thing in the world. And as I click send on the email with this file attached, I'm currently sipping a glass of wine with my wife as I watch my children run around on the beach in Portugal. I guess what I'm trying to say is, Ethan Knight, thank you.

DECEMBER 24TH

Today is the day I make my appearance on Patrick Miller's show. A moment I have dreamt of my whole life. Ethan is taking me to the demolition site of the hotel; romantic, I know. However, I want a million reassurances that everything will be fine and Ethan will return unharmed. After my talk with Eleanor yesterday, I haven't been able to stop thinking about what she said. *Is it true?* Ethan came home late, and we didn't really speak this morning because he had arranged for us to head straight over to the site once we were ready. He insisted we go in his car, but I insisted we go in my car. I won of course.

The site was overflowing with men and women wearing yellow and orange high visibility jackets, and white safety helmets. Ethan forced me to wear the same outfit due to *safety* reasons.

"Aw, you look so adorable," Ethan said.

"I hate you," I replied with a frown.

He took a step back, pulling out his phone. "Say cheese."

"No," I said, folding my arms and increasing my frown.

He smiled down at his phone after taking the picture.

"That's my new screen saver right there. I might even get it framed and put on the wall, you're so cute in your helmet."

I gazed upon him, straight-faced and uninterested. "I'm not five years old."

He passed his phone to a workman and asked him to take a photo of us.

"Stop being so stubborn!" he said before kissing my cheek for the photo. He patted my helmet after. "Right, let's go inside then, shall we?"

I rolled my eyes and rearranged my helmet. "Let's." I felt so stupid having to walk around in that ridiculous outfit. My helmet didn't even fit my head right, and the jacket was three times too big for me. I looked like the child of a builder who they had brought to work for the day. I don't know what Ethan was excited to show me; all that remained inside was concrete and a few chairs for the workers to sit on. It's so weird seeing the inside of the building when everything has been stripped from it. Lifeless. It's completely lifeless. I expected all the carpets and the furnishings to remain, but no, nothing, nothing to represent that this was once a hotel. Just cold, miserable, and dusty.

As we entered there were two young men sitting on a ruined sofa on their laptops, shouting at one another. Their argument faded as we approached them.

"These are two of the computer chaps who helped edit my show." Ethan slumped beside them on the sofa and put his arms around them. Strangely, they didn't say a word. They were just staring at me. I smiled, unsure how to react to such odd behaviour.

"Guys!" Ethan said clipping the back of their heads with his hands.

They jumped and stood up, extending their hands. "Yeah, we're his team who make everything happen. Hi, I'm Bryan," one said, rubbing the back of his head with a huge smile on his face. I shook his hand while keeping wary eye contact with him. These guys only looked the same age as me, maybe older, but they looked so young, it was tempting to ask them why they weren't in school.

The first was a tanned, chubby guy with glasses and long brown hair who wore a T-shirt with a picture of a slice of pizza on the front.

"Can I get your number?" the other snapped, extending his hand. He was the opposite of the first. Small, skinny, and as pale as a ghost, and had short spikey hair. I raised my eyebrow at him, avoiding the handshake.

"Toby, you're not having her phone number, sorry," Ethan said, standing and putting his hand on Toby's shoulder. "There are many reasons why, but I won't hurt your feelings by telling you them all."

"Sure," Toby replied.

"But the main reason is that she's too good for you, and she's my girl, chaps," he added. What did he mean *she's my girl? Can you be more specific?*

As I thought it over I started to sing: *I got sunshine on a cloudy day. When it's cold outside I've got the month of May.*

Ethan shouldn't have said that, now I looked like a lunatic randomly singing "My Girl" in front of two guys who helped run his show.

Ethan turned and gave me a puzzled frown, but a smirk replaced his frown. Our eyes instinctively knew what we'd have to do next.

"*I guess you'd say, what can make me feel this way?*" we sang in unison.

I sang the first, *my girl*, while Ethan carried on the next two that repeated.

"*Talkin' bout my girl*," we sang in unison again.

We both pointed to Bryan to sing the final, *my girl*, and he backed us up perfectly.

Ethan and I high-fived and laughed at one another for a good minute before we eventually calmed down. I apologise if we now have "My Girl" stuck in your head and you're singing it for the rest of the week.

"You're sleeping with that?" Toby then asked inappropriately, unimpressed by our excellent, synchronised, harmonised vocals.

It hurt a little because I thought Ethan would be lucky to be sleeping with someone as funny and hilarious as me. Not to mention a great spontaneous singer, too. Ethan's brightened mood dampened as quickly as it had been created. "Toby, I'm this close to firing you. You're in the presence of the most beautiful woman on the planet and you refer to her as *that*? Sit back down, please, before I get mad." He held his fingers no farther than an inch apart in front of his face.

Toby turned red and slouched onto the sofa, sulking and tapping away at the keyboard.

"Sorry about that. He's a constant pain in the ass," Ethan said. "I need to check on a few things. Are you ok to wait here for two minutes?"

I smiled. "Sure, I'm not going anywhere."

He stepped forward, stopping toe to toe with me, tucked my hair behind my ears, and then pulled a small section forward. "Elfie, think of a card and I bet you five bucks it's in your shoe."

"Ok," I said as he jogged away.

It was tempting to turn and ask Bryan, *You heard him call me the most beautiful woman on the planet, right? And you saw the spark between us there?*

Instead, I sighed, ruffled my hair, and sat down on the sofa, as far away from Toby as possible. I untied my white Converse shoelaces. My card was the king of clubs. Nothing. Bryan held the first shoe as I untied the second. It didn't surprise me to find a card facing down in the sole of my shoe. He'd become too good at it for me to doubt his ability. I reached in, and there it was. The king of clubs. I grinned.

"Is that the card you were thinking of?" Bryan asked.

"It is," I replied, placing my shoes back onto my feet.

"So, where's this tunnel?" I asked.

"Oh it's underneath there," he said, turning and pointing to a big white *X* painted in the centre of the floor of the dusty lobby.

I rose from the ruined sofa and observed the marking on the floor from what I thought was a safe distance. I couldn't see a door, but I guess that's the idea; otherwise, people would know it's there.

"What tunnel?" Toby asked.

I swivelled around and scowled at him.

"The one we were supposed to tell her about in which he escapes in, that one, remember?" Bryan replied.

"Oh shit, right, yeah, it's under the big white thing over there, yeah," Toby said, waving his hand at it.

I flicked my eyes between them. Bryan's expression dropped.

"There isn't a tunnel, is there?" I asked, lowering my head.

"Duh," Toby snapped.

I dropped my head farther and stared at the floor.

"Ok, Toby, you're done. Pick up your stuff and go. You're lucky other people are around you," Ethan snarled from over my shoulder.

My eyes filled up and my bottom lip trembled. How could I have been this naïve? Toby smacked down his computer screen and took off towards the exit. Bryan remained silent.

"August," Ethan said.

I took off my helmet and examined it before furiously throwing it to the ground as well as my stupid jacket and walked away.

"August, please wait."

I wiped my eyes as I paced to my car.

"August!" Ethan shouted again. He jogged behind me. "Where are you going?" He stopped in front of me, putting his hands on my shoulders.

"I'm not standing around and watching you kill yourself, Ethan!" I yelled, pushing his arms away and walking past him.

"August, please don't go." He groaned and walked beside me.

"You lied, Ethan! How do you expect me to react to this? I want no involvement in this, I'm going home."

The car was still another couple minutes' walk away, but I persevered at my fast pace.

"Why don't you trust me?" he asked, putting his arm around my shoulder.

I flung it off. "No! None of your stupid cuddling or kissing; it's either me or your stupid fucking trick. I'm sure Natasha will approve of it. See what she thinks about it!"

"What are you talking about? Is that what this is about? Natasha?"

I remained quiet and kept walking. I suddenly noticed he was no longer walking beside me. I glanced over my shoulder. He'd stopped and had his hands held in front of him. They were shaking. I stopped and watched him for a moment. He looked up at me and then walked back towards the hotel. Instead of making things worse, I returned to my car.

As it burst into life, I punched the steering wheel, setting off the horn, startling myself. I needed to be at Patrick's studio in a few hours, and now I felt so bad I didn't want to go. This wasn't an evening I could just avoid or postpone. The dust from the site made me feel unhygienic and clammy. So I told myself to take it a step at a time and just return home to freshen up. I ran my hands through my hair and fastened my seat belt, jolting it twice before it clicked into the buckle.

I drove home, upset and angry. I slammed my car door shut as I pulled up outside our apartment block and rudely threw the key at the man who parks the cars for us.

Ethan was already leaning against the sofa, waiting for me as I stepped inside. I rubbed my face, slamming the door behind me in frustration at his being home before me. Nevertheless, I walked straight past him.

"Are we going to talk about this?" he asked, following me.

"I have nothing to say," I replied, maintaining my course.

"August, don't make me leave like this," he said, still following me.

"I'm taking a shower and then heading over to the studio. You do what you need to do." I closed my bedroom door behind me and sat on my bed with my head in my hands.

The moment the shower water struck me I started to cry. The bathroom door creaked open not long after.

"August, there's something I need to say."

I sighed and wiped my eyes. "Ethan, what is it? Can't I have two minutes in the shower, please?"

Silence. The falling shower water echoed.

"I've been waiting twelve years to tell you. I think I've waited long enough," he then said, his voice sounding clearer than before. He must have stepped farther into the bathroom.

"I'm naked, this isn't the best time, Ethan. Just go."

The flow of the shower water suddenly slowed to a stop. The soft touch of his finger rose from the bottom of my spine, gently moving my hair off my back and placing it over my shoulder. A kiss pressed against my neck and another behind my ear. I closed my eyes as he rested his head on my shoulder. We deeply exhaled in unison.

"I love you... I've loved you from the moment I first laid eyes on you, and I will do until my dying day. I will always, always, always...love you. So badly, it hurts," he whispered into my ear, kissing it afterwards.

A smile developed into a grin as I opened my eyes. Ethan kissed my neck once more before the flow of water restarted. I glanced over my shoulder, but he was already gone.

The nerves inside me amplified as each second passed as I stood behind the set of Patrick Miller's show. Max and Eleanor were already sitting on the sofa waiting for me, after having a gossip with Patrick about their newfound love for one another. Despite Ethan telling me he loved me, I was still furious with him for lying about the tunnel. I just didn't want anything to happen to him. Especially with the whole world watching. I'm wearing a black shift dress with a collar according to my stylist lady. It's a very pretty dress, but it doesn't come close to my premiere dress. That's like the queen of dresses.

Time edged closer to the moment I'd always wished would happen. The churning butterflies in my stomach were making me feel like throwing up.

You'll be fine once you're out there, I told myself. *Focus on yourself for a moment. Ethan can take care of himself.*

"He'll announce you on any second," the assistant beside me said.

The moment has arrived. I'm sweating furiously. I looked up at the screen showing the live broadcast. Patrick rose from behind his desk.

"Ladies and gentlemen, it's the moment you've all been waiting for, the moment I've been waiting for. She's ruling the world right now, guys. AUGUST BISHOP!"

The lady with the headset on behind me placed her hand on my back and gave me a slight nudge forwards, breaking me from my trance. I forced myself forward, down the small tunnel towards the applauding audience. The studio lights blinded me as I took my first steps onto the stage I had heavily dreamt of stepping on. *Remember to smile…good. Now curtsy and wave to audience, perfect. Now walk over to Patrick and then sit down and relax,* my conscience helpfully instructed.

Patrick stood, open-armed. I walked over and embraced him. He smelt terrific, although the smell of hairspray was quite prominent.

"I can't believe I'm finally here!" I said into his ear.

"Please, please take a seat, August," he said, guiding his hand to the sofa occupied by my friends. Max and Eleanor smiled at me as I sat alongside them. They looked so cute. Max was wearing a smart suit and Eleanor was wearing a beautiful cream dress. I wished I could tell Max about my encounter with Ethan earlier, although it's not the time or place. No matter how quiet I whisper it to him, the microphone clipped to my dress would surely pick up what I was saying.

"It's great to have you on the show, August!" Patrick said.

I smiled at him and then the audience, allowing myself to soak in the atmosphere. "I can't tell you how long I've wanted to come on this show."

"Well, we've been dying to have you on here, haven't we, guys?" Patrick shouted to the audience, in which they replied with huge screams and cheers. It was so humbling to receive such a reception.

"It's a wonderful Christmas present having you on the show, August. So, first things first, we'll definitely be seeing you in another movie soon, won't we?"

I nodded. "Yes, for sure. People seem to like me, which I hoped for, and the parts have come flooding in for new films. So, you'll be seeing a lot more of me over the next year or two."

Patrick looked overjoyed; it was like he'd had horrible plastic surgery and it'd left him with a permanent grin.

Suddenly, a male shouted from the audience, "I love you, August!"

The audience burst into laughter. I gazed at Patrick and laughed at them.

"Thanks, Dad!" I replied.

My dad wasn't in the audience; I was just trying to be humorous. I'm sure he was snuggled up on the sofa with my mum, watching me right now. The audience and Patrick laughed as well as Max and Eleanor.

"On a serious note, tonight, yourself, Eleanor, and Max are here to support your good friend, Mr. Ethan Knight, who is performing something that is going to shake the world, literally. This guy is risking his life, doesn't that scare you?"

This was the question I was hoping to avoid; now I had to make up something to show everyone I had complete and utter faith in Ethan and everything was going to be fine, and we'd all live happily ever after.

Max answered first. "The guy is insane. He's taking magic to a whole new level. Personally, I've seen him produce the impossible many times, so each time he comes up with a new idea I don't doubt him for a second."

Patrick replied, "I understand, but for the world at home and for myself, we've only seen his series, performing cool, quirky card tricks and hand magic. This is a massively defining stage in his career, don't you think?"

Eleanor answered now. I couldn't produce a sensible sentence in my head. I *should* have thought of this before coming on. I've had weeks to prepare.

"Absolutely. I'm still getting used to his tricks, so I'm on the same page as everyone else. This is a gigantic moment. Max is so laid-back about it. He hasn't shown a second's doubt, which has helped settle my nerves."

Patrick nodded. "What are your thoughts about this, August? I know you and Ethan are close and have been for over a decade now."

I tucked my hair behind my ears and looked down. "Umm, he's my best friend, and I don't want to see him get hurt. I've always supported Ethan and I always will. But this is a little out of my comfort zone. In all honesty, I didn't approve of this trick and it has caused arguments, but he's my best friend and this is something he has to do, so I will show him my full support."

Patrick gave me a reassuring smile. "I would be the same if I was in your position, August. Dropping a building on top of yourself isn't the news any best friend wants to hear."

I raised my head and smiled in an attempt to show that it wasn't playing on my mind.

"So your first film, August, your first role with Eleanor. Any gossip to expose? What were your thoughts on your first part as the leading actress?"

I put my arm around Eleanor. "We clicked right from the word go. We had so much fun filming together. I didn't want it to end!"

Eleanor rested her head on my shoulder. "I feel like she's my momma goose, even though she's younger than me."

We giggled at each other. I guess it was kind of true.

"You appear like sisters! Which is great to see...because most people would assume there is a lot of intimidation between you. Did you guys not feel any of that at the beginning?"

I turned to Eleanor and we winced at one another.

"Naaah," we said, and giggled at each other once more.

"I mean... I was star-struck when we first met, but I soon settled down afterwards," I added.

"I thought you were a little nervous when you first spoke to me!" Eleanor replied and squeezed my arm.

All of a sudden a huge screen descended from the ceiling behind us.

"Right, everyone, I've been made aware we will be heading over to Ethan now so we can see how he is doing. We're approaching the seven-minute countdown." Patrick announced, walking towards the screen.

It flickered for a brief second before a view of the towering hotel was shown from a helicopter. It then switched onto Ethan, who was standing on the X in the middle of the once hotel lobby. I smiled at the screen when I caught sight of which tie he was wearing. My AB maroon and blue school tie. The first tie I ever gave him. His favourite tie.

"Hello, Ethan, can you hear me?" Patrick yelled to the screen.

"Hello, Pat, is that you?" Ethan replied, fiddling with his earpiece.

The audience laughed again at Ethan calling him Pat. Patrick shrugged at the audience. "Yes, Ethan, it's Pat. How is everything going?"

Ethan rotated in search of the camera positioned on the inside of the hotel.

"To your left," Patrick assisted, recognising what he was searching for.

Ethan looked up, spotted the camera, and pointed with his cuffed hands. "Oh thanks, I got you. Hi, everyone, everything's going well, I suppose. Not much to do...for a few minutes anyway. The explosives are set and I'm in the middle of them all. It's absolutely freezing here, though. I wish I'd worn a jacket."

Patrick laughed along with the audience this time. Our sofa remained silent. The throbbing in my ears was gradually building.

"Are my friends ok?" Ethan asked.

"Yeah, we're fine, bud," Max shouted at the screen.

"Good. August, are you ok?" he asked, readjusting his tie.

I grinned as I blushed at him. "I'm fine, Ethan. Nice tie."

He smiled and stopped fiddling with his tie. Patrick glanced at me, and then at the screen. From the expression on his face, I think he recognised the spark between us. I twisted back on the sofa to look at Max and Eleanor, who were already studying me. Max raised his eyebrow at me and I smirked, tucking my hair behind my ears. Max had definitely figured out what was going on. I'd completely forgotten where I was for a second and realised everyone in the audience and at home could probably see my feelings towards my friend. I raised my head and acted as if everything was fine.

"Ethan, we'll leave you to it, buddy. Make sure you come back in one piece," Patrick said. The camera returned to the helicopter's view of the hotel. Suddenly I felt sick; the size and weight that would be dropping on top of him worried me. *How many seconds would he have to escape?*

"Only four minutes and twenty-seven seconds to go, ladies and gentlemen," Patrick announced, reclaiming his seat.

I flicked my eyes back to the screen; thousands had gathered around the safe zone to stand and watch. A certain section was boxed off. I assumed that was the explosive controls area.

"Where do you think he will reappear after?" Eleanor asked.

We all pondered; none of us had stopped to think about that.

"I think the dust will settle and he'll be standing on the rubble once it clears, acting all casual," Max answered.

"I like that, standing like he's set foot on the moon!" Patrick added.

"Yeah, I didn't know if he would just appear from somewhere random and be like, I'm here, guys!" Eleanor said.

All three heads moved towards me in search of my thoughts on his reappearance.

"Max's idea sounds good," I answered.

We all nodded and glanced up at the clock. Two minutes and forty-six seconds to go. The churning inside my stomach had rejoined the throbbing in my ears. Eleanor grabbed Max's hand and rested it on her lap. The camera had now moved back onto Ethan, who was sitting on a chair on the X, biting his nails.

"We're taking a short break now, guys. Rejoin us with a minute to go!" Patrick circulated to the audience and to the cameras, broadcasting to the world. The lights dimmed and the makeup staff rushed onto the stage, dabbing the sweat off Mr. Miller's forehead. A few rushed over to us also, although now wasn't the time to be bombarded by makeup staff.

"Sorry, but now isn't a good time," I politely said to one lady dabbing at my forehead. She bowed her head and stood aside.

"Relax, August. You'll give yourself a heart attack," Eleanor whispered.

I smirked and gripped the sofa tightly with my hands. I shut my eyes in one desperate last attempt to calm myself.

"We're back in twenty!" someone shouted.

I sharply twisted around to see what was happening on

the screen. Ethan waved at the camera; it was almost as if he knew I was watching him at that moment. I felt like waving back, then I realised how pathetically stupid that would be. The studio lights ignited again. Patrick focused upon the rolling cameras. "Welcome back, everyone. One minute to go now on Christmas Eve, before we head on over to the demolition site. What emotions are you feeling right now, guys?" Patrick asked.

"Excited," Max replied.

"Yeah, me too," Eleanor added.

I paused. "Nervously excited."

Patrick rubbed his chin. "Yeah, me too. I'm dying to see where he will appear! Right! Without further delay, we're going back over to Ethan now with thirty-three seconds to go!"

Everyone's attention now focused on the screen and the studio lights dimmed to almost darkness. A great way to amplify my concern. I could feel my eyes welling up. Patrick sat on the armrest of the sofa, placing his hand on my shoulder. "He will be fine," he whispered.

The clock reached fifteen seconds. The chair Ethan was sitting on had vanished, and he was now planted in the middle of the *X*, alone. My hand started to shake. *Don't throw up*. The clock reached nine seconds. *Don't throw up*. The camera zoomed in on Ethan. He kept his sight fixed on the floor. Ethan's head rose with two seconds to go, and he winked into the camera. Then zero, the camera snapped to the helicopter's view, and the top floor of the hotel exploded. Within a few seconds the last floor blew, and the once grand hotel plummeted into a massive pile of dust and rubble. I closed my eyes, forcing a tear down my cheek. The crowd behind gasped. A huge cloud of dust still covered where the hotel had once been, blocking our view. Silence echoed throughout the studio as we waited for the dust to settle. I wandered my sight around the studio; all eyes remained on the screen. The dust had now settled, and the high visibility staff rushed towards the rubble. More tears rolled down my face as I watched the screen, waiting for him to reappear. The studio lights reignited. I squinted to allow my pupils to readjust to the light. I glanced over at Max. I could see the worry spread across his face as each second passed.

Patrick crouched down in front of me. "August, dear, don't worry, he's fine."

Eleanor placed her hand on my shoulder, squeezing it. A tear revealed itself and flowed down her cheek. Patrick clapped his hand three times and spun round towards the audience on the ball of his shiny black shoes.

"Do you want to know how I know Ethan Knight is ok, ladies and gentlemen?" he shouted.

Now most definitely wasn't the best time for him to be a chat show host; right now he needed to be a considerate man and respect his guests. I felt like charging at him. Patrick rotated towards me, staring into my eyes, pausing for a moment. I poop stared right back at him. Patrick raised his hand high above his head randomly. The whole world was watching, my best friend and the love of my life was probably dead, and this was the pathetic distraction he had created.

"The reason I know Ethan Knight is ok, ladies and gen-tlemen, is because..." Patrick started to say, clearly running out of ideas to draw the attention away from Ethan. He unbuttoned the top two buttons of his shirt. Great. He's stripping on global television on Christmas Eve. Exactly what we need. My opinion of Patrick lowered. I thought he was the third greatest person on the planet, behind Ethan and Dad of course. Patrick reached into his shirt and pulled his skin up. My face winced at whatever weird stunt he was trying to perform. But as he pulled on his skin more, I realised it wasn't skin, it was a mask. The mask slowly rose above his neckline. Suddenly everything appeared to pass by in slow motion. My heartbeat was pulsating, blocking out everything around me. The identity of the person hidden under the mask was revealed before it came off when Madeline's bracelet slipped down onto his wrist as he went to take it off. The mask flew off, and there he was. Covered in sweat and dust. He looked as if he'd been stuck up a chimney.

"The reason I know Ethan is ok, ladies and gentlemen, is because I am Ethan Knight." He winked at me before pivoting around to the audience, opening his arms to accept their reaction. The floor below us started to shake. Everyone jolted to their feet and erupted as if their favourite team had just scored. I casually smiled out of pure happiness and placed my head into my hands, wiping my eyes. The deafening roars and screams continued, and continued.

As I lifted my head Ethan crouched down in front of me.

"Hey, you," he said, wiping my cheeks with his thumb.

"Hey, don't you scare me like that again!" I replied.

He placed his finger and thumb on my chin, elevating it. My hair flicked forward from behind my ear. He smirked and combed it back behind my ear. My feelings couldn't be withheld any longer. I lunged forward, swinging my arms around his neck, and kissed him. It wasn't the most glamorous first kiss since his lips were dry and gritty and covered in dust, but it was still perfect.

"I love you so much," I whispered as we rested our foreheads together.

"Well, it's about time." He laughed.

While we were protected by our own little bubble, I hadn't noticed the crowd's uproar during our kiss. The real Patrick Miller then ran onto the stage. "How about that, ladies and gentlemen! Let's hear it one more time for Ethan Knight, absolutely phenomenal, absolutely phenomenal!" he shouted, jumping into the crowd and celebrating with them.

"Hey, guys," Ethan said to Max and Eleanor.

"Hey, bud. You had us worried for a moment there," Max replied.

A woman jogged onto the stage and handed Ethan a towel. He rubbed his face as he slotted himself beside me on the sofa, letting out a huge sigh of relief. He put his arm around me and kissed the top of my head once he was clean.

"Wasn't it just the greatest magic trick you'd ever seen in your entire life, though?" Ethan asked like an excited schoolchild.

"The best!" Max replied.

Ethan rubbed my chin and nose with the towel. "You gotta little dirt on your face... That's better," he joked.

"Thanks," I murmured from underneath the towel, unamused.

Patrick jogged up to Ethan, shook his hand, and applauded him as he returned to his desk. I found Patrick's reaction weird because he must have had a certain involvement in Ethan's trick. How much of an influence he had is another story. Maybe Ethan asked him to leave the stage during a certain point. However they did it, it would play on my mind for the rest of my life. Even if Ethan agrees to tell me how he did it, I don't think I would want him to. The secret to the greatest trick ever *should* remain a secret.

"Whoa!" Patrick shouted, slamming his hands on his desk. "How? How did you do that?"

Ethan grinned. "A magician never reveals his tricks, Patrick. You of all people should know that."

Patrick took a moment and looked at the audience with an open mouth. "I'm speechless. What is next for you? Surely topping that is impossible?"

"I've got to see what this one says first." Ethan squeezed my shoulder.

"Oh, so you two are like a thing now?" Patrick asked, eyebrows raised.

Ethan squeezed my cheeks together and kissed me.

"Just friends," he replied with a grin.

December 25th

"**M**erry Christmas," Ethan said, nudging me awake. I flung my hand at him and wafted him away. "Sleeping," I muttered.

Ethan then thought it would be a good idea to jump on top of me to get my attention. His head rested next to mine. "Wake up." He moaned. Blowing into my ear. My eyes took a moment or two to come alive. I feebly rolled over underneath him. His cheesy grin hovered over me. He was wearing the Santa Claus tie I got him for our second Christmas together. He's worn it every Christmas Day since.

"Morning," I groaned.

"You fell asleep in the car so I carried you up, ya little sleepyhead," Ethan said, tickling my feet.

I jolted upright and lightly punched his shoulder. "Why didn't you carry me to bed?" I asked, stretching out along the sofa.

"Oh I'm sorry, I'll make a note of your complaint and be sure to do so next time," he sarcastically answered.

I winced at him, then I realised I wasn't wearing my dress. I was wearing one of his T-shirts and his jogging bottoms.

"Why am I wearing your clothes?"

His face lit up. "Are you being serious? This is what I found in your wardroabe, my clothes you have clearly stolen!"

"Borrowed," I corrected.

He gave me a disinterested look. "Whatever. Your entire wardroabe is filled with my clothes. Don't ask how you got into them, I'm a magician, ok?"

I grinned at him while biting the sleeve of his jumper. I love stealing his clothes. "Where's my necklace? The one from Stanley?" I asked, gripping my neck.

Ethan flicked his hand towards the direction of the table. "I had to take it off while changing you because it would've caught on something and broke knowing me."

I sighed in relief and slumped back into the sofa.

"Now hurry and take a shower so we can open our presents. We need to be at Max and Eleanor's soon for dinner. You know how grumpy he can be when we're late!" he said, dragging me to my feet.

"Carry me, please, I'm too tired," I whined, clutching his neck and wrapping my legs around his waist.

"You're always tired," he muttered, walking towards the stairs.

"Why do you have to be so cute?" he mumbled.

I hummed into his neck as we climbed the staircase. I was still clutching him when he turned the shower on for me.

"August, stop being childish and get in the shower, please!"

I dropped my legs down and sulked at him as he grabbed me a towel.

"No sulking," he said, throwing the towel over me. I grabbed his wrist and pulled him back, kissing him firmly. "I'll be down in a minute," I said afterwards as we grinned at each other.

"Come on, you know I'm impatient to open my presents!" Ethan shouted as I took my time walking downstairs.

I fluffed his hair as I walked past him, and then kissed him. I love how I can stick my tongue down his throat whenever I wish. It's fun.

The tree had a pile of presents stacked next to it.

"Alternative gift swapping?" I asked.

Ethan stared at the presents.

"Ethan," I whispered, nudging him.

"I'm trying to figure out which one to give you first." He wandered over to the pile of presents and fetched them over to the coffee table, scattering them around. His presents to me remained on his side, my presents to him remained on my side. The first present I opened had *To, August/Ethan From, Ethan/August* written on the label. Confused, I ripped open the paper to find a men's tracksuit inside. "Let's hear your explanation then," I joked.

He laughed. "Since you're always stealing my clothes, I figured that this is really a present for me to wear for a day and then you can steal it...like every other item of clothing of mine."

I smirked. "Very clever. I was hoping for something designer, but you know, this is perfect."

"Well, before you're too conclusive...why don't you open your next gift from me?" He passed me a small long box.

"Ethan, if this is a pair of socks, I will punch you!"

"Just open it!"

I rolled my eyes at him and opened the box. It contained an Eiffel Tower pencil sharpener. I flicked my eyes up to him, awaiting his explanation.

"We're going to Paris, so you can go shopping for all your designer clothes and you can purchase whatever you like. I'll be your personal shopping assistant who will watch you try on all your clothes and carry your bags, and then we can explore the city."

"Yeah, I figured that's what the pencil sharpener indicated," I replied, raising a sarcastic eyebrow.

"I wanted to spoil you, you know. If I decided to buy you clothes instead of taking you to Paris and letting you select your own, then the apartment would be overflowing with bags and wrappings and labels. I mean, your happiness is priceless to me, August, and I will buy you as many dresses and clothes as you like until you're satisfied. But even then I know you'll still steal my clothes."

"God, I love you." I put my arms around him and gave him a big, hearty hug. *What more can I say?* He's perfect, he's honestly so perfect. I wouldn't change even the tiniest detail about him, and I question why I am so lucky to have him.

I got the satchel I wanted as well! It's a natural brown leather colour, and it has AUGUST etched into it in white and the buckles are golden. It's the most wonderful bag *ever.* It smells great, too. Much better than the one I used for college. I love it!

He also got me a magic set for beginners, which should be fun...

Ethan adored his new tie and his cards, especially the one with my face on, and our holiday to the Maldives.

He placed his arm around me and kissed my forehead. "You always get me the most thoughtful gifts, August."

We paused for a moment as we scanned over our gifts.

"Right, we better go now, we don't want to be late!" He patted my thigh, then wandered over to the mantelpiece, grabbing his clock.

"This still works?" he asked, surprised.

I nodded. "It hasn't stopped since the day you gave it me. I'm surprised you haven't noticed it before."

"The excellent craftsmanship made me think it was a high-quality clock!" He smirked and placed it on the coffee table. "I'll go and get changed, be back in two." He kissed my forehead one more time before rushing upstairs.

I placed my head in my hands and smiled, just smiled. I've never been so happy, and my life has never been so perfect.

I went to twiddle the necklace around my neck, forgetting it was on the coffee table. As I leant forward to pick it up, something clicked in my mind. I changed my sight to the clock. "No, it can't be," I said under my breath.

I turned around to check if Ethan was there. He wasn't. I shuffled forward, unfolding my legs and grabbing my necklace and my clock. Rotating the clock in my hands, I searched for the keyhole. I peered behind me again to check if Ethan was there. He wasn't. I ran my finger over the key slot in the clock and carefully placed the key from my necklace into it. It fit perfectly. I smiled, because for once, I was a step ahead of Ethan. The key was a lot harder to turn than expected and took a few attempts to turn the tiny key in the tiny lock on the tiny clock. The back popped up, startling me. I stuck my fingernail in, forcing the back off. Inside was a small black velvet box. Almost like one you would contain a ring in. I tilted the clock backwards, allowing the black velvet box to fall onto my lap. I looked over my shoulder one final time to see if Ethan was there. He wasn't. I gently placed the clock and its back onto the table. My heart started to race. I tried to open the velvet box, but failed since I was opening it at the wrong end. I giggled at my stupidity and then opened it from the other side. Inside was a diamond ring, an exceptional diamond ring. A gloriously huge, shining diamond ring. So many questions flowed through my mind, but there was no time to consider them. I removed the ring from its box and inspected it. It sparkled as the light from the balcony shined upon it. The silver ring had a small bracket connected to it to hold the mighty fine square diamond. I closed the ring in the palm of my hand and shut my eyes, appreciating its beauty. A hand placed itself on top of mine. I opened my eyes, and there he was. Knelt down in front of me, wearing a tie with the words *Will You Marry Me?* running down it.

"So what was the deal with Natasha?" I asked.

"She was helping me shop for your satchel, you moron."

He took a deep breath. "August, on April the sixteenth, twelve and a bit years ago. I met the prettiest girl I had ever seen in my entire life. She was so shy and sweet, her eyes captivated me and her smile, her smile was perfect. She was perfect, even when she spat black currant juice all over me. And every day since, I contemplated. *Do I tell her? How do I tell her?* That I'm so madly in love with her. To ask her to be mine. When I was in hospital and I found out you were seeing somebody else, it broke my heart because I thought I was too late. Too late to tell you that you're the first thing I think about in the morning, and the last thing I think about at night, and all the spaces in between. You were always meant to be with me, always were, always will. I'll never want to be with anyone else, never ever, ever. Before I ask my next question can I ask you something?"

I tried to compose myself, I tried, but tears kept flooding out of my eyes.

"Hey, hey, come here." He shuffled me forward and wiped my eyes.

"Can you remember when I gave you that clock?"

I flicked my eyes over to it. "My thirteenth birthday."

"Can you remember when exactly?" he asked.

I frowned. What did this have to do with him proposing?

"Well, you gave it me like a month late, *so* September?"

He nodded. "Correct. Do you know how long ago that was?"

My frowned increased. "Six years. Ethan, is this relevant right now? Can't I just say yes?" My tears stopped momentarily as I changed focus to his irrelevance.

"Last question, don't worry. How many months ago was that?"

I rolled my eyes at him and wiped my eyes while genuinely thinking of the answer. "Seventy-three...or seventy-four months ago?" As soon as I answered my eyes lit up. "No!" I shouted at him, placing my hands over my mouth and restarting my tears.

"Check your shoe," he replied smugly.

"No." I blubbered, wafting my hands over my eyes.

He rolled his eyes at me and slipped off my shoe, since I wasn't capable of doing so myself, and pulled out a card.

And there it was. The seventy-three of hearts. Well, the seven of hearts with his pathetic number three drawn beside the seven, signed by my six-year-old self with the smiley face. It still had the smudge from my chocolatey fingers. I could barely see the card through my flowing eyes.

"You kept it?" I asked, carefully taking it from him.

"Of course I kept it! There it is, August. There's the best magic trick you will ever see. No buildings being collapsed on top of anybody, and no switching seats in cars. To complete my magic trick, I need to ask you one final question."

Why couldn't I be stronger emotionally? Ethan constantly has me crying, it's not natural. I exhaled. "Ok."

He signalled down at his tie and wafted it. "August Victoria Bishop. Will you marry me?"

I've never cried and laughed and smiled and sulked and winced in such a short time. All these emotions were combining and I couldn't help but cry. I can't believe he kept that card. I can't.

I wiped my eyes and smiled, nodding my head. "Yes."

He quickly leant forward and kissed me. He had the biggest grin on his face. I'd never seen him so happy as he placed the ring onto my finger.

"It was my mum's. My dad bought it as soon as he won his first big payout. Growing up, my dad didn't give me much advice. But one day he crouched down in front of me and handed me the ring, telling me to give it to you when we were old enough. He said my mum would want me to have it."

I held his head next to mine and caressed the back of his neck. I held my hand up over his shoulder and admired the ring I possessed on my finger.

When he mentioned his mum though, it made me think of the letter. Maybe now I should give it to him, now is the right time. Leaving it any longer could only make things worse.

"Ethan, I need to show you something."

"Ok," he replied.

I rose from the sofa, seating him on it, and walked over to the cabinet I had kept it hidden in. I regretted keeping it from him for as long as I had. Still, I passed the box to him. The moment I gave it to him I think he knew who it was from. I sat quietly, allowing him to examine it in peace. Ethan removed the envelope containing the letter from his box and began to read it. I watched his eyes as they flicked along each line. Tears spilled down his cheeks as he folded the letter into the envelope and returned it to its box. I shuffled behind him and put my arms around his waist, resting my head against his back.

"I just wish she was still here, you know. To see how well I'm doing. To see you. It's not fair."

"I know it's not," I replied. "She'll be watching over you, and I'm sure she is so proud of you, Ethan."

We sat silently as he wiped his eyes.

"I'm such a baby! I don't cry my entire life and I've cried twice this year!"

We both giggled. I kissed the back of his neck and gave him a squeeze.

"Will you be ok?"

"I'll be fine, Mrs. August Bishop-Knight," he replied.

"Did you notice we kinda sound like the beginning of a chess set?" I asked with my cheek squished against him.

"Oh yeah," he replied with amusement.

NEW MESSAGE FROM MUM
A HOUSE! A BLOODY HOUSE! IS HE MAD? August, if you don't marry that boy I have failed as a mother! Tell him thank you, honestly thank you so much. Thank you for my shoes and the TV too. Madeline is running around like a lunatic and she went crazy over her presents. Your father cried, but he won't admit it. He also asked me to remind you to keep your tongue out of Ethan's mouth while on live television, lol! God, I need a lie down, it's too much to take in! All my love to you couple of goofballs, we love you so so so so much. Merry Christmas, my angel! Xx

I'm sure you can imagine my mum's overwhelmed reaction when I replied to her text with a photo of me and Ethan kissing as I flashed my engagement ring. Believe it or not, Ethan had already spoken to my dad about proposing to me. I didn't see that coming. When we arrived at Max and Eleanor's, Ethan introduced me as his fiancée. It was the strangest, most wonderful feeling, and I thought I was going to burst with excitement. Max and Eleanor were thrilled as I held up the *huge rock* on the end of my finger. My fiancé—wow, it's even more wonderful to say it—was creating our surprise dinner with Max while Eleanor and I enjoyed a glass of wine. Whatever it was they were making, it smelt great. The reason it smelt great was because when we sat down we had four pizzas waiting for us at our table. Eleanor and I were laughing for a good minute or two. Ethan and Max didn't find it too amusing because they had spent a long time preparing them for us. Pizza is hardly a traditional Christmas meal, but I'm glad we didn't have anything else. We sat and ate our pizzas prepared for us by our partners. Then I snuggled up into Ethan's arms on the sofa and we had a nap while Max and Eleanor did the same. I shuffled my head back and pouted my lips in an attempt to show that I wanted a kiss. I had to nudge him with my head before his hands grasped my cheeks and he kissed my pouted lips. We didn't stay much longer because Ethan was still a bit shaken by his mum's letter from earlier. I secretly made Max and Eleanor aware of it and they completely understood.

My fiancée had one more surprise for me as we reentered our apartment. He took my coat off me as I obliviously wandered straight past the gift he had hanging on the wall.

"August, you missed something, dear," he said, pointing to the wall.

I slumped my arms, as if to say, *How on earth did I walk past that without noticing it?*

I strolled over to him and gazed upon his final gift. It was a framed black and white photo of the moment he surprised me at my premiere. It was so pretty. He looked so smart and dashing in his suit, and I had the largest surprised smile on my face. And the flashing cameras were in the background. It would make the perfect movie poster!

He kissed the top of my head and put his arm around my shoulder as I admired the frame. "Do you like it?" he asked, resting his chin on the top of my head.

"I love it!" I don't know what happened, but as I said that a burp sneaked its way up and surprised us both. Ethan burst into one of his uncontrollable laughters, and I hid under my shirt in embarrassment.

"You're so adorable," he said, pulling my shirt from over my head. We laughed at each other again.

"I love you," he said, tucking my hair behind my ears, then bringing a small section forward. "My little elf."

I sulked at him. "I love you too."

Ethan placed his arm around me as we turned and faced the beautiful photo of us, newly hung on the wall. Nothing else was said, because nothing else needed to be said.

NEW EMAIL FROM ETHAN KNIGHT
October 31st
Leonard,

There's a solution, a simple one, to how we will resolve this matter. And that is no one will ever find out how it was done, not even me. Because I don't remember how I did it. There it is, the truth. However, the footage taken from the side of the vehicle where you would see how it was done is in my possession, or was, who knows. I had the tape in my hand, just like the footage I took from my college surveillance cameras when I broke a guy's jaw for hurting the girl I love. That's why August's parents didn't see the footage. This is irrelevant to you, but I wanted you to know why you couldn't get hold of the footage. No one needs to know the truth, Leonard. I thought maybe I did, so I placed the footage from the crash into the player. But then I removed it. Because I realised, maybe this should remain a secret from everyone. Even from the one who performed the act, and that's how it shall remain. I think we both know how I

did it, Leonard, but I think we both don't believe it because it is, as they say, impossible.
Ethan Knight.

60033343R00177

Made in the USA
Lexington, KY
24 January 2017